ROSINGS PARK
A PRIDE & PREJUDICE VARIATION

HAPPILY EVER AFTERLIFE
BOOK TWO

MARY SMYTHE

Quills & Quartos
PUBLISHING

Copyright © 2025 by Mary Smythe

All rights reserved.

This is a work of fiction. Names, characters, businesses, places, events, locales, and incidents are either the products of the author's imagination or used in a fictitious manner. Any resemblance to actual persons, living or dead, or actual events is purely coincidental.

No part of this book may be reproduced in any form or by any electronic or mechanical means, including information storage and retrieval systems, without written permission from the author, except for the use of brief quotations in a book review.

Generative artificial intelligence (Ai) was not used in the creation of this work.

No AI training. Without in any way limiting the author's [and publisher's] exclusive rights under copyright, any use of this publication to train generative AI technologies to generate text is expressly prohibited. The author reserves all rights to license uses of this work for generative AI training and development of machine learning language models.

Ebooks are for the personal use of the purchaser. You may not share or distribute this ebook in any way, to any other person. To do so is infringing on the copyright of the author, which is against the law.

Edited by Jo Abbott and Jan Ashton

Cover by Pemberley Darcy

ISBN 978-1-963213-67-6 (ebook) and 978-1-967030-00-2 (paperback)

To my meddling kids

TABLE OF CONTENTS

Chapter 1	1
Chapter 2	10
Chapter 3	19
Chapter 4	30
Chapter 5	41
Chapter 6	48
Chapter 7	53
Chapter 8	64
Chapter 9	69
Chapter 10	82
Chapter 11	89
Chapter 12	99
Chapter 13	107
Chapter 14	112
Chapter 15	118
Chapter 16	127
Chapter 17	134
Chapter 18	146
Chapter 19	157
Chapter 20	166
Chapter 21	172
Chapter 22	181
Chapter 23	187
Chapter 24	193
Chapter 25	203
Chapter 26	211
Chapter 27	221
Chapter 28	231
Chapter 29	241
Chapter 30	251

Chapter 31	257
Chapter 32	262
Chapter 33	268
Chapter 34	277
Epilogue	285
About the Author	291
Also by Mary Smythe	293
Acknowledgments	295

Elizabeth could not see Lady Catherine without recollecting that, had she chosen it, she might by this time have been presented to her as her future niece; nor could she think, without a smile, of what her ladyship's indignation would have been. 'What would she have said? How would she have behaved?' were questions with which she amused herself.

– *Pride and Prejudice*, Chapter 37

CHAPTER ONE

March 1813, Kent

"Dearest, we shall arrive shortly."

Elizabeth roused to the gentle murmur of her husband's voice against her forehead, his lips brushing her skin with each syllable. Her mouth curled up at the corners, and she snuggled deeper into his warmth. "Mm, wake me when we get there."

A soft rumble vibrated in Darcy's chest, and he pressed a kiss to her temple. "Come now, we are almost to the parsonage. I dare say we shall arrive at our destination within a quarter of an hour."

With a groan, Elizabeth complied, sitting up and stretching the stiffness from her limbs as she gazed out of the carriage window. The morning had begun fine, but somewhere along the road to Kent the sky had clouded over, and spattering drizzle had descended upon the land. It appeared to her that all the colour had been drained from the world, leaving behind a dull, dreary grey. The only brightness beyond the cosy confines of their conveyance was in the yellow daffodils growing in clumps along the side of the lane. Shivering, she rubbed her arms as a chill assaulted her through her pelisse. Outside the circle of her husband's embrace was far less pleasant than within.

They had travelled down from Pemberley the day after receiving Lord Matlock's letter announcing the unanticipated demise of Anne de Bourgh and were presently undertaking the final stage of their journey to Rosings Park to attend the funeral. Darcy had not wanted to go; he had not been on speaking terms with his aunt since she had learnt of their marriage and sent him an abusive letter denouncing it—or so Elizabeth assumed, having not been allowed to actually read the missive before it had been consigned to the fire—but at last he had been convinced of the necessity. Not only to pay respects to his cousin's memory and Lady Catherine's bereavement but also to uphold familial harmony.

On that score, Elizabeth had a delicate matter to discuss with her husband. "I have been thinking, and I feel we should keep my pregnancy to ourselves whilst we reside at Rosings. It would be awkward and unfeeling to announce that we are to have a child so soon after your aunt has lost one."

"On Lady Catherine's behalf, I agree. I would not wish to compound her grief. However, I shall likely inform my uncle and cousins, if only to explain why we shall not be taking part in the Season."

"Not that I am especially keen to be paraded about, but I do not mind attending a few soirées to please your family."

"Absolutely not!" Darcy looked aghast at the very thought. "London is a dirty, smelly place at the best of times, and I shall not have you exposed to it in your fragile state. What if the filth should harm you? Or the babe? To say nothing of the great burden upon your constitution from staying out till the small hours amidst the excesses of society. No, we shall adjourn to Pemberley once our duty to Lady Catherine is dispatched. There, at least, one can breathe freely."

Elizabeth took his nearest hand within hers and gave it a placatory squeeze. "There is no great need to argue your case to me, my love. I am perfectly satisfied to be at home for my confinement."

They fell into a comfortable silence after that, and Elizabeth turned her attention to the window to discern how close they were to the manor. She was just in time to see it appear like a withered apparition through the mist.

Rosings, unlike Pemberley, had always appeared incompatible with its environment. The woods surrounding the park were gloriously untamed and full of life, while the house gave a distinctly opposite impression of cold superiority. It relied entirely on the awkward taste of man instead of harmonising with the glory of God's creation, striking a discordant note.

The manor house stood three storeys tall, save for the occasional turret that rose above the main structure, and gave the impression of general stoutness. The facade was constructed principally of grey stone, beaten, stained, and discoloured by generations of weather. Prickly spires rose up to the sky, and along the edge of the roof at evenly spaced points, statues of snarling dragons stood guard over the mansion, rain dribbling from their open maws and falling to the ground below in a trickling cascade.

The windows were arched and pointed at the top, several of them boasting colourful panes in complex patterns. There was one particularly large, round window featuring some indecipherable tableau that had previously incited Elizabeth's curiosity. Unfortunately, it did not belong to any of the public rooms, so she had never been privileged enough to study it save from afar. Much as she could discern from a distance, a kneeling gentleman was presenting a flower to his lady, but without a closer look she could not determine which grand tale of romantic adventure it depicted.

The entrance was similarly arched into a point above a pair of doors. They were painted a vivid red, with great iron rings and nails as adornment. The knocker mimicked the menacing beasts on the roof, glaring at visitors and almost daring them to disturb the inhabitants within. Between the ironwork and the unwelcoming dragon warden, it reminded Elizabeth of nothing so much as the drawbridge to an ancient castle. *All the house is missing is a moat to keep the riffraff like me at bay,* she thought with wry amusement.

As the carriage drew to a stop at the foot of the steps, an austere butler emerged from the stronghold with an umbrella held aloft. Several footmen, also bearing umbrellas, followed him out and descended the steps to assist. After an agonisingly slow progression from the vehicle to the entrance hall, they at last made it inside where, after divesting themselves of gloves and hats in the antechamber, Darcy proceeded to fuss over the slight dampness of her attire.

"You will need to change immediately," he said, dabbing at her with a towel provided by a servant. "I will not have you catch your death of cold."

Elizabeth gently batted his hands away. "I have endured far worse than a light drizzle."

"That was before—"

The stilted voice of Lady Catherine echoed from somewhere deeper within the house, cutting Darcy's coddling short. "Is that my nephew at last? Send him in!"

Darcy's eyes closed for a long moment, and he breathed in a deep, steadying breath. Upon opening them, he said to Elizabeth, "Let me call for the housekeeper so you can be taken to your rooms. You cannot stand about in those wet clothes."

"Let us greet your family first. Then we may refresh ourselves together."

Darcy sighed. "But then I insist that you lie down until dinner."

Elizabeth was inclined to roll her eyes but subdued the impulse. Instead, she took Darcy's arm and did her best to appear demure for the sake of her new relations. As yet, she had not been introduced to any of the Fitzwilliams, save for the colonel and Lady Catherine, and she hoped to impress them with her gentility. Or if not impress them, at least force them to concede that she was not the horror they were expecting.

The interior of the house was divided distinctly in half, with two main corridors separated by a grand staircase—

also flanked by dragons in the form of newel posts and carpeted in a deep red. Above them, at the head of the stairs, was an enormous arched window and a line of lesser slender ones that provided light to the cavernous space. Below and to the left was the portion of the house she was most familiar with, but the right was something of a mystery to her. She knew the left to contain numerous parlours and the dining room, but she could not guess what was hidden down the other hall. A conservatory? A ballroom? More of the same? It was difficult to say in a house of this size and grandeur, but whatever mysterious chambers it possessed were not often revealed to visitors. *Or not to those beneath Lady Catherine's consequence, at least. A more elevated guest might be granted the privilege of a proper tour.*

They followed Percy, the butler, down the left corridor towards Lady Catherine's favourite drawing room. It was the one Elizabeth and Charlotte had previously dubbed the 'Throne Room' due to the enormous chair presiding over the rest of the furniture. It was a beastly thing of writhing swirls, gilded with ormolu and cushioned in carmine velvet. Elizabeth could not imagine it was especially comfortable but supposed that what it lacked in that regard it made up for in ostentation. Lady Catherine liked to sit upon it and issue orders or dole out advice to whoever happened to be at hand, exactly as a monarch was wont to do.

Inside, her eye was immediately drawn to where Lady Catherine, dressed in black, reclined upon her throne before the ornately rendered stone fireplace. Her bearing was regal, her person was dripping in gleaming ornamentation, and her fingers were intertwined atop the head of a silver-tipped cane that she seemed to go nowhere without despite having no apparent need for it —the lady was as spry as a woman half her age. Dressed head to toe in mourning black, she looked exactly as one might imagine the queen of the underworld would appear to her subjects. An enormous painting of King Arthur pulling Excalibur from a stone above Lady Catherine's head drew Elizabeth's eye. *Or perhaps Queen Guinevere.*

Her company was arranged about her in a semi-circle of matching lesser chairs and sofas upholstered in the same red velvet. The Fitzwilliams were a pale lot, their appearance lightened further by their distinctive white-blond hair. The family resemblance amongst them was remarkable; they shared the same general height, form, and colouring, and each of them, without exception, sported the grey Fitzwilliam eyes. It was rather unnerving to be assiduously peered at with the same gaze from so many alike, expressionless faces. Eerie, even. Although Darcy sported the same grey eyes, Elizabeth had never felt any creeping disquiet from any of *his* looks. *Then again,* she considered, *it transpires that he was always looking to admire rather than censure.*

Out of all the faces present, Elizabeth only recognised one aside from their hostess: Colonel Fitzwilliam. He stood apart from most of his family with his reddish hair, which Elizabeth supposed he must have inherited from his mother's side.

They collectively stood as the Darcys entered, observing the newcomers closely.

"I suppose this must be your...wife," said an older man, perhaps of around sixty years. He eyed Elizabeth askance as if expecting the worst.

Elizabeth felt Darcy tense beside her. "Indeed, Uncle. May I present my wife, Elizabeth Darcy?"

The gentleman, now confirmed to be the Earl of Matlock, snorted lightly but said nothing.

A glance at her husband proved that his jaw was tight with displeasure. Elizabeth placed her free hand upon his forearm in a comforting gesture, and he relaxed, if only slightly.

The rest of the introductions were made promptly. In addition to Lord Matlock, Darcy made known to her his aunt Lady Matlock and their eldest son, Viscount Marbury. The former was polite, if rather distant, while the viscount's lip curled in disdain as he muttered, "Charmed."

"And where is Georgiana?" demanded Lady Catherine, arching her neck and looking about as if she expected her niece to magically appear behind Elizabeth and Darcy.

Elizabeth bit her lower lip to prevent a smile from sprouting upon her face. Georgiana might have accompanied them to pay her respects to Miss de Bourgh were it not for the abject terror she felt towards Lady Catherine. Darcy had made a weak attempt to persuade his sister out of her fear but ultimately had not the heart to defend their aunt. As a result, Georgiana remained in London with the newly married Bingleys, happily assisting Jane in the decoration of their recently acquired lodgings on Brook Street until the Darcys returned to collect her.

"She remains in town. I thought her constitution too delicate for such a sorrowful occasion," Darcy replied stiffly. Just as Lady Catherine opened her mouth, presumably to object, he continued, rather brusquely, "My wife requires a chance to rest and refresh herself. Might we be led to our rooms?"

Lady Catherine scoffed. "You have only just arrived."

"Yes, and we are fatigued from the journey. Do not forget that we have travelled all the way from Pemberley."

Lady Catherine barked at the footman on duty to fetch her housekeeper, Mrs Knight. The lady appeared and was given orders to show the Darcys to their guest chambers, to which she curtseyed and complied.

CHAPTER TWO

At the top of the stairs was the large, arched window Elizabeth had seen from below. It featured the de Bourgh crest—a yellow flower that might, or might not, have been a rose crossed with a sword—and was flanked on either side by six tall, slender apertures that ran the length of the landing corridor. The dim light from without cast long bars across the floor, and Elizabeth wryly imagined that the housekeeper was leading them to some sort of dank cell.

A curious glimpse through one of these narrow windows showed her a view of a private courtyard with a fountain placed precisely in the middle of the space. It must have been grand at one time, though it did not appear functional any longer. The basins were stained with algae, and any water collected therein was a dirty brownish colour. At the pinnacle of the many tiers was a regal couple, their faces worn to indistinction as they presided over the enclosed garden, raindrops dripping from the points of their chins.

When Darcy came to an abrupt halt, Elizabeth's attention was called back to the interior. "Where are you taking us? The family wing is the other way."

The housekeeper paused at the open throat of the hall to the right. When she turned round, her face was as emotionless as the sculptures outside. "Her ladyship has instructed me to house Mrs Darcy in the guest wing. For her comfort."

Elizabeth could feel Darcy stiffening beneath her grasp again, and she lightly stroked his arm. It was not enough to quell the indignation simmering in his voice. "Mrs Darcy is family. She ought to stay in the family wing."

Mrs Knight's placid demeanour did not waver in the face of Darcy's mounting affront. "Those were not my instructions."

"That is outrageous—"

"I do not mind," Elizabeth interjected, wary of instigating a dispute. She felt the offence to herself but was not inclined to bait a woman so recently bereft of her only child.

"Absolutely not. You are my *wife* and will be treated as such. You will stay in the family wing, and that is my final word on the subject."

"I am afraid that, with so many others in residence, there is no place to put her," said Mrs Knight.

"Nonsense. There are more than enough rooms in the family wing to house a dozen guests. There ought to be something suitable for Mrs Darcy."

"Many of them have been shut up for years and are not presently habitable."

Elizabeth could have sworn she heard Darcy growl under his breath. "Are my usual chambers prepared?"

"Of course."

"Excellent. Then Mrs Darcy will share with me."

At last, a response from Mrs Knight: her eyes widened the slightest of increments. "I do not think Lady Catherine would approve—"

"Lady Catherine has no say in this instance," Darcy firmly interjected.

After several long seconds of contemplation, Mrs Knight nodded once and began walking down the opposite hall.

Although Elizabeth had seen various public rooms during her previous stay with the Collinses, she had never been above stairs at Rosings before. She discovered that the ornate style prevalent on the ground floor carried to the upper as well; the corridor was nothing if not richly appointed. Its walls were covered in a striking red silk with a raised pattern of *fleur de lis*, and it boasted, as Darcy had contended, a great many doors along its considerable length. The intervals between said doors contained shallow alcoves housing suits of gleaming armour, their swords pointed to the floor but at the ready—rather inhospitable, in her opinion. Above their heads, exquisite golden vaulting fanned out across the ceiling like swathes of overlapping lace. One's eye did not quite know where to look, and the combination of colours, patterns, and textures was liable to induce a headache if endured for longer than it took to reach their chamber. On the whole, it was vastly overdone.

"Here we are," announced Mrs Knight, stopping outside a room at the far end of the hall. Elizabeth noted that it was situated to the immediate right of a prominent pair of double doors that presumably obscured the mistress's chambers. "I shall have Mrs Darcy's things brought up to this room. Will you be requiring anything else?"

"No, that will be all," Darcy curtly replied. "You are dismissed."

The housekeeper dropped the shallowest possible curtsey and departed.

Fortunately, the bedchamber was not as outrageously decorated as the hall. It was appropriately spacious, yet not cavernous, and the only sign of medieval fashion was the fireplace, which was turreted on either side and flanked by yet another pair of knights. These held flags —sporting the de Bourgh crest, Elizabeth noted—rather than weaponry, which was at least somewhat more friendly.

She crossed to the bank of windows and knelt upon the padded bench there to look out. The view was far lovelier without the manor house in her field of vision. If she craned her neck to the left, she could just see the church spire, and that curl of smoke almost certainly originated from the parsonage. Slightly to the right of the Collinses' residence, and above the trees, she spotted the crenellated top of a structure she did not recognise; did the park boast an actual castle on its grounds?

"I will be speaking to my aunt about her treatment of you. Trying to place my wife in the guest wing!"

Elizabeth turned to see Darcy tugging ferociously at the knot in his cravat. In his frustration, he appeared to be tightening rather than loosening it. "I beg you would not. It serves no purpose to antagonise Lady Catherine."

"It serves the purpose of forcing her to show you greater respect."

"I sincerely doubt you will achieve such an end. If anything, you are likely to deepen her resentment of me."

Darcy scoffed, and the movements of his hands became more urgent yet less successful in his tussle with the neckcloth. "So I should say nothing and allow her to mistreat you?"

"For now, it is the best course," Elizabeth said, her voice lowered to a soothing register. "Remember, your aunt is not only angry at being denied her favourite wish of uniting your two households but also mourning the loss of her only child. I cannot even imagine the things she must be feeling—sorrow, anger, disappointment, and more. Have the compassion she has not shown me and let it lie."

Sighing, Darcy disentangled his fingers from his cravat and approached. He sat beside her in the window seat, cupped her jaw, and drew her in for a sweet kiss. "You are right, of course. Lady Catherine is not an easy sort on the best of days, and this is far from the best. I shall try to be more understanding of her grief, but know that I shall still stand firm if I feel she, or anyone else, has crossed a line. Having compassion does not require me to sit back and accept any form of treatment."

"That is fair."

"Even if I must be lenient with Lady Catherine, I shall at least have a word with my uncle and Marbury on this subject. They have not her excuse to be so cold and inhospitable."

"If you must, but I ask that you at least approach the subject gently. I should not wish for them to despise me more because they feel I have complained about them."

"Worry not, my love. I shall be diplomatic."

"Oh dear." Elizabeth nibbled on her lip to prevent a saucy smirk from emerging. "I am not certain whether your style of diplomacy will improve the situation or worsen it. I beg you, do not be too honest with them and insult their consequence."

"Tease." He leant in to kiss her.

It was the work of a single fluttering beat of her heart before Elizabeth's amusement faded away in favour of headier feelings. Half a year into their marriage, these sensations were no longer alien to her but familiar and welcome. Between learning of Anne's death, nights spent on the road, and various other concerns, it had been unreasonably long since her husband had touched her in this way. She had been deprived of the passion she was accustomed to, and she was eager to renew her acquaintance with it. She sank her fingers into Darcy's hair and tilted her head to deepen their kiss, opening for him when his tongue sought hers. A stifled groan, rumbling up from deep within his chest, was her reward.

Just as her hands dropped to the knot in his cravat, determined to untangle it where he had failed, Darcy jerked back and held her away from him. His eyes were wild with desire, but there was some other emotion she could not quite place lurking in their depths. Whatever it was, it banished the stirring of lust in the pit of Elizabeth's stomach and replaced it with a clench of unease.

"We…ah, I should call for your maid. You cannot lie down in damp clothing."

Affixing a smile to her face that had always tempted him in the past, Elizabeth coyly suggested, "You might help me undress. Then we could lie down together."

"No," Darcy said so quickly that she felt a pang. He then extricated himself from her entirely and stood, putting yet more distance between them. "No, you require rest. I would not wish you to overtax yourself."

"Overtax myself!" she exclaimed, indignant. "I have only just woken from a nap. I am perfectly able to enjoy your attentions with no risk to my wellbeing."

"I am glad to hear it," he said, though he sounded anything but. The way his gaze darted away from her and he fiddled with his signet ring further disclosed his unease; he was only inclined to such fidgeting when attempting to hide some sort of distress. "Even so, I would still prefer it if you were to lie down until dinner. You cannot be too careful in your condition."

Elizabeth opened her mouth to argue with him further, but he was already halfway across the room to the bellpull, which he impatiently tugged thrice to call forth the servants. There was no point in quarrelling with him any longer; Blake and Bailey would be there at any moment to destroy any chance of marital intimacy. Crossing her arms over her chest, Elizabeth slumped into the window seat and returned her gaze to the misty scenery outside.

Although Elizabeth had submitted to his cajoling reluctantly, she was at last tucked safely into bed where Darcy could keep watch over her. He was ostensibly attending to his correspondence, but even if the weak light cast by the cloudy sky had suited his purpose, his attention would have been invariably drawn to where his wife restlessly lay.

When Elizabeth had first told him of her pregnancy, Darcy had been overjoyed to learn that he was going to be a father. He retained fond recollections of Georgiana's early childhood and knew, with no doubt whatsoever, that he would cherish his son or daughter from the moment of their birth.

But.

That same evening, as his wife had tossed and turned next to him in a fruitless effort to find repose, worry had begun to seep in. Memories of what his own mother had suffered to bear children had given rise to a darker anxiety. She had only successfully managed to do so twice, once for him and then again nearly twelve years later for his sister. The latter event had taken her life. In between, a series of miscarriages had weakened Lady Anne's constitution and, in the physician's learned opinion, resulted in her ultimate demise.

When Darcy had eventually fallen asleep that night, he had dreamt of terrible things—Elizabeth sobbing piteously, torn and bloodied sheets, and yet more sinister imaginings that were better left forgotten. Since then, these dreams had tormented him frequently, and even though he had scolded himself repeatedly that his fears were largely baseless and that Elizabeth was a hardier sort of person than Lady Anne had ever been, it was to no avail. His nighttime fantasies continued to haunt him with all the worst things his mind could possibly conjure.

During his waking hours, he could not help following his wife with his gaze, studying her closely for any sign of illness or frailty. What he witnessed was not at all comforting, even if Elizabeth and the midwife—called immediately to Pemberley before they left for Kent at his staunch insistence—both assured him that fatigue, aches, and even clumsiness were to be expected and nothing to be concerned about. Even so, he could not shake the sense of impending doom that had settled over him.

He had not touched his wife intimately since, and even recoiled from her attempts at seduction upon any flimsy premise that occurred to him, but truly he was wretched with guilt. Had he not been so...*enthusiastic* with his ardour, Elizabeth would not be facing childbirth so soon into their marriage. *Could I not have abstained from her bed for even a single evening?* His selfishness was reprehensible.

A rustling of the bedclothes and an impatient huff disrupted that maudlin train of thought, which was for the best. Darcy looked to Elizabeth, who had flopped inelegantly onto her opposite side and was presently pummelling her pillow into a different shape. He did not like to confine her against her preference, but he felt he had no choice. *What shall I do if...?*

No, he would not think that way. So long as precautions were taken, so long as he was vigilant, Elizabeth would be well. He could abide nothing else.

CHAPTER THREE

At the sound of the dinner gong, Elizabeth kicked back the ivory-and-blue-patterned covers in relief. If she had to lie there even ten minutes longer, the tedium would drive her to madness. Even the prospect of dining with her husband's disdainful relatives was more favourable.

Darcy had demanded she 'rest' some hours ago, and given that she had already napped in the carriage that morning, Elizabeth had lain back and stared at the intricately wrought de Bourgh coat of arms imprinted upon the ceiling above her. She traced the design until she had memorised it, then began counting cracks in the plaster —there were forty-two of them—before resorting to tapping out the fingering of a Scottish jig against the quilt.

She might have read a book to entertain herself instead, but her husband had insisted upon dimming the room as much as possible and standing guard over her as if to ensure she did not endanger herself by moving about. Any attempt to draw him into the bed with her and coax him back into the passion they had stirred up earlier had been met with a stern admonition to preserve her energy, so she had given it up as a lost cause. Darcy had occupied himself by sitting at the desk directly beneath a pair of the smaller windows and attending to his correspondence.

Just as Elizabeth's bare toes touched the carpet beside the bed, her husband stood from his chair. "You need not get up, Elizabeth. I can have a tray sent to you later."

"If I lie here any longer, I shall be fit for Bedlam! I shall go down to dinner with you. Ring for Blake, will you?"

Darcy, while simultaneously attempting to back her towards the vacated mattress, replied, "You have had a strenuous day. I think it best for you to remain abed until tomorrow, at least."

She planted her hands upon her hips, squared her shoulders, and arched her neck back to stare him directly in the eye. "I am not an invalid. Now, unless you would prefer for me to appear downstairs in my shift, I am going to call for my maid." So saying, she stepped past her husband and stalked to the bellpull herself, giving it a hearty tug.

With a weary sigh, Darcy abandoned his objections and moved to the desk to tidy his correspondence. They were silent as he put away his writing implements and she sat down at the dressing table and began unpinning her hair. The tension was blessedly alleviated, albeit not entirely dissipated, when their personal servants arrived to dress them for the evening.

Elizabeth's irritation with Darcy only lasted for as long as it took to don a fresh gown and put up her hair. She was not especially concerned with being *au courant*, but a change of clothing often changed one's aspect, even when garbed in mourning attire. The black did little for Elizabeth's complexion, but the dress—one of three hastily dyed before leaving Pemberley—was a more fashionable cut than she could have afforded as one of the Miss Bennets of Longbourn, and it became her well. It was growing somewhat tight in the chest, but Blake assured her that it could be let out before she wore it again.

When Darcy appeared over her shoulder in the mirror, bent to kiss her neck, and called her "the handsomest woman of my acquaintance," her charity with him returned in full. *He cannot help himself,* she thought, reaching back to stroke his cheek. The other was pressed to hers as they gazed upon one another's reflections, and his cologne pleasantly tickled her nose. *He is protective by nature.*

They went downstairs without further quarrel, arriving in the Throne Room in good time. All but Viscount Marbury were present and situated as they were before, with Lord Matlock at his sister's right hand, his wife across from him, and Lady Catherine seated in her imposing chair at the centre. She and the earl were either so caught up in their bickering or so genuinely indifferent to their presence that they did not acknowledge the Darcys as they entered. Darcy scowled at his relations but blessedly kept any commentary to himself.

Colonel Fitzwilliam was placed as far from the elder

generation as possible, planted in a single chair along the fringes of the circle. He winked at Elizabeth as she and her husband approached and seated themselves on a sofa near him. "There you are. I worried that Darcy might have locked you up in a tower to keep you all to himself."

"Do not think the notion did not cross my mind," Darcy quipped in return. It was said in his characteristically dry style, but there was a hint of a smile about his mouth that belied his amusement.

"I dare say he could not keep me there for long, Colonel. Unlike most helpless maidens, I am not afraid to dirty a frock to make my escape."

He laughed at her jest. "My brother will be here shortly. It takes him far longer to beautify himself than it does me."

A loud, disdainful sniff sounded from the doorway as the viscount entered. Indeed, it appeared that he had taken some time to improve his appearance, for he was dressed foppishly in a maroon tailcoat with a great deal of lace hanging from his sleeves and his cravat tied in a ridiculously intricate design for a family meal. A black armband was fashioned around his sleeve as a nod to Anne, but otherwise he would not have looked out of place in any London soirée. Caroline Bingley would have liked him very much, and Elizabeth wondered whether she ought to introduce them.

"Only because you do not bother yourself at all," the viscount drawled. "I should be ashamed to leave my chambers dressed as you are. I shall direct my valet to have a word with your batman over the state of your cravat."

The colonel pressed a palm to his chest and cried, in a fashion one would usually find on Drury Lane, "Wounded! By my own brother!"

There was nothing wrong with his appearance, in Elizabeth's opinion. His coat might have been a duller colour and unadorned—all the more appropriate to the occasion—and his cravat tied in a simpler style, but it was impeccably tailored and suited him well. If anything, had he been wearing his brother's attire, it would have clashed horribly with his red hair.

Turning her gaze to Darcy, who looked both understated and elegant in a black jacket and a silvery-grey waistcoat that reflected his eyes, Elizabeth thought he truly was the most handsome man she had ever known and seemed to grow more attractive by the day. Of course, her opinion was highly biased in his favour.

Percy entered behind the viscount and announced that dinner was served, causing those within the room to rise. Lady Catherine led the procession on her brother's arm while Marbury escorted his mother. The colonel offered his elbow to Elizabeth with a flourish, only to be shooed away by Darcy. She indulged in a quiet giggle as her husband led her out.

As they drew closer to the dining room, a pungent odour that had barely been noticeable in the front part of the house grew far stronger. It was an odd mix of flowers and some other redolence that Elizabeth could not name. For a moment she believed she might cast up her accounts right there on the carpet, but she managed to suppress the impulse, choking it down with deep breaths.

Near the very end of the hall, Elizabeth espied a

preponderance of daffodils that glowed against the gloom. They were crowded around one door in particular, nearly blocking it, and it suddenly occurred to her what the mysterious stench must be. *Miss de Bourgh is laid out in that chamber.*

She shuddered.

"Are you well?"

Tearing her gaze from the flowers, she turned it towards her husband, who was regarding her with an expression wreathed in concern, bordering on alarm.

Although she did not trust herself to open her mouth at that particular moment, Elizabeth forced a smile onto her face and nodded at him. Thankfully, they crossed the threshold into the dining room seconds later, and the door closed behind them, blocking out the worst of the smell. Once she was able to gain enough control of herself to actually speak, she reassured him, "Only some slight nausea, but it has passed. It is to be expected on occasion."

Elizabeth had dined at Rosings with the Collinses on her previous visit, and the dining room had always struck her with its need to impress. It was a grand chamber that resembled nothing so much as an ornate, oddly symmetrical cave, with the walls painted a dark claret hue and ornate carvings dripping from above like stalactites. She distantly wondered whether there were bats hidden in the nooks and crannies created by the ribbed vaulting that spread across the ceiling, though comforted herself that Lady Catherine would never suffer an infestation of that sort.

Lady Catherine took her place at the head of the table, and Lord Matlock traversed the length of the room to sit at the other end as host. Lady Matlock and Viscount Marbury were seated on either side of Lady Catherine, while Colonel Fitzwilliam sat beside his father. When a servant pulled out a chair at the centre of the table for Elizabeth and attempted to direct Darcy to sit across from the colonel, her husband put on his fiercest scowl and made a great show of placing himself beside her. He then turned his glare towards his bereaved aunt, who returned it with venom.

Elizabeth suppressed a sigh. Between her new relations' determination to give offence and her husband's inclination to play the white knight and defend her honour, this visit was sure to be a trial.

Dinners at Rosings Park had never boasted the boisterousness of those at Longbourn, but an attempt at polite, if stilted, conversation was always made. With Lady Catherine presiding, one could expect to hear strictures on any number of subjects—few of which she could claim any true expertise in—but on this occasion she, and everyone else present, was pointedly silent.

Darcy might have thought the lack of communication a symptom of mourning, but this particular stillness was palpably hostile. Rather than sporting airs of melancholy, most of his kin, save for Fitzwilliam, glowered at their plates as they sawed at their beef. Lady Catherine liked her meat rare, so this was a gruesome business.

And what was their complaint? That he had married a woman outside their sphere. Elizabeth herself was everything lovely, but they would not condescend to know her any better than 'that girl you married'. It was insulting to her but also to Darcy himself; he was his own man and perfectly capable of making his own choice of wife, without regard to people who, while his closest connexions, had only their own interests at heart. He had married to please himself, not them, and they could not abide the notion that their counsel went disregarded. Their injured pride thus led them to snub the most delightful woman he had ever had the pleasure to know. He was ashamed to admit, if only to himself, that before meeting Elizabeth he would have felt similarly had the situation been reversed.

His greatest concern was how his family's disdain was affecting his wife. She was made of sterner stuff than most ladies, it was true, yet Darcy would defy anyone to feel completely at ease while surrounded by so many antagonists. *And in her condition too!*

Darcy's eyes continuously strayed to Elizabeth's plate, observing her appetite. He was not at all pleased by the amount of beef remaining there; it appeared barely touched. Her face alarmed him more, for her complexion was far less glowing and robust than he was used to seeing. "Elizabeth, are you well?"

His wife, who had just speared a potato on the tines of her fork, looked to him without consciousness of any sort. "Perfectly well."

"You have hardly eaten anything."

She placed the potato in her mouth with deliberation, chewed, and swallowed it down. "I am eating well enough."

"Your meat is all but untouched."

Her nose wrinkled delicately, and she glanced at the

beef in question before returning her gaze to him. Quietly, so that only Darcy could hear, she replied, "It is a little rare for my tastes, but you need not be concerned. I have potatoes and Brussels sprouts to fill me."

"You must eat, my love."

"I *am* eating."

Darcy was just reaching for another serving platter, hoping to tempt her with something else, when Lady Catherine called out, "Miss Bennet, is the food not to your liking?"

"Everything is perfectly delicious," Elizabeth replied evenly.

But Darcy could not let the insult pass. "*Mrs Darcy* is feeling unwell this evening. I am trying to tempt her with something that will not disagree with her."

Lady Catherine's resulting smile, which seemed more like a sneer to Darcy, suggested that she was unsurprised at Elizabeth's lack of sophistication. Or such was his interpretation. "Not everyone is suited to fine French cuisine. I am sure she is used to simpler fare at her father's table."

"At Pemberley," Darcy shot back, "we employ an English cook, as we have done my entire life. French chefs might be all the rage, but their outlandish style cannot compare to good, hearty fare."

"We have a French chef in town," said Lady Matlock, her gaze flitting anxiously between Darcy and Lady Catherine, "but we have an Englishwoman in the country. There is something to be said for each."

Lord Matlock concurred with his wife with a grunt,

while the viscount offered, "Is not that dull, Darcy? Surely you keep a French chef in London, at least."

"I can answer for that," interjected Fitzwilliam with a wary glance Darcy's way. "Mrs Allen is an absolute wonder in the kitchen, and Darcy would be mad to let her go for some uppish Frenchman. I have never had better sweet rolls anywhere."

"They are superb," Elizabeth agreed, smiling at the colonel. "Her biscuits are divine as well, particularly with a cup of chocolate. Tell me…"

And so the conversation was rescued from devolving into an outright dispute. Even so, Darcy could not help but dart another fierce glare at Lady Catherine, one she returned with equal ferocity.

At the conclusion of the tediously protracted meal, Lady Catherine rose and regally led the way out of the dining room with Lady Matlock and Elizabeth trailing after her. They were a silent procession with nothing to say to one another, like ladies-in-waiting on hand to serve a queen.

Creak.

Elizabeth stopped short in the middle of the carpet as the squeal of a hinge echoed along the corridor. Was it really so loud, or did she only imagine it so?

Slowly, with her pulse steadily picking up speed, she pivoted to look over her shoulder. When she discovered the door concealing Anne's body propped open, her heart nearly stopped entirely.

A moment later, a maid emerged from the room carrying a pot of wilted flowers in the crook of one arm.

She turned and pulled the door closed behind her before hurrying off in another direction and disappearing from sight.

Goodness, Lizzy, she chided herself as she scurried down the hall after her aunts-by-marriage. *Ever since last summer, you are beginning to see ghosts everywhere.*

CHAPTER FOUR

Darcy rose from his chair alongside Elizabeth, intending to follow her out, but his uncle called him to order. "Sit back down, Darcy, and leave the women to their conversation. I have a few things to say to you."

Elizabeth discreetly squeezed his hand before adjourning with the ladies. Once the door had closed behind them, Darcy turned to Lord Matlock. "That is well, for I have a few things to say to you also."

His uncle grunted and reached for the decanter of brandy that had just been set out. "Yes, yes, I am certain you do. Now sit."

It was a handful of long minutes before the gentlemen seated round the table had served themselves their beverage of choice and the servants had withdrawn. Once this much was accomplished, Darcy launched immediately into his complaints. "I would have thought, with all your blustering about familial harmony, you would have treated my wife with greater respect. I am not unconscious of your disappointment that I did not marry into the uppermost levels of society, but that gives you no right to be so dismissive of Elizabeth. She is my wife and ought to be treated as such."

Marbury, who had already imbibed more glasses of wine at dinner than the rest of them combined, swallowed back a mouthful of brandy. "If you wanted us to treat your wife with respect, then you ought to have married a *respectable* one. There are any number of suitable ladies in London—*my* betrothed, for example."

Darcy had the questionable honour of being acquainted with Lady Susan Cliffton, and he could not agree with his cousin that she was in any way 'suitable' other than being wealthy and well connected. She was a higher-born Caroline Bingley with more beauty than brains, and even then not much of either. "I prefer a wife whose company I can tolerate for more than a few minutes at a time, thank you. Not only do I love Elizabeth, I *like* her as well."

Marbury's laugh was interrupted by a hiccup. "One is not meant to *like* their wife, Darcy. That is the role of a mistress."

Disgusting. Darcy had never thought well of men who bound themselves body and soul to one woman, only to give their heart—assuming they had one—to another. Knowing his uncle also kept an actress, Darcy held his tongue rather than deliver a stinging retort to the viscount.

Lamentably, Marbury had not finished disparaging Elizabeth. Waving his glass in Darcy's direction, the contents of which sloshed onto the tablecloth, he declared, "Miss Bennet is a nobody."

Darcy's response was forced through his clenched teeth. "She is my *wife*."

"She used her arts and allurements to elevate herself to that position."

"I am a gentleman, she is a gentleman's daughter. We are equal."

"She might be a gentleman's daughter, but who was her mother? Who are her uncles and aunts? You are now kin to attorneys and tradesmen!"

"The Bennets have resided at Longbourn for nearly as long as my ancestors have held Pemberley, and they are due a greater modicum of deference than you have shown. They are respectable people with an honourable lineage. Let us not forget where the Fitzwilliam line began." According to lore, the first Fitzwilliam was the by-blow of one of the Tudors—a dynasty begat on the wrong side of the blanket.

"Better the bastard of a king than a lowborn—" The word he used to describe Elizabeth did not bear repeating.

Darcy immediately burst out of his chair and made to leap at his cousin across the table, but Fitzwilliam intervened and held him back. "Outside! I shall have my satisfaction!"

Marbury, already red from a great deal of liquor, swore at him with words that ought not to be spoken outside a gaming hell. Even Fitzwilliam, accustomed to the worst sort of language bandied about by soldiers, shouted his outrage as he fought to restrain Darcy.

"Enough of that!" thundered Lord Matlock, standing from his seat at the head of the table. "Sit down, Darcy, for God's sake. There will be no satisfaction other than an apology from my idiot son." Turning to Marbury, he continued in a repressive tone, "There is no call to speak so commonly, or to insult your cousin's wife in such a disgusting manner. What is done is done. Darcy is right. We ought to put aside our personal feelings about Mrs Darcy and welcome her to the family properly. We must provide a united front for society because nothing sets tongues wagging quite like familial discord. Now, apologise."

Marbury's only response was to glare unrepentantly at Darcy, who returned the look steadily. Should the viscount not offer amends—not that such a gesture was nearly enough—he was prepared to walk directly out of Rosings and never return, taking his wife with him. If he did not, he could not be held responsible for the violence he might succumb to.

"Apologise, or I shall dock your allowance. Do not test me, boy."

At last, and with his reluctance on full display, Marbury muttered, "I am sorry I insulted your wife, Darcy. Do forgive me." To his father, he asked in a sullen tone, "Ought I to get down on my knees?"

Lord Matlock disregarded his son's last flippant remark and lowered himself back into his chair; Darcy and Fitzwilliam did likewise. "Very good. Now, I did not wish to speak of Mrs Darcy but rather Anne."

Darcy's temper was immediately smothered at the mention of Anne. He had been so wrapped up in his wounded pride over how his relatives had been treating Elizabeth that he had nearly forgotten why they had travelled to Rosings in the first place. He could see that Fitzwilliam and Marbury appeared similarly abashed.

Swallowing down the lump in his throat with a mouthful of port, Darcy asked, "How did she die? Was it one of her usual attacks?"

Lord Matlock nodded, his expression grave. "As far as we can tell, yes. According to Catherine, Anne had been doing poorly since before Christmas, but nothing to give her true alarm. When she fell ill one evening after dinner, it seemed naught but what she had endured countless times before. She was discovered the next morning, cold in her bed."

How horrible. Darcy had seen Anne in the throes of one of her attacks many times and knew it could not have been an easy death. He rested his hand above his eyes and squeezed them shut against the image of her face contorted in a rictus of pain.

"Why was the doctor not called?" demanded Marbury. "Our aunt pays him well enough. He ought to be at her beck and call."

Fitzwilliam snorted with derision, and Darcy was in charity with his feelings on the matter. "Nichols? Better he stayed at home else he likely would have hastened her demise. The man is a charlatan."

Darcy dropped his hand into his lap, blinking dark spots from his vision. "What of her companion? Where was Mrs Jenkinson during all this?"

Lord Matlock shook his head. "Mrs Jenkinson was dismissed a month or so before Anne's final illness."

Darcy was not alone in his surprise at this pronouncement, for Fitzwilliam also cried out, "Dismissed! Whatever for?"

"I asked my sister that very question, but all she will

say is that Mrs Jenkinson did not know her place, whatever that means." Lord Matlock rolled his eyes, an unusual gesture for him. "In any case, a new companion had not yet been retained, leaving Anne more vulnerable than ever. I know not what Catherine was thinking, going so long without someone to help care for Anne, but there is no point in chastising her over it. What is done is done."

Darcy could not help recalling that Lord Matlock had spoken of his marriage in the same fashion. He forced that resentful thought aside to say, "She has certainly been punished enough for her oversight."

"Indeed. Of more urgency is Anne's will."

"What about it?"

"It cannot be found."

Darcy was taken aback by this news. Although he had been intimately involved in the business of Rosings Park for many years, he had never had cause to seek out Anne's will before. It had been written and signed during his father's lifetime and was thus not a matter that required any action on his part. George Darcy did not leave loose ends. "What do you mean, it cannot be found? Is it not with her solicitor?"

Lord Matlock threw his hands up in a gesture of exasperation. "I have told Catherine time and again to send her business to my man in London, but she has always insisted upon using a local attorney, some fool in Hunsford village."

"Even a local attorney would retain records," said Darcy, striving to keep his tone reasonable. His uncle had left the business matters of Rosings to him for the last five years, at least, but surely he had not waited for his nephew's arrival to approach Mr Stephens. "Has his office been searched?"

"As to that, Catherine informs me that there was a fire some months ago that destroyed the law office. All the records—gone. The attorney himself, a Mr Stanton—"

"Stephens," Fitzwilliam corrected, hand cupped around his chin and his eyes narrowed in thought.

"Stephens, then. He perished as well. Trapped inside, the poor fellow. His clerk survived, but he knows nothing of the will or even whether it was held at that establishment. For all anyone knows, Anne did not even have a will, however much Darcy—your father, that is—and I insisted she have one written up after she inherited." Lord Matlock steadily shook his head back and forth, patently disbelieving. "This is exactly why women should never be left in control of these things. They always make a hash of it."

Darcy overlooked his uncle's editorial comment on the efficacy of women in legal affairs; he had heard it all before, and there was no changing the earl's mind on the subject, even though Anne herself had been eminently capable. It was merely the weakness of her body, not her mind, that had prevented her from taking the reins of Rosings from her mother. Instead of tilting at that particular windmill, he focused on the dilemma at hand. "If the clerk did not know of Anne's will, could she have possibly retained the services of a London attorney after all?"

The earl absently swirled his brandy, thoughtful. "I cannot see how, but I shall investigate the possibility when we return to town after the funeral. Perhaps your father's man would know something of it. Darcy was at least as forceful on the subject as I at the time."

"I am sad to say that Mr Pickering died last year, but his son took over the practice and might be of assistance. I have used his services since his father's retirement, and he is a capable man."

"Very well, I shall begin there. If nothing else, I shall ask him to look into the legalities of where the estate devolves to next, should the will never be found. There is no apparent heir since she never married nor bore children."

Anne had come into her majority and inherited Rosings Park several years ago, per the dictates of her late father's will. As the last of the de Bourghs, an ancient though untitled family, the next in line to inherit was not clear. They would have to confirm that the de Bourghs were, indeed, defunct before determining who was entitled to Anne's assets. One might rightly assume she had left her holdings to her mother, but without a will stating so explicitly, there was no telling where the estate would devolve. It was imperative that they discover it, should it exist, else Lady Catherine might find herself amongst the hedgerows—though, of course, she would be immediately taken in by her Fitzwilliam relations should it come to that.

"I have a task for you," continued Lord Matlock. "While I engage representation in London, I would like you to have a look about the house"—he vaguely indicated the cavernous room surrounding them with a haphazard wave of his free hand—"and attempt to discover a copy. Should you find it, many problems would be resolved."

Darcy rubbed his temple. His uncle's inclination to foist every responsibility onto his relations was wearisome. "Have the household papers not already been searched?"

"My sister has never been especially gifted in overseeing her household. What papers we have been able to find have not been in good order—ripped, stained, pages missing, and such—and none of them were to the point of our search. Her steward was no help—the man has no more sense than this table." Lord Matlock rapped upon the wooden surface before him, visibly exasperated.

Darcy, who had dealt with Mr Cummings himself, could not dispute this characterisation of Lady Catherine's idiot steward. He was of the same ilk as Mr Collins, and blind obedience to his mistress seemed to be his only qualification for his position. Darcy had urged his aunt to dismiss the buffoon numerous times over the years, but she had adamantly refused, fond as she was of unquestioned reverence. Every man under her employ seemed to be crafted from this same mould, from stable boy to steward.

"We have looked in every reasonable place one might keep documents," Lord Matlock continued, "only to come up empty. I am hoping that it might be tucked away in some unorthodox location, waiting for someone to stumble upon it."

"Very well, I shall do my best."

"Good, good. You may keep Richard here with you to assist, for he is on leave from his regiment until next month. Lady Matlock, Marbury, and I shall return to town on Monday."

Darcy looked to the colonel, who raised his glass in confirmation.

Swallowing the last of his brandy, Lord Matlock pushed back his chair, which squealed unpleasantly against the stone floor. "Well, with that sorted out, I suppose it is time to rejoin the ladies."

"Not just yet," replied Darcy, holding up a staying hand. His uncle halted his rise, waiting for more. "I have an announcement to make. Before I say more, I must have your solemn promise to reveal nothing of this to Lady Catherine. Given the circumstances, it would be unfeeling to mention it."

Lord Matlock and Fitzwilliam frowned with concern, while Marbury refilled his glass, disinterested.

"I have recently learnt that Elizabeth is…ahem, she has informed me that I am to be a father sometime over the summer."

Fitzwilliam slapped Darcy on the back hard enough to cause him to jerk forwards. "That was quick! You have only been married for—what? Four, five months?"

"Six. Since the end of August." Though it felt like the blink of an eye to Darcy. How had it already been more than half a year since stumbling across Elizabeth at Pemberley? He recalled with warm fondness the wide-eyed surprise on her face when he had emerged from the lake like a ravenous sea monster. It had not been many moments later that he had recognised the second chance presented to him and devoted himself to winning her affections at last. They had been married less than a month after that encounter.

"Always efficient," Fitzwilliam concluded with a snigger and a congenial shake of his head.

Marbury lifted his glass to his mouth and grumbled something nearly indistinct against the brim. "The lower classes do breed like rabbits."

Darcy clenched his jaw, inclined to call out the viscount after all, but this impulse was forestalled by Lord Matlock's congratulations. "That is excellent news. I am glad to hear that Mrs Darcy is mindful of her duty."

Darcy could not call the pleasures they had discovered in the marriage bed a 'duty', per se, but he supposed any praise for Elizabeth from his uncle ought not to be criticised. It was enough that Lord Matlock was willing to allow she had merit. *For now*.

"Yes, well, I should very much like to return to her, if there is nothing else."

So saying, the gentlemen set their glasses aside and rose, moving towards Lady Catherine's favourite drawing room. Darcy was in the lead, eager to see his wife, while Marbury tottered along drunkenly at the tail.

CHAPTER FIVE

No matter what she had said to Darcy before, Elizabeth could not deny that fatigue was setting in at last. Ever since falling pregnant, it had become a difficult task for her to stay awake late into the evening, and she generally tucked herself into bed by nine o'clock. A glance at the time from beneath her drooping eyelids told her that it was not yet eight, and already she found herself suppressing a yawn every couple of minutes. She was determined to wait for Darcy to appear before escaping upstairs. Should she make her excuses before then, her husband was liable to send for a physician. *Or confine me to bed until I am delivered.*

With Lady Catherine and Lady Matlock content to exclude her from the conversation, she amused herself as best she could by taking in the decoration of the room. It was as gaudy and uselessly fine as the rest of the house and boasted the same strong medieval aesthetic. Even the panelling on the walls was composed of golden spokes, which, upon closer inspection, proved to be miniature swords. This realisation served to make Elizabeth smile. *Sir Lewis certainly kept to his theme.* Although he had clearly taken minute care with the renovation of his home, she regrettably felt he should have used his money more wisely; she had never seen a place so gilded in her life, or a colour palette so hurtful to her eyes. The whole was quite ugly, in her opinion.

Of the greatest interest to Elizabeth were two matched portraits: one of Lady Catherine in her youth and the other of a balding gentleman she supposed to be the Arthurian-inspired Sir Lewis. Wedding portraits, she further presumed, since they were dressed in complementary garments of crimson and gold. The gentleman's eyes were a warm chocolate brown and shone with kindness, while the lady's were a gleaming silver and devoid of any identifiable feeling. As Elizabeth had suspected, Lady Catherine had been quite handsome once upon a time with her strong Fitzwilliam features and pale delicacy. The resemblance to her sister, Lady Anne, was quite striking, though the elder sister's portrait was lacking a certain *something* that was present in the younger's. She could not put her finger on exactly what that something was, but she suspected it was some intangible quality that made Lady Anne's early death so lamentable. Despite their physical similarities, the sisters were seemingly quite disparate from one another in essentials.

The door to the hall opened, and Elizabeth perked up, eagerly watching for the entrance of Darcy. Instead, it was Percy, who announced, "Mr and Mrs Collins."

The anticipation of being in her friend's company again reinvigorated Elizabeth as she stood to greet the

Collinses, whom she had not seen in person since her last visit to Kent. She had corresponded with Charlotte, of course, but it was not at all the same as being together. Besides, she strongly suspected, from hints her friend had laid, that Mr Collins also read her letters, preventing Elizabeth from being truly open in her wording.

Mr Collins scurried into the room with a bundle of daffodils cradled in his arms. Charlotte followed in his wake at a more reasonable pace, tossing a smile at Elizabeth on her way past. They stopped in the middle of the seating area, where Mr Collins bowed low over the flowers, partially crushing them to his chest, and Charlotte dipped into a proper curtsey. The scene looked like nothing so much as a pair of peasants presenting themselves to the queen. "Lady Catherine, how are you this evening?"

Lady Catherine sniffed disdainfully at the parson, and Elizabeth could not entirely blame her. *What a stupid, unfeeling question!* "As well as one can be expected the night before her daughter's funeral. Ring the bell for a servant and request a vase."

While Mr Collins stammered his apologies to Lady Catherine, with Lady Matlock looking on in disgust as he prostrated himself without dignity, Charlotte pulled the cord and moved to greet Elizabeth. They embraced and sat down upon the sofa.

"It is so good to see you again," Charlotte said, taking both of Elizabeth's hands within hers. "It has been nearly a year since we last laid eyes on one another. Not since you stayed with us last Easter."

"I am sure you must be correct. Oh, how I have

missed you!" Elizabeth squeezed Charlotte's hands in lieu of another embrace, which would not go unnoticed a second time. With a glance at Lady Catherine, which proved her still occupied with her fawning parson, she quietly enquired, "How are you, my friend? Truly."

"Truly? I am content. Fatigued and often overwhelmed, but content. The life of a parson's wife is full of responsibility and tribulation. Death, illness…there was a fire in the village not long ago that cost a man his life. Luckily, it was contained before anyone else could suffer substantial harm, but it has cast a great pall over the community. Mr Stephens was well-liked."

"My goodness," replied Elizabeth, affected by her dear friend's difficulties. "I am so sorry for you. Between that poor man and Miss de Bourgh, your duties must be quite wearing on you."

Charlotte's expression transformed from one of sadness to warm satisfaction. "I would not have you believe I am unduly burdened by recent events. There has been tragedy, certainly, but there have also been great blessings. Becoming a mother…oh, Eliza, the joy is indescribable."

Her own face stretching in a smile, Elizabeth enquired, "How is baby Cathy? Is she much grown since your last letter?"

"I dare say she is, for I swear she always appears bigger every time I look at her. Such a remarkable child."

Miss Catherine Collins had been born four months previously and, by her mother's accounting, was a healthful, thriving bundle of cooing joy. Mr Collins was understandably disappointed not to have sired an heir yet but had consoled himself by naming his first born after his beloved patroness. On Charlotte's side, she had written that she had no real concerns over producing a male child eventually; the Lucas clan was even larger than the Bennets and could boast four sons to a mere two daughters. No doubt little Cathy would have a brother ere long.

Elizabeth could not help but wonder whether or not she was carrying the Darcy heir—and whether or not her husband had strong expectations of one. All gentlemen hoped for a son to whom to pass their holdings, but Darcy had assured her that Pemberley was not entailed, so a boy was not required to protect their assets; he could just as well leave the estate to a daughter, as the de Bourghs had done. Still, would her husband be disappointed if their firstborn was female in the same fashion as Mr Collins? Much as she despised comparing the gentlemen in any way, she could not be entirely certain.

After canvassing the perfections of little Cathy, Elizabeth and Charlotte shared news of their mutual Hertfordshire acquaintance. Elizabeth was pleased to describe her sister's plans for decorating her new London home, and the pair of them quietly tittered at Jane's relief in avoiding unwanted direction from Miss Bingley. Apparently, the lady was too busy hunting for a husband to be underfoot.

Amidst an anecdote relating to the local washerwoman's reported sighting of the famed ghostly goat at Netherfield Park, Elizabeth happened to overhear Mr Collins say to Lady Catherine, "I assure you that everything is quite in hand for tomorrow. You need have no worry on that score. And my dear Charlotte, of course, will personally sit vigil with Miss de Bourgh tonight."

Elizabeth looked in surprise at Charlotte, who nodded her head in a single affirming bob. "I am honoured to be of service."

Lady Catherine waved a jewelled hand in Charlotte's direction. "Yes, yes, good. Now, I want you to ring the bells at precisely…"

In a lowered voice, Elizabeth asked, "You are to remain here overnight? What about little Cathy?"

"She is with her wet nurse, of course," replied Charlotte. "Lady Catherine recommended Betsey to us, and she has been a godsend."

"And you do not, um, mind sitting vigil?"

"Oh, I have been in charge of the body since we learnt of Miss de Bourgh's death. I share the responsibility with Mrs Knight, as a favour to Lady Catherine."

"Is that not …" Elizabeth wanted to say 'unreasonable' but settled for, "unusual?" Generally, a body was cleaned and cared for before a funeral by her relatives and house servants, not the parson's wife. It was rather presumptuous of Lady Catherine to order Charlotte about the same way she did her housekeeper.

"I am perfectly content in my role. Lady Catherine is my husband's patroness—it is the least I can do to show our gratitude." This was said with such gentle firmness that Elizabeth desisted. She would certainly never demand such a thing as mistress of Pemberley, but then it was not difficult to believe that Mr Collins may have volunteered his wife without Lady Catherine even condescending to ask. It not being her place to object, she let the matter lie.

It was not many minutes later that the door opened again, this time to admit the gentlemen. Darcy stalked ahead of his uncle and cousins and made directly for Elizabeth.

"I see that I am about to become *de trop*." With a wink, Charlotte dismissed herself to speak to Lady Catherine and left her open cushion to Darcy.

CHAPTER SIX

While Collins droned on about the minute details of Anne's funeral, Lady Catherine observed her nephew as he fawned over that upstart he had married. *Look at them over there, speaking only to one another in intimate whispers. And his countenance! I dare say he would kneel down and kiss her slippers should she ask it of him. Shameless.*

They were on a sofa with their fingers tangled together between them and likely thought they were being discreet, but anyone could see what they were about. *And in a public room too!*

Seeing Darcy so slavishly besotted with *that girl* was an insult to Anne's memory. Had the chit any regard for the wishes of his friends or his closest kin, she would never have quit the sphere in which she had been brought up. Instead, Lady Catherine was forced to endure her as a niece and pretend to accept this horrid farce for the sake of her brother, who would brook no opposition on the matter of a family schism. *Men and their politics! What of our dignity?*

She could not conceive of what arts and allurements Miss Bennet—she would never acknowledge that unrepentant strumpet as Mrs Darcy—had used upon Darcy to achieve her ends, but no doubt they were disgustingly wanton to turn her most sensible nephew's head. If only Anne had followed her example and ensnared him before it was too late. It would have been nothing to sneak into his bedchamber whilst he stayed with them, as he did every Easter, and cement her position as his partner in life. But no, Anne had not wished to resort to such 'extreme measures', as she called them, and Lady Catherine had been forced to punish her daughter for such wilful disobedience. And then to keep her quiet.

Perhaps she had been a touch heavy-handed, but how was she to know that beforehand? It had been Mrs Jenkinson's job to oversee Anne's care. Regrettably, there had been no choice but to dismiss that slanderous, ungrateful witch—*Who is she to question the commands of her betters?*—leading to unfortunate results.

In the end, Lady Catherine laid the greatest portion of the blame at the feet of the scandalous Miss Bennet. It was *her* fault for snatching Darcy away from Anne. Had it not been for her interference in Catherine's best laid plans, everything might have turned out differently.

When the mantel clock chimed nine times, Lady Catherine glanced at its face, narrowing her gaze as she read the time. It was not even half past eight! She would task a servant with seeing it repaired.

"What do I care? Darcy's bit o' muslin will hear worse in London."

Lady Catherine, as well as everyone else in the room, diverted her attention to Marbury, who sat sprawled in his chair like a common labourer at a tavern. *Loathsome boy!* This disgraceful behaviour was one of the many reasons she had pursued Darcy as Anne's husband rather than her brother's heir. On top of being far wealthier, Darcy never appeared slovenly or ridiculous as Marbury was prone to be.

Fitzwilliam hushed his brother harshly. "Do you want Darcy to call you out after all?"

Darcy, from where he sat, glowered at his elder cousin from across the circle. "Were you not in your cups, I should insist we meet outside this moment."

Miss Bennet clutched at his arm. "Mr Darcy, no!"

How tragic it would be for her to lose her dupe so soon after ensnaring him. She is unlikely to meet with such success a second time.

"Marbury," broke in Matlock, his voice a stern lash. His son sat up as if struck by it. "Go to bed."

Although still grumbling belligerently under his breath, Marbury struggled to his feet and moved towards the door on unsteady legs. On his way, he stopped before Darcy and his lowborn wife and executed a deep, mocking bow. Catherine smiled in dark amusement. "I have yet to offer you my congratulations, Mrs Darcy, on both trapping my cousin and begetting his whelp so quickly. You have my undying admiration for your wiles, madam—the ladies of the *ton* could learn much from you."

Darcy was on his feet the next instant and grabbing Marbury by the lapels of his coat. Only the intervention of Fitzwilliam, who had wisely followed closely upon his brother's heels, prevented violence from breaking out.

While the men brawled and Collins expressed his long-winded concerns, the meaning of Marbury's verbal attack sank into Lady Catherine's brain. *'Whelp'? Does that mean...*

Her eyes immediately found Miss Bennet's midsection, which the girl cradled defensively with one hand while utilising the other to reach for her enraged husband. Although it was difficult to tell through the volume of her skirts, one could see a slight protrusion beneath her palm if one looked closely enough.

If it were not bad enough that Darcy had married a common country chit behind her back, destroying all her grand plans of uniting Rosings with Pemberley, now his wench carried the Darcy heir within her womb? This girl, this nobody, had taken everything from her—from Anne—and now flaunted her success in their faces? This was not to be borne! What had happened to Anne had been unfortunate, but what would befall her usurper would be nothing less than justice.

Lady Catherine was startled from her plotting by a loud rattling, a cold splash on her arm, and a shout. Whipping her head in the direction of the disturbance, she found Collins grasping at the urn of daffodils that had nearly toppled into her lap, congratulating himself on rescuing her gown. "Did you see that? It began tilting over, all by itself. Thank goodness I was here to catch it or else—"

"Had you not been standing so close, it never would have fallen over in the first place," Lady Catherine barked, darkly pleased when her parson flinched. "Get a maid to clean this up. Now!"

Collins scuttled off to do as bid, and Lady Catherine's viper gaze reaffixed itself to Miss Bennet. She was coaxing Darcy to sit as Marbury was hustled out of the room—and nearly overset by Collins rushing past him, calling for a servant—still cradling her belly. She whispered softly in her husband's ear as the red flush drained slowly from his face, and within minutes, they were back to fondling on the sofa as if nothing had ever happened.

Despicable, abominable girl. I shall rest easier once the world is rid of you.

CHAPTER SEVEN

Elizabeth awoke with a start, blinking into the pitch darkness as the hall clock struck midnight. The babe in her belly fluttered wildly as if also jolted awake, and she pressed a hand to the slight rise beneath her nightgown.

The only mystery was what had disturbed them both. She had a notion that she had been dreaming but could not recall the content. There was a flickering in her mind, sparks of images she could not entirely make out, each quickly snuffed. Whatever her brain had conjured, it was gone now—dissolved into the ether in a coil of smoke.

Even with no tangible recollection of the dream, Elizabeth felt…unsettled. Disturbed. There was no rational explanation for it, but she could not help the deep sense of unease that beset her. She shuddered; whatever it was, perhaps it was best that she could not remember it.

Beside her, Darcy snored lightly. She considered waking him but decided against it. Not only would it be unkind to disturb his rest, but she did not relish the probability that he would coddle her more than she liked. It would be better for them both to let him sleep.

Elizabeth reclined again into her pillow and tried to will herself back to the realm of Morpheus, but her mind would not quiet itself enough for the task, and the baby continued to dance a merry jig within. She lay there for what felt like an eternity, shifting back and forth in the hope of magically soothing herself and her child, but it was no use.

I wonder whether Charlotte is awake. She knew, from Mr Collins's earlier announcement, that her dear friend was enlisted to sit with Anne's body overnight. It must be a dull task with only servants and the dead to converse with, so Charlotte might enjoy company.

Decided, Elizabeth conceded defeat and sat up. Careful not to disturb her husband, she slid from beneath the counterpane and lowered her feet to the floor. Each movement was slow and deliberate so as to avoid Darcy's notice; he would undoubtedly prevent her going if he could, so it was best he never know. *I shall sit with Charlotte for a short while, then return without his ever being aware.*

Elizabeth swiftly donned her robe and slippers and lit a candle in the low-burning fire. She then made her way to the door and reached for the latch, only to draw back from the sharp coldness of the brass. She had not considered the night especially chilly, but then it was only early March.

After steeling herself for the unpleasant sensation, she delicately released the latch and egressed into the hall—*How absolutely frigid! No wonder the fixtures are so cold*—shutting the door silently behind her.

On the ground floor, Elizabeth followed the corridor she knew to lead to the chamber holding Anne's remains. As she drew closer, she was required to cover her nose with the sleeve of her robe so as to dampen the overpowering stench of death and daffodils.

She stopped midway down the hall, just before the dining room, and fought the inclination to retch. *Perhaps this was not the best idea*, she admitted to herself. After quelling the uprising in her stomach, however, she determinedly moved forwards; she had already come this far, and it would be a shame to miss her chance to speak to Charlotte.

Reaching her destination, she rapped lightly on the door and awaited an answer. With a muffled rustle of fabric and the light tread of footsteps, it opened on a squealing hinge to reveal her friend's surprised face. The wave of odour that poured out forced Elizabeth to cover her mouth and nose again.

"Eliza, what are you doing up?"

"I could not sleep, so I thought I might keep you company."

Charlotte looked over her shoulder into the room where Anne was laid out upon a long table, surrounded by yet more clusters of daffodils. She clutched a posy of wood anemones against her abdomen, looking every inch the macabre princess in a fairy tale waiting for a kiss to rouse her. She appeared much as she had in life: waxy, listless, unmoving. It pained Elizabeth to think so, especially of a young woman cut down too soon, but it was the truth that Anne de Bourgh had been a wraith long before she died. *How tragic.*

"Come," said Charlotte, taking Elizabeth by the elbow and turning her back the way she had come. After closing the door behind her, she urged her friend into motion. "You cannot stay here and make yourself ill. We shall sit in the library."

With that, Charlotte led her past Lady Catherine's Throne Room, across the vast entrance hall to the opposite side of the house, and finally down the mysterious corridor Elizabeth had never been privileged to tread. A little way down was a set of yew doors that were surprisingly unadorned. She was unsure whether this lack of ornamentation predicted a sad, uninspired library akin to the one at Netherfield or conversely implied that it had been left unspoilt by the gilded touch of Lady Catherine.

When she entered, Elizabeth found herself overcome by awe; the plain doors disguised the entrance to a magical realm. The library was flooded with moonlight, enabling her to see nearly as much detail as she might during daylight hours. This was a blessing, for the decoration, far from the grotesque taste of the rest of the house, was absolutely enchanting. Nowhere else in the manor was the Arthurian theme so prevalent or exquisitely done. Numerous tall shelves of light-coloured stone had been elaborately crafted to emulate the mythical Camelot, their dividing columns wrought into spires that truncated in crenellated moulding where the wall met the ceiling. The ceiling itself was a fresco of King Arthur seated at his famed round table, surrounded by his knights and lifting the Holy Grail in tribute.

Best of all, in Elizabeth's giddy opinion, she espied the stained-glass window she had oft wondered about set within the outer wall, the one she had only been privileged enough to observe from afar. The moonlight filtering in through its coloured panes created a dappled mosaic effect upon the hardwood floor, almost as if a giant rose were blooming there at her feet. It was flanked on either side by half a dozen tall, pointed windows filled with plain glass, allowing light to pour in unobstructed, brightening the space, and she had no doubt that the aspect of the park would be magnificent.

She moved closer and peered out onto the shadowy grounds. Close to the house were the formal gardens, of course, but fortunately they did not spoil the view of the woods farther afield. A glint of brightness above the tree tops caught her attention—the same white-stone tower she had spotted from her bedchamber earlier. She was determined to find it before the end of their stay and have a closer look.

Putting those fancies aside, Elizabeth stepped back a few paces so she could more fully gaze upon the ornate window that had so captured her imagination. It was enormous, at least ten feet across and equally tall, and was encircled by a thick border of pale stone bricks in alternating sizes. There was elaborate scrollwork carved into the masonry along the casement, like petrified vines encroaching on the glass. It was almost as if it had been set back in a pile of prickly brambles.

The image itself was largely what she had gleaned from a distance, but on closer inspection the details gave her a greater understanding of the significance of the tableau. It was clearly a depiction of King Arthur—no, wait, perhaps Lancelot—proffering a golden flower to Guinevere. The flower might have been a rose, as suggested by the thorny growth that intruded upon the scene, or possibly a daffodil by its rendering. The lady appeared pleased with the gift; her angular face wore a faint smile as she reached out to accept it. *Absolutely lovely!*

From behind her, Charlotte's voice lightly echoed out of the shadows. "This room is quite something, is it not?"

"'Tis marvellous!" Elizabeth exclaimed, returning to the centre of the room and spinning about in the colourful mosaic cast by the window. It was magical; she felt as though she were dancing inside a brilliant jewel.

Charlotte, still standing near the doorway, laughed. "Lady Catherine does not visit it often, as she is not a great reader like her husband was, but it is well worth seeing."

"If I lived at Rosings Park, I doubt I would ever leave this place." Elizabeth paused a moment, then admitted, "Save to walk the grounds. Kent is the Garden of England, after all." *And I must find that tower!*

"Once you have gaped your fill, do come and sit with me."

Elizabeth pulled her gaze from the magnificent window and turned it to Charlotte, who was strolling towards a set of comfortable-looking chairs near the hearth.

Sinking down into the seat across from Charlotte's, Elizabeth emitted a contented sigh. "Do you think Lady Catherine would mind if we took these chairs back with us to London? The ones in the library there are not nearly so delightful."

"I dare say Lady Catherine does not enter this room more than once in a decade, so you are likely safe."

"Such a waste!"

"Now that we are settled"—Charlotte leant more deeply into the corner of her chair as she said this—"why do you not tell me what has you up at this hour?"

"I had a dream. I think."

"You think?"

Elizabeth shrugged, feigning nonchalance even as a creeping sense of disquiet tingled in her limbs. She rubbed the resulting goose-skin absently. *My, but it is rather cold in here. I ought to have worn a more substantial robe.* "I cannot recall the particulars of it, but I awoke suddenly and in such a dither that I cannot but suppose it was an intensely unpleasant sort of dream."

"Why did you not go to your husband?" Charlotte's mouth curled with wry amusement. "Or do you not know where Lady Catherine has put him?"

"Oh, I know very well where my husband is." Elizabeth explained the circumstances of their arrival, Darcy's near apoplexy at being informed that she was to be housed in the guest wing, and his subsequent demand that they reside together.

"I suppose Lady Catherine is not yet inured to your marriage, then. It is no wonder, given how dedicated she was to seeing her daughter united with him. She spoke of little else besides his 'betrayal' after receiving word that he had married you."

"Mr Darcy assures me that he was never engaged to

Miss de Bourgh, nor did she expect his addresses. It was all in Lady Catherine's mind, nothing more."

"I believe you. However, that does not alter Lady Catherine's belief, so her resentment is perhaps understandable."

"Quite understandable, but also entirely un*reasonable*."

"That as well, yes." After a slight pause, Charlotte asked, "If your husband was with you, why did you not wake him? Not that I am unappreciative of your company, mind you."

Elizabeth sighed. "Lately, he has been so consumed with worry over my 'delicate condition' that he barely allows me to walk on my own. I did not wish to worry him, or vex myself, by waking him with any sort of problem."

"It is not unusual for a husband to coddle his wife once he learns that she is expecting. They cannot take on the burden themselves, so they like to assist in any way they can, even when it is inadvisable for them to do so. Mr Collins took to following me about like a puppy when I told him I was pregnant with Cathy."

Elizabeth grimaced at the image of Mr Collins scampering about on the trail of Charlotte's skirts. "I cannot imagine that was especially pleasant."

"I shall admit that he was rather underfoot, but he settled after a few weeks once he realised that I was as hale and hearty as ever. I was sure to be firm with him when he was too much in my way—a lady does not require her husband's care while bathing, after all—but generally his anxiety eased by itself."

Biting her lip, Elizabeth refrained from mentioning

that a husband could, in fact, be an asset while bathing in the right circumstances. Then again, not every household was blessed with a copper tub large enough for two. Or a husband like Darcy.

"And how do *you* feel at the prospect of becoming a parent?"

Elizabeth blinked, surprised. No one had yet asked her that question, merely assumed that she was overjoyed to be on the brink of motherhood. It was the duty of every wife to provide children, and she was no exception. "Ah, happy, naturally. How else might I feel?"

Her friend's smile softened to one of sympathy. "You might be feeling many things, most of them contradictory to one another. With Cathy, I was elated, yet also anxious and fearful. It is no small thing to bear children, even when the blessing is desired."

Elizabeth was silent as she examined the contents of her heart. She was glad to be with child—she genuinely was, without question—but closer consideration revealed other emotions clinging to the fringes of her joy. She was eager to hold her babe in her arms and dote endlessly on him or her, but she was also afraid of the accountability of seeing this precious little creature safely to adulthood. Was she really prepared to become a mother? Her own mother had been—and continued to be—a mixed blessing, often more burden than boon. Was she destined to be the same?

She placed a wary hand upon her abdomen where her child slumbered, vowing silently to them both to do her best. *I hope it is enough.*

"Forgive me. I had not meant to upset you."

Withdrawing from the boggy mire of her thoughts,

Elizabeth shook her head to banish them. "You did not, I promise. I suppose I never truly considered it before—not consciously, at any rate—but I *am* nervous. It is a great responsibility, is it not? I can only hope I am up to the task."

Charlotte reached out and grasped Elizabeth's free hand, giving it a squeeze. "It is natural to worry about your performance, but this very worry is what will make you an excellent mother. The most important element of being a good parent, as my own mother told me, is loving your child and being willing to do anything for their wellbeing. From there, all else falls into place."

Elizabeth squeezed Charlotte's hand in return. "Your mother is an excellent example, so I am sure she must be right." For all her faults, no one had ever accused Lady Lucas of being anything but a devoted caretaker of her six children.

Mrs Bennet, meanwhile, had neglected to so much as hire a governess, and she absolutely forbade her daughters from setting a single slippered foot in the kitchen, avowing that the Miss Bennets were far too elevated for such work. Given that their futures were hardly secure due to the entail, it would have perhaps behoved her to think otherwise, but she had done as she thought best and cultivated her girls into what she believed high-born gentlemen would want in a wife. To a degree, she must have been correct, for both Elizabeth and Jane had married well above reasonable expectations—though Elizabeth was unsure whether this was the result of intent or chance. Bringing them all out at fifteen had been another questionable decision, one made more out of fear of the future than rational consideration. Had she done so to advance her daughters' or her own interests? It was difficult to say. Much as Elizabeth knew Mrs Bennet loved her and her sisters, she could not help but wonder at the choices she had made as their mother.

Elizabeth was about to turn the conversation when a movement in the corner of her eye caught her attention. She whipped about, and her breath hitched at the same moment her heart stopped beating—there, framed in the doorway to the hall, was a looming black silhouette.

CHAPTER EIGHT

With a loud gasp, Darcy sat straight up in bed. His heart was beating aggressively against his ribs, and his body was covered in a sheen of perspiration. Spots flashed before his eyes against the background of general darkness, popping like champagne bubbles as he adjusted to his sudden wakefulness.

Tangling the fingers of both hands deep within his disordered hair, Darcy leant forwards to prop his elbows upon his knees and concentrated his attention on slowing his pulse. *Blasted dream!* He had not suffered one so terrible in quite some time, not since just after Elizabeth had soundly rejected his first proposal. Then, he had heard her echoing voice berating him endlessly, calling him ungentlemanly and unfeeling, declaring that he was the last man in the world she could ever be prevailed upon to marry.

This latest dream also featured Elizabeth, he was fairly certain, yet it was somehow worse than before.

The previous spring, Darcy had been consumed by his own failings, but he could at least be assured that she was alive in the world somewhere, presumably thinking ill of him. This dreadful vision…he shuddered to even think of it.

Unbidden, the image of a ghastly pale woman cloaked in a gown of deepest cobalt swam before his mind's eye. Her features were indistinct, but Darcy was confident that she was his wife and that she was in some sort of danger. The harrowing element of the dream was that he could never quite reach her even as he gave vigorous chase; she slipped out from beneath his fingers time and again until she simply melted into the mist. Gone, leaving him alone and cold without her.

A surge of irrational alarm rose within Darcy, and he reached blindly for Elizabeth across the mattress. When his hand met with emptiness, he employed the other to more thoroughly search the bedclothes, but his increasingly frantic exploration turned up no sign of his wife.

"Elizabeth?" he called out, then waited impatiently for her reply. Silence. "Elizabeth? Are you there?"

When Darcy's second entreaty was met with no response, his mind began conjuring all sorts of calamities that might have befallen her. With shaking hands, he scrambled to untangle himself from the sheets, intending to conduct a thorough investigation of the bedchamber; perhaps she had moved to one of the sofas and fallen asleep? The low light cast by the dwindling fire showed no sign of her, but he would tear apart the room until he discovered her and confirmed she was still with him.

Ding. Creak.

Somewhere in the darkness, a bell rang out and a hinge squealed. He turned to the door, which he only just noticed was propped open; a sliver of light from one of the wall sconces lining the hall was visible.

Well aware of his wife's penchant for wandering about Pemberley when she could not sleep, Darcy felt he now knew where she had gone. He breathed a sigh of mixed relief and irritation before rising, donning his banyan, and rushing out after her. He was beset by a wave of cold as he departed and made a point of pulling his robe more tightly closed.

Darcy conducted a thorough search, beginning with Lady Catherine's favourite withdrawing room and continuing along the corridor of various parlours and dining spaces, peeking into each in case his wife happened to be within.

He even peered into the room in which Anne was laid out, but there was no one present—save the dead. Anne herself was stretched out across the table, surrounded by dozens upon dozens of flowers and blocks of ice, appearing pale and wan. She looked just as she used to when she lived, which was unsettling, and he almost thought she might simply wake at any moment. Her perfect stillness ultimately convinced him that she would not, and a tightness formed in his throat.

What if Elizabeth is taken in childbed? Will she be laid out in the same fashion?

Darcy's entire body quaked violently at the errant, tormenting thought. *She will be well...she* has *to be well. I could not bear it.*

After whispering a quick prayer over his cousin, he backed swiftly out of the parlour and closed the door. He felt inexplicably more at ease with a barrier in place between himself and Anne's body.

Once that part of the house was eliminated, he moved on to the opposite side. He took the corridor leading to the library and his uncle's study; had the layout of the manor not been dated prior to his marriage to Lady Catherine, Darcy might have supposed that Sir Lewis had arranged it so as to avoid her. *Perhaps it was she who instigated the division.*

A sound tickled Darcy's ear, and he stopped in the middle of the hall, listening. Soft whispers floated towards him on the still air, light and feminine. The relief he felt was staggering; he had found his missing wife.

In retrospect, Darcy ought to have gone to the library first, knowing how much Elizabeth favoured the one at Pemberley, but he had no notion that she even knew where it was when he began his search. He arrived at the doorway and peered inside. The moonlight pouring in through the windows revealed her position immediately; there she was, seated with Mrs Collins near the fireplace. His shoulders sagged as if some invisible string holding them taut had been cut.

He was about to call out to her when Elizabeth emitted a sharp gasp and jerked in her seat, a hand rising to clutch her heart. Darcy crossed the threshold, immediately concerned that she was in some sort of pain. "Elizabeth, are you well? What are you doing out of bed?"

"I could not sleep, but I am perfectly well. I came downstairs to sit with Charlotte."

Darcy nodded at Mrs Collins, who acknowledged him

in like fashion, before returning his full attention to his wife. "You ought not to be roaming the house in the middle of the night. What if you were to take a spill on the stairs? Or get lost?"

Even in the dim lighting, which cast shadows upon Elizabeth's face, he could see a scowl forming. "I am perfectly capable of walking down the stairs, and I was never in any sort of danger."

Not that I could possibly have known that. Disregarding her protestations, Darcy reached down and grasped Elizabeth's hand, tugging her to her feet. She followed his direction reluctantly. "Come back to bed. You require your rest."

"If I must." Turning to Mrs Collins, Elizabeth said, "Apparently, I am for bed. I thank you for sitting with me."

Mrs Collins also stood. "It was a pleasure. I shall see you in the morning, while the gentlemen are at the church."

"Will you not require rest after sitting up with Miss de Bourgh?"

With a glance at the clock, Mrs Collins assured them both, "Mrs Knight will relieve me in a quarter of an hour, then I shall sleep. I bid you both a good night and pleasant dreams."

Darcy mumbled his own goodnight before leading both ladies out of the room and towards the entrance hall, where they parted. Mrs Collins disappeared down the darkened corridor, while Darcy led Elizabeth up the main staircase towards the family wing. The newel posts at the base, a pair of dragon busts, winked impudently at him as they ascended.

CHAPTER NINE

The morning of Anne's funeral dawned more cheerfully than Darcy felt was appropriate, given the circumstances. The sky was a soft blue, there were no clouds to mar it, and the sun provided a pleasant warmth. The top of Anne's tower could be seen peeking above the trees, enchantingly whimsical as ever. It was not at all the sort of farewell he had hoped for his cousin, whose death ought to be mourned by the world itself.

As Darcy approached the lych-gate where Collins stood ready, his uncle and male cousins proceeding ahead of him, the church bell began tolling. It rang in the usual pattern—twice, twice again, twice a third and final time—before counting out the years of Anne's short life with a succession of individual strikes. By the time he and his kin had reached the unctuous parson, only a light echo lingered on the air.

The sight of Anne's coffin, settled under the awning of the lych-gate, caused Darcy's throat to tighten. It was so odd to consider that his dear cousin was inside that box, and soon, within the hour, she would join her father in the de Bourgh vault. Life would then proceed almost as if she had never been amongst them. Her family would wear black in her honour for a period of weeks, maybe less, before returning to the colours they preferred. She would be mentioned occasionally, but not often, and then it was entirely possible that they would cease to think of her at all. For such a kind-hearted, gentle young woman to have amounted to so little in the hearts of those who ought to have loved her best was a travesty of the highest order.

And yet, Darcy knew that he himself would likely fall into the same pattern. He would always recall Anne with fondness, but he would continue to live—God willing—and thrive with his growing family long after his beloved cousin was interred. He might think of her in the spring, when he always used to see her, but he had other concerns to tend to: the demands of Pemberley and various social obligations, to say nothing of Elizabeth and any children they might have.

Darcy swallowed hard against the lump in his throat as his fears for Elizabeth's wellbeing rose up and joined his grief for Anne in attempting to choke him. He squeezed his eyes shut and breathed in deeply through his nose and out of his mouth, struggling to quell the mounting panic.

Mr Collins bestowed upon them an expression he must have thought to be sympathetic. "A solemn and most mournful good morning to you, gentlemen," said he with a deep bow at the waist. How one could have a 'solemn and mournful good morning', Darcy could not say, but Collins rarely appeared to consider his words before speaking. "You have my most heartfelt condolences. Miss de Bourgh was a jewel among women, a noble and gentle beauty, the pinnacle of her sex—"

"Yes, yes, now let us begin before the rest of us expire as well," interrupted Lord Matlock. Unlike his sister, the earl had no patience for sycophants.

"Of-of course," Collins stammered, staring at the earl with bulging eyes. "This way."

The parson turned and all but scampered towards the church, tripping once on the hem of his vestments. His uncle and cousins followed without a glance at Anne's coffin, but Darcy paused a moment to touch it with reverence before continuing on his way.

※

Inside the church, Darcy sat in the family pew and directed his unfocused gaze to Collins while he droned on from the pulpit. Funerals were meant to be a straightforward sort of ceremony, but Collins could never resist an opportunity to exalt his beloved patroness—even when she was not present.

Darcy was not pleased with Lady Catherine for how she had spoken of and treated Elizabeth, but he ought to remember that her daughter's funeral was taking place before his eyes and abstain from his bitterness for the present. For all her faults, Lady Catherine had loved Anne—no doubt loved her still, as even death could not take that from her—and wanted the best for her, even when that desire conflicted with what Anne had wanted for herself.

Poor Anne, constantly under her mother's well-meaning but unrelenting thumb. Once, not long after his father's death, when Darcy had foreseen no possible happiness in his own future, he had offered to rescue his cousin from Lady Catherine's reign.

It was the first Easter after George Darcy's death and likewise the first journey to Rosings Darcy had undertaken without him. In previous years, whenever Lady Catherine would begin badgering the younger Darcy to marry her daughter, the elder would put a stop to it.

"It is Fitzwilliam's choice, and I am certain he will make a good one when the time is right," George Darcy would say with a stern and knowing expression meant for Lady Catherine. "As for this notion that my wife supported the match, she never said as much to me, so I will thank you to stop bandying that about."

That year had been different. Lady Catherine's arguments were no more convincing than before, nor did Darcy feel any change in sentiment towards Anne, but with his father gone and the future bleak, he was inclined to make at least *someone* happy. Not his aunt, but rather his cousin; Anne was miserable at Rosings, and he had the ability to remove her. If he could improve her lot in life, did he not have the obligation to do so?

The only potential drawback—apart from taking on Lady Catherine as a mother-in-law—was that Anne had always been of indifferent health, and there was no guarantee she could bear children safely. With that in mind, as well as what had happened to his own mother, Darcy was inclined to forgo procreation entirely. Pemberley was not encumbered by entail, and he was perfectly amenable to settling his assets on Georgiana and any children she might one day have.

He found Anne seated with her mother in the drawing room, slowly drifting off to sleep before the fire as Mrs Jenkinson fussed over her and Lady Catherine snapped orders at her daughter's increasingly flustered companion from her ugly gilded chair. It pained him to witness such a scene, but Darcy reassured himself that it would not be thus for long.

"Anne," he called out, startling her into full wakefulness. "It is a fine day out. Why do we not take a drive?"

Lady Catherine's face lit with unholy glee, and she pounced on the idea. "Yes, yes, a drive is just the thing. It will do wonders for your complexion. Up, Anne—up I say! Your cousin is waiting."

Darcy bit his tongue against bidding his aunt to let Anne rise at her own pace, knowing anything he said would only enflame Lady Catherine's badgering.

In relatively short order—impeded rather than assisted by his aunt's meddling—he had loaded Anne into her phaeton and taken up the reins. Once they were out of sight of the house, he attempted to pass them to his cousin, who was an excellent driver, but she shook her head. "I thank you, no. I ought not to be driving in my condition."

Concern furrowed Darcy's brow. "Are you unwell? Should I take you back to the house?"

"My stomach hurts, and I am a mite dizzy, but it will pass. The fresh air is already doing me some good."

Although he remained ill at ease, he overlooked it; she hated it when he and Fitzwilliam coddled her, and he had learnt to abide by her wishes. Instead, he guided the horses to Anne's favourite place on the grounds, the ruins her father had built at the height of his daft renovations to the manor. Later on, when Anne had taken a liking to the tower, Sir Lewis had repurposed it to her tastes, creating a haven for his beloved daughter where her mother could not be bothered to tread. Back then, she had delighted in his stories about King Arthur's noble deeds and had dreamt of living in a castle of her own. In Darcy's opinion, Rosings already looked rather like something sprung from the pages of a storybook, but Anne was not satisfied, and her indulgent father had taken great pleasure in gifting her the palace of her dreams—or a piece of one, at any rate.

Anne's tower was set within the woodland just far enough to be obscured by the trees, all save for the turret at the top. It was roughly three storeys tall, made of local stone that was intentionally roughened to look weathered by age, and had a single room at the top for Anne to hide away in whenever she pleased. It looked as if it might fall over at the slightest gust of wind, but then it was meant to; inside, it was structurally sound and comfortably furnished. Lady Catherine did not like it, declaring that she preferred to have her daughter safely at home under her supervision, but Sir Lewis had never been much in the habit of listening to his wife.

Darcy tugged the horses to a stop before the artfully crumbling structure and gazed up at it, looking back into the past. It was not so long ago that he and Fitzwilliam had gambolled about the base, battling invisible enemies in defence of their stronghold. Anne would lean out of one of the smaller windows, waving a handkerchief and wailing for them to rescue her from some imaginary foe, usually an ogre, dragon, or evil witch. They always managed their daring feats by dinner time, then rushed back to the manor as champions. Now it was time to play hero again.

"Anne," Darcy began, then cleared his throat. He was unaccountably nervous, doubt niggling at the back of his mind, but continued regardless. "I have been thinking that your mother's desire for us to marry is not such a bad notion after all. What do you think?"

Anne, who had been staring inattentively at the wood as they drove through it, whipped about and fixed him with a look of utter revulsion. "I think you have lost your senses."

Straightening his spine, he fixed his cousin with the famed Darcy glower. "I am of perfectly sound mind, thank you. What about marrying me strikes you as so unpalatable?"

"You are nearly a brother to me," replied Anne with a droll twist to her mouth. "Have you thought about what it would be like to kiss me?"

Darcy could not help it; he felt the muscles of his face contract with disgust. He straightened his expression again quickly, but Anne had already seen and laughed at him.

"If you cannot even countenance the prospect of a kiss, then what hope do you have of taking me to the marriage bed? I cannot say that I know precisely what it entails, but the village women are quite clear that it is more than kissing."

"Forgive me, I had not meant to insult you. There is naught wrong with you on that score." So he said, but in truth Darcy did not find Anne attractive. She was extremely thin and had a waxy pallor that did not appear healthy. Her pronounced features might have been handsome with some flesh on her bones, but the sunken quality of her cheeks only emphasised the sharp angles in an unflattering way. Her white-blonde hair not only never held a curl but fell lank about her face like tattered curtains. She was far from the sprightly brunettes he tended to prefer.

Anne waved her hand at him as if it were nothing, though it must have stung. "Never fear, I do not find you particularly attractive either."

This took Darcy aback. He did not like to consider himself vain, but he had mirrors and was reasonably assured that he was a handsome gentleman. He was tall, of an athletic build, had all his teeth, and his hair was thick upon his head, to say nothing of the strong patrician features he had inherited from his father. Part of the reason he was so desirable to unmarried ladies lay in the prospect of bedding a suitably wealthy man who did not look like their grandfathers. Or Marbury, who was growing increasingly doughy about the middle.

Anne laughed again, and while it was nice to hear, it did not soothe his ruffled feathers. "Do not look at me like that. Even were you not my brother in nearly every way, I do not care for tall, dark gentlemen who scowl at everything that moves. I prefer a more cheerful aspect."

"Like Fitzwilliam?"

He thought he saw a light flush rise on Anne's cheeks, but it was difficult to tell in the shade of her bonnet. "I am not inclined to marry him either. I am not suited to marriage for the simple fact that I am not healthy enough to carry children, and men require heirs.

Even when they do not, I am told they come in any case."

"I think you mistake me. I am proposing that we do not...that we never..." Darcy huffed in frustration at his own babbling. "Blast, this is an awkward business. Suffice to say, I shall not expect any children from you."

"You would deprive Pemberley of an heir?"

"My estate is not entailed, and I can dispose of it how I wish. I have no need of a child of my own blood."

Anne's expression was unmistakably dubious. "You say that, but I cannot believe you mean it. You truly do not wish to have children?"

After witnessing his mother slowly losing her strength from miscarriage after miscarriage only to die in childbed with Georgiana? No, he could not say he was inclined to inflict that sort of misery upon any woman.

He did not wish to share such maudlin thoughts with his delicate cousin, however. "Not especially, no. What I do require is a wife, preferably one with good connexions and healthy assets, to shore up my own finances. Georgiana's dowry is thirty thousand pounds, so I shall need to replace that with my marriage."

"And you would rather marry me than some lady whom you love?"

"I *do* love you."

"You know what I mean."

"I know you have not had a Season in town, but let me assure you that there are no *débutantes* there whom I could see myself marrying. They are all insipid, grasping, and vicious, not at all the sort of person I would wish around my sister. It would be far better to marry a woman whom I know I can tolerate and who has been a good friend to me."

"A woman whom you can 'tolerate'?" Anne shook her head. "That is not the compliment you think it is, Cousin."

He stiffened. "I beg your pardon?"

"You ought not to be so jaded about your prospects at only two-and-twenty. What if, a few years from now, you actually did meet a woman whom you could love? What then?"

"You have been reading too many novels. I sincerely doubt that my perfect match is out there somewhere, waiting for my addresses."

"Do not disparage my novels!" Anne cried, pinching his arm. Despite her size and the thickness of his coat, many years of practice had enhanced her technique enough to cause pain. Darcy jerked away even as she proceeded to scold him. "You read them all before you pass them along to me—do not deny it."

He rubbed at the sore spot she had inflicted as he said, "I do not deny it, but I shall say that they are not realistic. Have you ever met a woman who combines taste, beauty, wit, and charm? One who is also suitable for a man of my stature and comes with a healthy dowry?"

"No, but then you have always been unreasonable in your demands. Perhaps the perfect woman for you is out there, but poor and unconnected."

"Then she is not the perfect woman for me."

"Fie on you, Fitzwilliam Darcy!" Darcy shrank back, sure she was about to pinch him again. Anne merely crossed her arms and fixed him with a blistering scowl instead. "I thought you better than that. You ought to realise that a woman's worth is not in her purse but in her personality. Do not disregard a lady merely because she cannot enrich your coffers."

"Even if such a mythical creature should exist, and I doubt very much that she does, it would not matter because I would be content in my attachment to you. A marriage is not about affection, it is about—"

"Siring heirs?"

Darcy tipped his head back, searching the heavens for patience. "I was going to say that marriage is about cementing connexions and acquiring assets, not romantic whimsy. Even if your mother goes about it in the wrong way, she is correct in that our alliance would be the envy of many. Just think of it—Pemberley and Rosings united."

Anne sighed and looked down at her lap, shoulders hunched. "If you will not listen to anything else, at least hear me on this: Rosings Park is not the boon you think it is."

"What do you mean?"

"My mother misrepresents our wealth. If something is not done soon, we shall be forced to retrench."

"How do you know?"

"I overheard your father and Uncle Matlock confronting my mother last spring about her spending habits. They insisted upon taking control, but she refused, declaring that she has everything well in hand. Look at the estate books, and you will see."

Darcy was astounded that his father had never mentioned this to him. In thinking back, however, he could see how this might have slipped the elder Darcy's mind; between the demands of Pemberley, his son away at university for most of the year, raising a daughter on his own, and his prolonged illness, the tribulations of Rosings Park would not have been at the forefront of George Darcy's mind. Darcy himself was entrenched in his father's former responsibilities now and knew he was not handling them efficiently.

Shaking off his shock, Darcy said, "My offer still stands. I shall assist Lady Catherine with estate business regardless, for that is a familial duty, but if we were to marry, I could more reasonably devote a greater portion of Pemberley's wealth to the endeavour. Eventually, it could be made to turn a profit, I am sure."

"And my answer still stands—no, I will not marry you. I thank you for your kind offer, but I am not inclined towards matrimony now or ever. Even if I were, I cannot deprive you of the chance at a happier union or saddle you with the expense of saving Rosings. You may consider your duty to me fulfilled."

He might have pressed harder for a different outcome, but his heart was not in it. "Very well, I comprehend your feelings. Should you change your mind, you have only to let me know."

"I shall not, but I thank you for your devotion. You are the best of men, Darcy, and some fortunate lady will happily accept you as her husband one day. No matter what you say, I am convinced that she is out there, and you will not be able to resist her."

Darcy snorted and took up the reins, clucking at the horses to drive on. Anne was not well enough to climb the spiral staircase that day, but she could still enjoy the blooming daffodils along the lane. "We shall see."

Darcy was abruptly withdrawn from his reverie as the congregation stood, chanting "Amen" as a single voice. He belatedly joined them, earning a sympathetic grimace and slap on the shoulder from Fitzwilliam. He alone seemed to understand Darcy's grief, having been one of Anne's former playmates himself.

He and his cousin followed the other pallbearers out of the church and back to the lych-gate, where Anne's body awaited them. It was time for the final farewell.

CHAPTER TEN

Elizabeth had held the unreasonable expectation that such a sad day must have weather to match the melancholy of the occasion. Instead, it was the finest day she had yet experienced since her arrival, and she was a touch insulted by it, however irrational that was. Or perhaps she was experiencing another of those inexplicable mood shifts that had beset her lately; the midwife had assured her that such was perfectly natural, but it was disconcerting and exhausting to cry over burnt toast or feel prickly about a beautiful day.

To distract herself from her unfounded annoyance, Elizabeth withdrew her gaze from the window and looked about the withdrawing room instead. In the brightness of the unreasonably pleasant morning, the Throne Room was not nearly as impressive as it appeared in evening shadow. Its grandeur was fading like an ageing *débutante*; the walls were peeling along their seams, a tapestry to her left did not entirely cover a spreading water stain, and even the fireplace that Mr

Collins liked to remind them cost in excess of eight hundred pounds was cracked and patched in places. She rather doubted that any significant work had been done on the estate since Sir Lewis's time.

She, Charlotte, and Lady Matlock were forming the usual half circle with their hostess presiding over them from her throne. The tea table in the centre held the vase of daffodils given by the Collinses. The arrangement sat high enough to obscure her friend from view and prevent any attempt at conversation. Lady Matlock sat just below Lady Catherine, and neither of them was speaking either. It was a miserable occasion, and they were only gathered together to await the return of the gentlemen from the churchyard where they would inter Anne; and so they sat like a silent murder of crows while the bells tolled their sorrowful melody against the expanse of a flawless blue sky.

Poor Darcy was utterly distraught by his cousin's death, and it had been all she could do to give him a small measure of comfort before he departed for the church. For reasons unfathomable to her, he seemed to feel as if Anne's demise was somehow his fault, as if he could have prevented it had he only done…something. Even he did not seem to know what that something was, but such did not lessen the guilt he professed for not being at hand to effect some sort of change in events. Elizabeth had assured him that he took far too much upon himself, but there was no reasoning Darcy out of his feelings on the subject. He was, as she knew well, prone to blaming himself beyond his due.

And how must Lady Catherine feel? A glance at her ladyship did not reveal any particular sensibility other than ennui, but Elizabeth was sure she must be deeply affected by Anne's death. Whatever her faults of temper and understanding, she had been a devoted mother and was surely desolate without her daughter. *I cannot even imagine what it must be like to lose a child.*

Without conscious purpose, Elizabeth's hand moved to cup the small bump hidden beneath her gown. She could not call herself a mother quite yet, but fears aside, she had already formed such a sincere and intense attachment to the child growing within her belly as to ache at the thought of losing him or her. Tears welled in her eyes, and she furiously blinked them away; she did not wish to burden Lady Catherine with her overwrought emotions when the lady was so encumbered by her own.

Beneath her palm, the babe fluttered. Elizabeth wondered whether it could feel her sadness and sought to comfort her.

"I suppose congratulations are in order."

Elizabeth started and turned her attention to Lady Catherine, who watched her with a sharp eye. Her ladyship nodded at Elizabeth's midsection, where her hand still rested. Quickly, she returned the appendage to her lap. "Darcy must be gratified. Every man wants an heir."

"Oh, yes. We are both quite pleased."

"You have our congratulations as well," said Lady Matlock with a regal nod to Elizabeth. "It is well that you know your duty to your husband. Some brides are far too missish about such things and put it off for as long as possible. Now you need only take steps to ensure the child is a boy. I have heard that most of the best opportunities occur *before* conception, but I suppose there is no helping that now. And I am sure you will be wanting a recommendation for an *accoucheur*."

"Um...I thank you, but—"

Lady Matlock pushed on, apparently unaware that Elizabeth had made the effort to speak. "Lady Bertram's daughter—the younger, *respectably married* one—recently endured her own confinement. I shall ask whom they used."

"Nonsense," said Lady Catherine, also apparently unconscious of her niece's intentions to speak for herself. With a quiet sigh, Elizabeth relented and let the lady have her part in the conversation. "Why should you trust the recommendation of a woman who could not contain the baser impulses of her own daughters? The younger might be married, but whether or not the arrangement is 'respectable' is up for debate. They eloped, you know."

Lady Matlock's lips pressed into a thin line. "I cannot see what that has to do with a recommendation for an *accoucheur*."

"Why, the entire family's good sense is called into question by their horrid behaviour. One daughter ruined forever, the other only barely respectable, a son recently wed to a penniless cousin... No, I would not stand for any of *their* lot to advise me. Nichols will almost certainly know of a worthy candidate."

"But all the best physicians are situated in London. We ought to seek one out there."

"Mr Darcy prefers that I take my confinement at Pemberley," Elizabeth interjected. Both of her aunts-by-marriage turned to her with queer expressions, almost as if they had quite forgotten she was in the room. "He says the local midwife there is excellent."

Mrs Green was a delightful woman, and one who had served Lambton well for more than twenty years. The ladies thereabouts swore by her methods, and by and large, most had healthy children to show for it. Those that did not...well, Mrs Green was not God. Some things were simply out of mortal hands.

Lady Catherine sniffed. "As if men know anything of female matters. No, my sister is correct—you will require the attendance of a capable London physician."

Elizabeth abstained from mentioning that the *accoucheur* would be a man also. "I would, of course, welcome your recommendations and will pass them to Mr Darcy." If it would appease her husband's family, she would pretend to consider their advice, then continue as she had before. It was certainly an improvement over their studied indifference.

"In the meantime," Lady Catherine continued, an oddly fierce glint in her eye, "you ought to ensure your own health. There is a particular tonic that I recommend for ladies in your condition. One that will ensure a strong child and robust vigour for yourself. Your symptoms will simply disappear."

"Oh, my nausea is all but gone now and—"

Lady Catherine flicked her hand at Charlotte. "Mrs Collins, ring the bell for tea. I shall have the tonic brought up now. It is best taken with a beverage."

Full of umbrage that Lady Catherine, yet again, was treating her dear friend like a servant, Elizabeth protested, "Truly, it is not necessary. I had some slight discomfort early in my pregnancy, but it has been many weeks since I last felt truly ill."

"I insist. Mrs Collins, the bell." Again, Lady Catherine waved at Charlotte in that dismissive, insulting way, riling Elizabeth's temper.

"Really—"

"It is well, Eliza," said Charlotte, rising from her chair above the towering bouquet of daffodils. Once her face was visible, Elizabeth could see that her features were rendered in placatory lines. "I do not mind." So saying, she carefully stepped round the table and made for the gold-tasselled bellpull over by the window.

Outside, the church bells began ringing again, signalling the end of services for Anne. This timely reminder of Lady Catherine's grief cooled Elizabeth's temper even as the baby, perhaps feeling its mother's irritation, jumped and wriggled. She placed her hand upon the curve of her belly and stroked it in soothing circles. *There now, little one. All is well.*

When Charlotte was already halfway across the room, Elizabeth heard a shuddering rattle. She turned to the tea table just in time to see the vase of daffodils tip over, spilling flowers and water everywhere. The vase itself—an ugly thing with a busy pattern of red and gold flowers on a black background—practically burst upon impact, breaking into dozens of tiny shards that could not possibly be fitted back together again. It was no great loss to good taste, though it more than likely cost a ridiculous sum.

Lady Catherine was on her feet and pointing a shaking finger in Charlotte's direction a blink later. "You clumsy girl! That vase was an heirloom worth more than your entire house."

Lady Catherine continued to shriek invectives at Charlotte for upsetting the arrangement, though Elizabeth did not see how her friend could possibly be blamed; she was the farthest from it and certainly had not upset the tea table on her way to the bell.

Perhaps it had been a draught? Or an unseen presence...

Do not be absurd, Lizzy. Just because Miss de Bourgh recently died, it does not necessarily follow that her spirit lingers.

Such silent admonitions did not entirely banish Elizabeth's inexplicable suspicion that Anne was with them. She shivered and rubbed absently at the goose-skin prickling her arms as an army of servants, heralded by Lady Catherine's shouting, arrived to clean up the disorder.

CHAPTER ELEVEN

"Look at the time." Lord Matlock muttered unintelligible imprecations to himself as he snapped his watch closed and slipped it back into his waistcoat pocket. "I expressly told them to be ready to depart at nine o'clock."

Darcy could understand his uncle's desire to be away from Rosings. Anne had been laid to rest two days ago, on Saturday, and the day in between had been a dull struggle of dreary company. None of their party had anything to say that anyone else wished to hear, and their moods had all been so dark as to make the general atmosphere oppressive. The only brightness was Elizabeth, who did her best to cheer them, but his kin remained obstinately inured to her influence.

He looked down to where she stood at his side, her hand resting in the crook of his elbow, and was dismayed to find her burrowing deeper into her shawl as if chilled. The day was pleasant enough, but there was a nip in the air largely unfelt through his coat, and he worried that she would suffer for it. *Where the devil are my aunt and cousin?*

Lord Matlock addressed Darcy. "You will write to me immediately if you discover any documents of import."

"I know what needs to be done."

Beside him, Elizabeth pressed her hand to his forearm in a silent plea that he calm himself.

"Good, good." His uncle seemed not to realise Darcy was reaching the edge of his patience as he examined the time on his fob watch again. "What is keeping them? It is not like Eleanor to be so tardy, and Marbury was eager to return to town."

Darcy was inclined to frown but kept his countenance carefully blank. He knew very well what had delayed his aunt and cousin and could not comment upon it without being churlish. Marbury, the intolerable sot, had spent the greater part of yesterday drinking himself into a stupor and was undoubtedly suffering for it this morning. Had the earl truly expected his son to be up and about before noon? Last Darcy had heard, Marbury was proving difficult to even rouse, and Fitzwilliam had gone upstairs to help his brother's valet hurry things along. He could not know for certain where Lady Matlock was, but Darcy presumed she was also lending a hand to the Sisyphean endeavour.

"There is a reasonable explanation, I am sure," Elizabeth lightly commented when the pause in conversation grew awkward.

"Hmph," was all the earl said in return, snapping his timepiece closed. Only by actually biting his tongue could Darcy remain silent. *Keep the peace for Elizabeth's sake.*

The double front doors of the manor swung open at last, and Marbury, flanked by a pair of hovering footmen, tottered out. When he tripped upon the first step, his brother was there to grab his coat from behind and prevent him from taking an injurious spill. The footmen took hold of both his arms, propping him precariously upright.

"Marbury, are you hurt?" cried Lady Matlock, scurrying out, one glove haphazardly on and the other forgotten elsewhere. Behind the countess, Darcy could see the black-clad wraith of Lady Catherine lingering just inside the house. She watched the scene with a sneer for a few seconds before turning and disappearing in a swish of dark skirts.

"I am dying!" proclaimed Marbury in a carrying voice. "Do not let that idiot Collins preside over my funeral else I shall haunt you all—"

Fitzwilliam clapped a hand over his elder brother's mouth. "He is perfectly well, Mother, merely a touch out of sorts this morning. Some sleep will put him to rights."

Lady Matlock, a surprisingly devoted mother despite her disinterest in most areas, followed her drunken son and his retinue down the steps, alternately cooing soothing words at Marbury and admonishing the footmen to handle him with care. The colonel brought up the rear of their procession, full of bonhomie and more patience than Darcy could have summoned in the circumstances. But then, Fitzwilliam was often thrust into the role of diplomat; his father had a habit of ordering them all into harmony, while his son actually saw it done.

"Finally!" Lord Matlock stepped aside so the servants could load Marbury into the waiting carriage. He did not otherwise offer any assistance. "It is about time you graced us with your presence."

The earl's bluster was largely disregarded, and once Marbury was settled and his mother had climbed in herself to see to his immediate care, they were ready to leave. Lord Matlock called out of the window as the wheels began rolling, "Make sure to search the house for a safe. Rosings is a funny old place, and it might be well hidden."

Fitzwilliam, who stood on Elizabeth's other side waving to the departing carriage, sniggered. "I cannot decide whether he believes us to be idiots or he simply could not be bothered to look for a safe himself."

"Either supposition is likely."

"What does he have you searching for?" Elizabeth asked, tilting her head at a curious angle. "It must be important for him to harp on it so."

"We have not yet been able to find Anne's will," said Darcy, turning them to face the steps. "The local attorney's office burnt down some months ago, apparently, and Lady Catherine swears that Anne did not take her business to London. We hope to find a copy somewhere in the house, but my aunt has never been especially adept at estate management, and her papers—those we can lay our hands on—are not in any conceivable order. Fitzwilliam and I have been tasked with the search."

"Herculean task, you mean," his cousin quipped as they began their steady ascent.

Elizabeth hugged Darcy's arm tightly. He felt her slight shivering and drew her yet closer. "Where is the study? My explorations have yet to yield that information."

"It is off the library," replied Darcy, surreptitiously surveying his wife from top to toe. Her colour looked off to him, she was leaning rather heavily upon his arm, and there were dark circles beneath her eyes. *She ought to be in bed.*

"I was in the library just last night but saw no sign of any study."

Darcy opened his mouth to explain but was forestalled by Fitzwilliam's eagerness. "That is because it is hidden behind a secret door," he said, voice lowered to a mysterious cadence. "It is only accessible to those who believe it exists."

"Or those who pull on the lever disguised as a copy of *Le Morte d'Arthur*."

"You are entirely devoid of whimsy, Darcy."

"And you are entirely devoid of wit."

Elizabeth interrupted their petty squabble with, "Now, boys, no need to resort to insults."

"He started it," Fitzwilliam protested with a whine so petulant that it could not have been serious.

Darcy smirked and returned, "It was not *I* who implied that our uncle's former study was a wizard's den."

"The pair of you, honestly." Elizabeth rolled her eyes, though she smiled throughout. "I would be happy to assist you in your search, if you like. I may know little about legal documents, but I am certain I could spot one."

"That will not be necessary, my love. I would much rather you rest."

Elizabeth's brows drew together, and she leant away from him. Darcy was inclined to bundle her back up in his embrace, but by the look on her face he felt it might be unwise to risk her ire. "Surely you do not believe I shall overtax myself leafing through papers."

"We shall have to ransack the entire house, drag out old boxes, and search under furniture, to say nothing of the dust… You need not subject yourself to all that."

"You cannot be serious." Elizabeth's tone was incredulous, and even Fitzwilliam was staring oddly at him as if he could not quite understand Darcy's reasoning.

"Perfectly so." To his cousin, he said, "Fitzwilliam, I shall meet you in the study once I have seen my wife to our rooms."

Fitzwilliam saluted him with two fingers before turning on his heel and marching away down the hall that led to the library.

Although she protested all the way up the stairs, Darcy at last prevailed and saw Elizabeth tucked safely into bed. With a peck to her furrowed brow, he left her to rest.

※

After a monotonous Sunday cooped up with a coddling Darcy and his haughty, dour relations, Elizabeth was eager for some fresh air. More than that, she was ready for a change of scene and society, and thought a visit to the parsonage was in order.

Her husband had practically ordered her to rest, but Elizabeth was full of energy and could not remain abed. She had tried, truly, but had eventually succumbed to the lure of a nice long walk. No matter the debatable taste of the manor, the park around Rosings was delightful, especially once one ventured beyond the formal gardens and into the woods that separated the estate from the lane. She only required a companion before beginning her jaunt.

"Freddy!" she called once she reached the courtyard where the Great Dane and a handful of spaniels were gallivanting about. Poor Freddy was not allowed inside the manor house at Rosings as she was at Pemberley and so had been relegated to the kennels with the other dogs. Lady Catherine was of the mind that animals were filthy and unruly so had no place in respectable households. Elizabeth could not agree, but she respected the lady's ruling.

Upon hearing her name, Freddy pricked up her ears, swung about to face Elizabeth, and barked with joy before loping towards her mistress. The spaniels halted their frisks a moment before resuming, content amongst themselves alone.

Elizabeth held out her hands and greeted Freddy like the dear friend she was, scratching her head and babbling nonsense at the dog that she was sure neither of them understood. "Do you want to take a walk with me?"

Freddy barked again, spun in a circle, and bounced on her paws like an impatient racehorse. Elizabeth laughed at her antics.

"Come on, then, let us take the path through the woods. You can sniff about the garden while I speak to Charlotte." Mr Collins, to no one's surprise, was of the same mind as his patroness regarding pets. Knowing this, Elizabeth might have left Freddy behind, but she felt her dear canine friend deserved the freedom to roam every bit as much as she.

As if Freddy understood, she took off in the direction of the tree line, leaving Elizabeth to trail more sedately in her wake.

~

Elizabeth peered into the basket at Charlotte's feet where her tiny daughter slumbered in a bundle of blankets. The child snuffled in her sleep, which somehow enhanced her charm and caused Elizabeth's stomach to flutter. "My goodness, you are such a pretty baby!"

And it was true; little Catherine Collins was far prettier than she had any right to be as Mr Collins's child. Charlotte herself was accounted as plain, but there was an understated beauty in her face. It occurred to Elizabeth that her friend's looks might have been enhanced by her happiness, for Charlotte had never looked so well as she did since removing to Hunsford. Elizabeth might not have been able to countenance Mr Collins as a husband, but Charlotte thrived as the mistress of her own household.

"I know I ought to humbly deny any extraordinary merit," said Charlotte, smiling fondly down at her daughter as she absently knitted a hat, "but I cannot bring myself to do it. She is perfect."

"She is," Elizabeth agreed, withdrawing the hand that had lightly stroked the baby's cheek. "Even so, I know it cannot be easy, especially with your first. How do you do it?"

"I have help, of course," Charlotte said with a shrug, returning her full attention to her work. Her fingers moved deftly in a well-practised pattern, forming the miniature white hat almost without conscious thought; she had always displayed a knack for useful endeavours. "My mother stayed with me for the first two months, and the nurse tends to Cathy at night, though I shall say that motherhood is a responsibility I was not quite prepared for. I do not believe anyone is until they have experienced it themselves."

Elizabeth chewed on her lip, now watching little Cathy with something more like fretfulness than reverence. "That is what I fear for myself. What if I am not naturally inclined to motherhood?"

"None of us are naturally inclined to it, not really," said Charlotte, her eyes still fixed upon her knitting. "Certainly, there are those women who desperately want a child and are eager to love one, but it can be difficult, particularly when you are new to it. But you will learn, as all of us do."

"What if..." Elizabeth swallowed, her throat suddenly dry. "What if I do not learn? What if I am not capable?"

Charlotte lifted her gaze and turned it to Elizabeth. There was something emphatic about it as she said, "Do not fret, Eliza. I have every confidence that you will make an excellent mother."

Inhaling a deep, steadying breath, Elizabeth banished her fears to the darkest reaches of her mind. There was no use dwelling upon it now. "And Darcy will make an excellent father." She winced. "Assuming he ever reconciles himself to the notion."

"I am certain he will. Men are different from us—they often learn to care for their children after they are born, not necessarily before. Until then, they are merely a concept—one that makes his wife sick and miserable, which in turn makes him sick and miserable as well." Charlotte laughed at her jest and returned to knitting.

"I just wish—"

Elizabeth was interrupted by a loud shriek coming from outside, one which startled poor little Cathy awake. Charlotte immediately lifted her daughter out of the basket and cradled her to her bosom, hushing and bouncing the child in her arms, while Elizabeth bounded to her feet and raced to the window. She peered out into the garden and gasped, covering her mouth at the scene unfolding before her.

"What is it?" Charlotte asked over Cathy's wailing cries.

Elizabeth did not immediately have the words to describe what she was witnessing—the horror was too fresh. All she could think to say was a breathless, "Oh my…"

CHAPTER TWELVE

Mr Collins's lamentations followed Elizabeth and Freddy as they departed the parsonage and could, in fact, be heard well into the woods. It was several yards before the trees muffled his diatribe to the point of escaping it, by which time it was Elizabeth's turn to make her displeasure plain. "Had I known you were going to dig up Mr Collins's daffodils, I never would have brought you with me. You never behave this way at Pemberley. For shame, Freddy!"

The dog, plodding along at her side with muddy paws and a lolling tongue, merely tilted her head at Elizabeth in an affectedly innocent manner.

"Do not give me that look!" Elizabeth scolded around a laugh. "You know very well what you have done. I shall have to tell Darcy, and then you must face the consequences."

Freddy's head lowered, and she emitted a pitiful whine. Her pace slowed from a jaunty walk to a trudging crawl as if she intended to delay the inevitable punishment. Elizabeth continued at her usual pace, expecting her friend to follow rather than be left behind.

Just as she was reaching the final bend that would bring the manor house into view, Freddy barked to garner her attention. It sounded from such a distance away that Elizabeth halted on the path and turned round, perplexed. Freddy was lingering several yards back, standing to attention with her ears pricked up into sharp points and staring at her mistress expectantly.

"Come," called Elizabeth, lightly patting her leg.

The dog barked again, wagging her tail and prancing on her forelegs. She remained otherwise stationary, as if expecting Elizabeth to come to her.

"*Come*," Elizabeth repeated with firm emphasis.

Freddy twirled about in a circle then lowered her front to the ground, backside jauntily propped in the air and wiggling playfully. She barked again from this position as if enticing her mistress closer.

Elizabeth raised her gaze to the heavens, begging for patience. "Do come along now, before Darcy realises I am gone—*Freddy*! Where are you going?"

In the middle of Elizabeth's speech, Freddy had apparently grown impatient and darted off into the woods. Picking up her skirts, Elizabeth dashed back the way she had come. She dearly hoped she would not have to resort to wading into the weeds and brambles in order to retrieve her canine friend.

When Elizabeth reached the spot Freddy had fled from, she peered into the trees for any sign of the animal. To her surprise, she discovered signs of a rutted lane, largely overgrown, leading deeper into the woods.

Some distance along it, Freddy stood watching her and wagging her tail expectantly.

"How odd," Elizabeth commented, largely to herself. As these words drifted gently from her lips, her feet began moving towards the newly discovered passage of their own volition. "I have walked this way numerous times before and never noticed this path."

Freddy spun in another circle, bouncing and barking happily at Elizabeth's approach. The next moment, she bounded off again, tunnelling her way through the detritus of dead leaves, wilted grass, and newly sprouted wildflowers that had sprung up along the path. The greenery was dappled in sunlight through the canopy above, casting a mystical air about the place as she followed the canine deeper into the trees. With wood anemone growing in abundance and birds lustily twittering their songs above her head, Elizabeth almost felt as if she were being shown the way into the Faerie Queen's bower.

After a short distance, the trees opened up into a large circular clearing. She halted at the edge of the mottled shade and brought her hand to her mouth, which had hinged open on a gasp. *A castle!*

It was not a castle, of course, not really. It was a round stone tower about three storeys tall, standing directly in the centre of the clearing—presumably the one she had spotted from her chamber window. Elizabeth's eyes scaled the length of it from bottom to top, taking in the weather-beaten stone that seemed prepared to crumble at the lightest touch and the ivy that appeared to bind it together. It was turreted at the top, hence her initial impression of it belonging to a castle, and boasted at least a dozen slender windows ascending its face at an angle. Just below the line of the roof, a large round window of stained glass was sunken into its face. Around the base were various shrubs and wild greenery, which clung to the tower in a manner that suggested it had sprung up amongst them like one enormous flower.

She followed the lead of her curiosity and slowly perambulated about the tower, investigating it from a closer aspect. There were various rocks and boulders scattered about, though without any clear origin. They matched the structure, yet there were no breaks in the masonry or any other indication that there had ever been more to the building than she presently observed. She could see no sign of crumbled walls, discarded artefacts, or exposed rooms—it had always been, as far as she could discern, a single tower standing sentry amid the trees.

With that, Elizabeth thought she knew the truth of the matter. It had been fashionable once to build false ruins upon one's grounds, a silly fancy meant to pretend antiquity where there was none. It had no doubt cost a great deal to construct yet served no purpose. Even so, she was admittedly impressed by the tower, which had been rendered so lovingly and so completely as to be a work of art. She was certain that Sir Lewis had not regretted the expense.

Directly below the stained-glass window, at ground level, was a whitewashed wooden door with a brass ring. A pair of stone steps, artfully worn, led up to it, tempting her to go inside and explore more thoroughly.

Elizabeth bit her lip with indecision; ought she to trespass?

Freddy appeared to have no qualms on that score. After she had thoroughly sniffed about the shrubs around the base of the tower, frightening at least one squirrel out of its wits, she scampered up the steps and began scratching and whining at the door.

"Stop that, Freddy," Elizabeth cried, lunging to pull the dog back by her collar. "You will damage it."

Freddy looked up at her with what Elizabeth swore was incredulity. In fairness, the paint on the door was already peeling and distressed, warped from many years of exposure to the elements. Even so, it was not their place to invite themselves in.

"We ought to go. We do not belong here." As Elizabeth moved to leave, a sweet spring breeze pressed into her back, urging her forwards instead. She closed her eyes and inhaled; it smelt of wildflowers and fresh damp. She could not be certain, but she thought she also heard the light jingling of bells tickling her ears, though she had no notion where they might originate from. *Birdsong, undoubtedly.*

By the time she opened her eyes again, she had experienced a change of heart. "I suppose it would not hurt to look inside. It is not as if anyone lives here." *Or so I hope.*

Grasping hold of the brass ring, Elizabeth gave the door a tug. It budged, but only a little, so she added her other hand to the effort and leant her weight into it. The door gave way with a squealing protest, and she stumbled back a step. Once she had caught her balance, she was free to enter.

Inside the tower it was cool and full of cobwebs, and Elizabeth saw no sign of recent human habitation. The thick layer of undisturbed dust on the flagstone floor attested to that much, as did the musty scent assailing her nose. She left the door ajar to allow in the delightful spring breeze that had encouraged her exploration.

The inner walls were more structurally sound than the outer, further bolstering Elizabeth's theory that Sir Lewis had erected the tower rather than it belonging to any of his ancestors. It was a singular round space, about the size of her mother's favourite parlour at Longbourn, and a spiralling staircase was its primary feature. It twisted upwards towards a distant ceiling comprised of wood and stone and was illuminated at evenly spaced intervals by the slender windows she had observed from without. She could not see the inside of the round window, so she presumed it must exist beyond the ceiling above her.

Freddy, her nose to the ground, was already proceeding up the staircase, enraptured by some scent that her human companion could not discern. Carefully, Elizabeth placed one booted foot upon the lowest stair and tested its strength; it did not give way or even bend, though there was a slight creak when she applied pressure, so she proceeded upwards at a careful pace.

By the time Elizabeth reached the uppermost landing, she was breathing heavily. Pausing, she looked up, and just above her at the top of a smaller set of stairs was the outline of a trapdoor. She climbed these as well and pushed against it. The trapdoor opened easily under her persuasion, allowing her entry to the floor above.

As she climbed through, Freddy at her side, Elizabeth

looked about in wonder. It was a sitting room—one which was richly furnished in the style of a lady. There was a large, round carpet upon the floor in a deep primrose hue with a pair of armchairs and a sofa, all upholstered in complementary blush, settled upon it. A small fireplace was set into the wall next to the seating area, flanked by short, whitewashed shelves filled with various well-loved tomes. There was even a rosewood desk and matching chair perched under the round window she had been searching for. Due to the sunlight streaming in through the stained glass, the entire space was cast in a delicate pink glow flecked with golden glimmers. On either side of this incredible casement, a pair of tall, arched windows allowed in natural light to brighten the room. Aside from being horribly dusty, the place looked recently abandoned by a gentlewoman of delicate taste.

Elizabeth spun about in the centre of the room—careful to avoid the open hatch in the floor—and took it all in. "How wondrous! I wonder whether Darcy knows about this place."

Elizabeth began moving from one object to another in the room, trailing her fingers lightly across each as she approached for a closer look. On the surface of the desk was a set of carved initials set into the lower right-hand corner: AdB. *Anne de Bourgh.*

Elizabeth's fingertips traced the embedded initials as a wave of sadness washed over her. She lamented the opportunity she had missed to know Anne. She had assumed, wrongly, that the young woman was as haughty and disdainful as her mother, but her husband had assured her that such was not the case. Anne, by his report, had been a soft, gentle creature who was easily cowed by the stronger personalities surrounding her, though by no means lacking in her own opinions. Her health, too, made her less inclined towards conversations and making friends, being sadly deficient in the energy required for such endeavours. Elizabeth pitied Anne for her sickly constitution and her loneliness and wished that she could make amends, but it was far too late for that. "You poor thing."

Creak.

Elizabeth inclined her head towards the unexpected sound and discovered one of the smaller windows listing slightly open. Her brow furrowed. *How odd. I was sure it was closed a moment ago.*

A sweet breeze wafting into the room through the mysteriously ajar casement brought with it the loud clang of the church bell, which signalled three o'clock. With a frantic glance at her watch, Elizabeth winced; how had it become so late without her noticing?

"Come, Freddy," she commanded, swiftly but carefully quitting the room via the floor hatch. While the dog passed her on the stairs, Elizabeth lingered a moment longer to look about. With a sigh and a promise to herself to return, she lowered the trapdoor and began her descent.

CHAPTER THIRTEEN

After hours of fruitless, dusty searching that aggravated Darcy's nose, he and Fitzwilliam sat in the leather armchairs inside their late uncle's study sipping glasses of port in weary silence. It was astonishing how much paper a single room could contain while offering up nothing useful.

"Do you suppose Anne even had a will? I am beginning to seriously doubt it," Fitzwilliam commented, swallowing back his final sip of port.

Darcy swirled the dregs of his drink in the bottom of his glass, staring morosely at the drops of tawny liquid. "One must assume that she did. My father tended to Rosings's business when Anne came of age and would have seen to it."

"Then why can we not find the blasted thing?"

"Perhaps it is hidden elsewhere in the house, somewhere we have not thought of yet. Or perhaps Lady Catherine did not retain a copy of her own and it was destroyed in the fire that took the attorney's office in the village. It might even be in the custody of some unknown solicitor in London, though I do not think that likely, given how infrequently our aunt and cousin left Kent."

"Could it be at Darcy House or Pemberley?"

Darcy shook his head. "No, I would have come across it at some point in the years since my father's death. He also would have mentioned it to me, were it in our safekeeping. If the will exists, it must be here at Rosings Park."

"Well, we can be sure it is not in *this* room," Fitzwilliam groused, waving his free hand at the disarray they had created. Stacks of papers littered the desk, floor, and bookcases, sorted into dozens of piles based on their contents. There were receipts for laundry, decades-old correspondence, outdated tenant leases, invitations to dinner parties from years ago, scraps of terrible poetry in his uncle's hand, and even a copy of Sir Lewis's will—long since executed—but no sign of Anne's.

"Tolerably so, yes." Darcy exhaled harshly, frustration high. "I have been in this study so many times over the years, especially since my father's decease when I took up Lady Catherine's affairs, but I had no notion that it was so poorly organised. The estate books were always readily at my disposal, so I never looked inside the desk, save to search for a quill. How does our aunt ever find anything?"

"I sincerely doubt she ever enters this room, or even this part of the house. She leaves all the accounting to her housekeeper and male relatives and only concerns herself with badgering her tenants into her way of thinking. The place has been sorely neglected since Sir Lewis died."

Recalling the state of Rosings's finances and the stern lectures he foisted upon his aunt every year, Darcy grimaced. "I cannot disagree. I, and my father before me, have done my utmost to improve things, but the estate is crumbling. The house is in dire need of repairs, the tenants are unhappy, and there is hardly any money left to fix anything. It might be a kindness to the heir, whoever they may be, to let Anne's will remain lost."

Fitzwilliam laughed darkly at that and stood, moving to the decanter behind Sir Lewis's desk. "I am sick of this subject. Let us choose another." He took a sip of his refreshed drink, released a gasp of appreciation, and returned to his seat. Crossing his feet before the empty hearth, he raised his glass at Darcy and said, "Cheers to your impending fatherhood."

Darcy hid his grimace by standing and repairing to the decanter himself.

"Why do I get the sense that you are not happy about this?"

Still refusing to face his cousin, who he knew could readily read his expressions, Darcy replied as lightly as he could, "I am happy. It is joyous news."

"Which is why it is odd that you do not wish to speak of it. Whenever the subject of Elizabeth's pregnancy is raised, your spirits take a decided plunge. Why is that?"

"I have no notion what you are talking about."

"I know when something is bothering you, just as I am certain your wife does. If you could bear to look at her when speaking of the baby, you would see that she is confused and hurt by your reticence."

Darcy clenched a fist down by his side. "You have barely known Elizabeth for a year. What makes you think you understand her looks?"

"Because, unlike you, she has an expressive face," Fitzwilliam replied, quite reasonably. "Her eyes, especially, reveal exactly what she is feeling, as I am sure you are well aware."

Of course he was aware of it. He drained half his glass before admitting, "I am frightened, Richard. For her."

A beat of silence. "Because of what happened to your mother?"

"She is hardly the only woman to have died in childbed. It is exceedingly common, you must know that, and my concern for Elizabeth's welfare is well founded."

"You must remember that Lady Anne was always delicate and sickly. Elizabeth is a hale, hearty girl with five sisters—she has as good a chance as anyone of being delivered safely."

Darcy set his glass aside and tangled his fingers in his hair, leaning back against the bookcase. "I cannot help worrying, nor can I help blaming myself for putting her in this position, in this *danger*. I have only just convinced her to love me, and now I could very well lose her forever. Is our time together to be so short?"

Fitzwilliam was up and across the room before Darcy had finished his speech, grasping his cousin by the shoulders. "Look at me, Darcy—*look at me*. You have not endangered your wife any more than any other husband.

The begetting of children is a consequence of marriage, you know that. There is no blame to be ascribed to you for any of it."

Darcy swallowed against the tightness swelling in his throat. "I cannot lose her. I could not bear it." He pressed his thumb and forefinger against his eyes, suppressing the tears that burnt behind his eyelids.

"Elizabeth is strong, and she will likely give you an equally strong brood of children before all is said and done. I expect at least one of them to be named after me, by the bye. Perhaps two. But I absolutely forbid you to call any of them Frederick."

A watery laugh escaped Darcy, splintering the worst of his anxiety and reestablishing his reason. When he had collected himself, he dropped his hand and blinked away the last of the moisture obscuring his vision. "That moniker is already taken, as you well know. Much to your brother's chagrin."

"He is only jealous that your dog bears it with more dignity than he does."

At one time, Darcy might have defended his elder cousin on this charge, but Marbury's most recent behaviour did not allow for it. "Indeed. I suggest that we take a break from our search"—he indicated the piles of paper surrounding them—"and return to it in an hour or two. I should like to see Elizabeth."

"If you are not careful, you will send your dear wife to Bedlam with all your cosseting."

Darcy scoffed but joked, "At least there she cannot wander off."

CHAPTER FOURTEEN

Darcy's hands shook as he fumbled with the spine of *Le Morte d'Arthur*, and he swore in frustration. At last, he managed to engage the mechanism that operated the hidden door, and it opened for him. He had burst through it and into Sir Lewis's study before the gears stopped whirring. "I cannot find her anywhere!"

Fitzwilliam sat up straight in his armchair, fully at attention. "What do you mean? Cannot find whom?"

"Elizabeth!" cried Darcy, stalking across the floor to stand immediately before his cousin. "I have looked everywhere. She is not in our chambers, she is not sitting with Lady Catherine, she is not in the gardens—she is *missing*."

Fitzwilliam stood, set his port aside, and held both his hands out to Darcy in a placatory manner. "You know how your wife likes to walk. She is very likely in the grounds somewhere. If not, I dare say we can find her in Mrs Collins's parlour."

"I have already been there! Mr Collins went on and on about Freddy turning up his bloody flowers before I could get him to tell me anything of the whereabouts of my wife. His only suggestion was that she must have returned to Rosings, but I met her neither on the way there nor on the way back." Darcy's panic was mounting at the recitation of each salient fact; he had never felt so helpless, not even in the wake of learning of Elizabeth's pregnancy. *Where can she be?*

"There are numerous paths through the woods. She might be strolling along any of them."

"She ought not to be walking here, there, and yon in her condition! She did not even take her maid with her."

"She is with child, not an invalid. Has she not been walking about Pemberley these past months?"

Darcy tunnelled his fingers through his hair and grasped it in frustration. It was becoming more difficult to breathe as his heart raced ever faster. "That is neither here nor there. We must focus our attention on the present. Elizabeth might be in danger."

"In danger from what? It is a pleasant spring day, warmer even than one would expect this time of year, and no highwayman who valued his hide would dare set foot at Rosings Park."

"She is not as familiar with the countryside hereabouts as she is at home. She might get lost, or injured, or suffer some other calamity without anyone nearby to assist her. Anything could happen."

"True, but she might as easily get struck by a carriage crossing the street in front of Darcy House. So might you or I for that matter." Fitzwilliam was admirably maintaining a low, soothing tone as he addressed his distressed cousin. "We cannot allow ourselves to fear the unknown, else we might never set foot outside our homes. Even there, your house might catch fire, or a bookshelf might topple over on you—"

"*Fitzwilliam.*"

"My point being, you cannot control the world around you. There will always be some chance of ill luck no matter what you do or where you go. You cannot coddle Elizabeth to such a degree that you deny her any freedom, else you will make her miserable."

Darcy readily recognised that his cousin's advice was sound, but he could not regulate the hysteria that was overtaking his composure. "I will not rest until we find Elizabeth."

Sighing and shaking his head, Fitzwilliam straightened the lapels of his jacket. "Lead on, then."

※

As Elizabeth and Freddy crossed the vast, fastidiously maintained great lawn of Rosings Park, they were hastily met by Darcy and Colonel Fitzwilliam. The former was dashing across the grass and leaping over shrubs in a manner that almost certainly would give the head gardener the vapours, while the latter jogged at a more reasonable pace in his cousin's wake.

"Elizabeth!" Darcy cried once he had reached her and enveloped her in his arms. Freddy barked and leapt upon them, but Darcy waved her away with one hand while cradling Elizabeth's head against his chest with the other. From the corner of her eye, she witnessed the colonel take the dog by the collar and tug her out of the way.

Elizabeth gasped at the sudden and fierce embrace. "What is wrong?"

Without releasing her, Darcy scolded, "Where have you been? I have been looking for you everywhere."

"I went to the parsonage, then I took a walk through the woods. You never mentioned the tow—"

Darcy set her away from himself, his expression dark and lightning crackling behind his eyes. "Without telling anyone where you were going? Without taking a maid with you? What were you thinking?"

"I was thinking that I am a grown woman who is free to do as she pleases, within reason. I cannot see how taking a walk is *un*reasonable. I have done it before, I dare say I shall do it again, and I do not understand your objection."

"You are *with child!*" he hissed, as if that resolved the matter. Perhaps it did to his satisfaction, but not hers.

She strove to speak with patience. "I was in no danger at any time during my excursion. I walk frequently—"

"Not at Rosings Park, you do not."

"I shall remind you, since you have apparently forgotten, that I was much in the habit of walking the groves hereabouts last spring, and no harm ever befell me then. You ought to recall it well since you frequently sought my company on those rambles. The only difference between then and now is the child I am carrying, but that is hardly reason to confine me to the house."

"I disagree." Darcy's nostrils flared as if he were an antagonised bull. "Anything might have happened to you, and you would have had no recourse. Did you think Freddy would come and fetch someone from the manor if you suffered an accident?"

Elizabeth glanced at Freddy, who was still being held back by an uncomfortable colonel a few yards away. She was a sweet, clever thing, but still a dog and not a fit companion should anything befall her mistress. However, she could concede nothing of the sort to Darcy. "You are being ridiculous. You do not even know what you are afraid of other than some unknowable calamity."

Darcy's response was like the harsh lash of a whip, swift and brutal in its delivery. "I am not being ridiculous. I am being properly cautious. You ought to learn a little something of caution before becoming a mother—do you not agree?"

Elizabeth felt this admonishment as a physical blow, which stung enough to bring tears to her eyes. It was one thing to fret internally over whether or not she would be a good mother but another entirely to hear her husband question her competency. Whatever small confidence Charlotte had inspired crumbled into dust.

Blinking rapidly, she stepped back and out of Darcy's hold. "I see. The reason you treat me like a child is because you doubt my ability to raise one."

"That is not what I meant—"

Elizabeth swiftly held up a hand—one which trembled with contained emotion. Her voice shook likewise. "I clearly have no notion of my own strength and am completely incapable of behaving responsibly. I ought to go indoors before I harm myself or the baby. Every moment I stand here I increase my risk of potential tragedy. What if a bird should fall from the sky, knock me on the head, and render me senseless?"

"Now who is being ridiculous?" Darcy lifted his hands only to drop them back to his sides, looking helplessly exasperated. "You have twisted what I said into something absurd."

"Not absurd at all—perfectly rational. Anything could happen. Excuse me, I ought to go and lie down before I collapse or fall into a hole in the lawn."

As she turned, Darcy reached out and lightly grasped her elbow, halting her. His expression was penitent, yet he still retained his air of righteousness. "I did not mean to be so harsh, but you must understand that you are no longer responsible only for yourself. There is our child to think of, and—"

She snatched her arm from his keeping and resumed stalking towards the house, calling out to him with her back turned, "I beg your leave, sir, for I am too enfeebled to continue in my condition. Do apologise to your aunt for me."

CHAPTER FIFTEEN

Elizabeth spent the remainder of the afternoon 'resting' in the bedchamber she shared with Darcy, blessedly alone. He had attempted to look in on her a couple of hours ago, but she had instructed Blake to send him away under the premise that her indolence was not to be disturbed. She had felt it prudent to brood a bit longer before attempting any semblance of dispassionate discourse lest it devolve immediately into another argument. *A short respite is all I need.*

Even so, it was time to come down from her high horse and prepare for dinner. The gong had sounded a quarter of an hour ago, and despite her lingering irritation, she had instructed Blake to dress her for the evening. Darcy had already come and gone, offering to make her excuses to Lady Catherine, and she had snappishly sent him off with a word over her cold shoulder.

He lingered just outside their bedchamber, standing

as stiffly as any of the suits of armour about them. "Are you certain you are well enough to go down?"

"If I feel faint, I shall signal you to fetch my salts."

Darcy muttered something indistinct under his breath and held out his arm for her. She took his elbow, and he led them both downstairs.

Their party was greatly diminished since last evening, what with the greater portion of the Matlock contingent returned to London and the Collinses at their own home. A glance at Anne's empty chair, placed near the hearth with a screen nearby to protect its absent owner from the heat, increased this sense and beset Elizabeth with palpable heartache. *What will it be like for her ladyship when the rest of us leave?*

Darcy led Elizabeth to a sofa, but she manoeuvred herself into a single chair. He breathed a subtle sigh and settled himself in the one beside her.

Lady Catherine looked at Elizabeth down the slope of her prominent nose. "I see you have finally decided to grace us with your presence, Miss Bennet. Were you really so unwell after your ill-advised walk that you required the entire afternoon to recover?"

On the edge of her vision, Elizabeth saw Darcy's jaw tighten. She laid a staying hand upon his clenched fist, forced as pleasant a smile as she could muster, and spoke quickly. "I am afraid I overestimated my stamina today. I am much refreshed now."

"You look lovely and refreshed to me, dear cousin. Far too good for the likes of Darcy," said the colonel from across the circle with a wink. She appreciated his attempt at levity, even if no one else did, and thanked him for the compliment.

"Balderdash, she is all peaky," declared Lady Catherine with a regal sniff. She then leant in and employed her spectacles, which hung about her neck by a chain, to observe Elizabeth more closely. "Are you positive you are well?"

My, but she does love to flatter me. "Perfectly so, your ladyship."

"Nonsense, you do not look healthful to me at all. You ought to partake of that tonic I recommended to you the other day to improve your constitution. Fortunately, I have taken the liberty of having some made up for you." Lady Catherine waved to a small phial of sickly yellow liquid on the tea table before her. Somewhere within the house, a bell jangled sharply.

"What is in it?" Darcy queried, eyeing the tonic with a suspicious tilt to his mouth.

She disregarded her nephew's query and addressed Elizabeth directly. "It is meant to be taken with tea to make it more palatable. Anne always said it had a bitter taste."

Elizabeth's uneasy gaze darted between the phial and her hostess. "Miss de Bourgh used to take this tonic?"

"Yes, twice daily. It did wonders for her."

Wonders, indeed! Right up until she died. "I thought… forgive me, I thought you mentioned before that this tonic was meant for women who are with child."

Lady Catherine waved her hand dismissively. "It is good for anyone, but especially those who suffer from weakness."

Somehow, Elizabeth doubted that very much. She did not think there was much comparison between her own condition and the late, poorly Anne's. "I thank you, but I truly do not require a tonic. I am quite well."

Lady Catherine scoffed. "If you were as well as you purport, you would eat my dinners. Do not think I am blind to the fullness of your plate every evening."

If Lady Catherine were to employ her memories of last spring, she might recall that Elizabeth had disdained her table then too. Rich sauces and tough meats had never been to her tastes, and being *enceinte* only increased her disgust of them.

"I shall admit to a sensitive stomach these days, but—"

"Ah, here we are." They all turned as the drawing room doors opened to admit a maid burdened with a tea tray. It boasted a pot as well as a single cup and saucer, making Elizabeth believe that it had been arranged just for her.

That mysterious bell chimed again out of sight, somehow louder and more urgently than before. She instinctively turned, searching for the source, but naturally one was not apparent from her position.

"It is best to take it before a meal, so it has a chance to improve your appetite."

The tray was placed upon the table between them, and the maid set about pouring a single cup of the steaming beverage. Into the brew was added, by Lady Catherine's own hand, a generous dose of the yellowish tonic, turning it a jaundiced tint. There was nothing else she could do when Lady Catherine all but thrust it into her hands; it was either take it or suffer an unpleasant burn.

When Elizabeth brought the steaming beverage up to

her face, she gagged as an acrid aroma filled her nose. She disguised it as a cough, but only after setting the tea away from her.

Darcy was immediately upon her, stroking her back. For once, she was pleased by his attentive ministrations. "Elizabeth, are you well?"

She blinked the sting from her eyes and nodded. When she spoke, her voice emerged as a croak. "Quite well."

He took up the teacup himself and proffered it to her from his own hand. "Drink your tea."

When Darcy lifted the cup to her lips, Elizabeth's stomach threatened to rebel again, and she pushed it aside. "N-Not just yet, thank you."

Darcy's eyes darted between his wife and the tea, and Elizabeth could practically see his brain making the connexion. After smelling the beverage himself, his expression shifted into one of subtle revulsion. He set the cup and saucer aside on the table. "I do not think Mrs Darcy ought to partake of this. It seems more liable to make her ill than give her strength."

"I agree," added the colonel, siding with his cousin. His face bore the faint signs of detecting a foul odour. "One cannot be too careful."

"It will help, I say," Lady Catherine impatiently snapped, her face turning a blotchy red. She then fixed her imperious stare upon Elizabeth and demanded, "Go on, drink it."

"You need not," countered Darcy, moving to push the cup farther away from her.

Even if the concoction smelt vile and she was sure she

could not possibly drink the entire cup, Elizabeth was willing to choke down a sip or two to preserve the peace. If she allowed Darcy and Lady Catherine to carry on like this, the breach they all sought to avoid would become imminent. "If it means so much to Lady Catherine, I shall try it."

Elizabeth lifted the tonic and brought it to her lips. Just as she was about to take a tentative sip, she was once again distracted by the chiming of bells. This time, it was a number of them, and they were jangling a frantic tune. She set the cup back in its saucer and frowned thoughtfully. "Do you hear that?"

"Hear what?" Darcy asked.

"The bells."

Their party was silent for several seconds, allowing the persistent jingling to fill the room. "That is odd," said the colonel, brow furrowed. "Why would they be ringing like that?"

"What difference does it make?" demanded Lady Catherine, slapping the arm of her golden throne. "Drink, girl!"

Before the porcelain could so much as touch her lips, the cup was somehow wrenched from her fingers and flung away from her. Elizabeth turned her head to follow the sudden motion and observed with wide, aghast eyes as it landed in Lady Catherine's lap, soaking her skirts and bodice. Not unreasonably, her ladyship shrieked at the sudden assault.

Both Darcy and Fitzwilliam were on their feet a moment later, rushing to their aunt's aid. She pushed them aside and stalked away, screeching invectives as she swept from the room in a cloud of black bombazine.

The maid who had poured the tea scampered after her, calling for Mrs Knight.

The bells slowed their tolling and at last grew silent.

Could it be...? Elizabeth's eyes darted about her, half expecting to see an inexplicable shadow, perhaps in the form of a slender young woman, looming over the back of Lady Catherine's throne. She saw nothing out of place aside from the overturned teacup.

It was an accident, nothing more. There are no spirits lurking about and abusing the crockery. Such she told herself, yet she was not wholly certain she believed it.

"Elizabeth, are you burnt?" Darcy asked, kneeling next to her chair.

"No, not at all. Merely confused. I do not know what happened."

The colonel, who stood watching her with mild concern over her husband's shoulder, admitted to his own bafflement. "It looked almost as if the cup were wrested from your hand and flung at Lady Catherine."

"I swear I did not intentionally target her."

"No, of course not," said Darcy, shooting a glare at his cousin.

"I did not mean to imply you had," the colonel said with an apologetic bow. "It is just so strange."

"Elizabeth has been rather clumsy of late," Darcy said, eyeing her speculatively. "The midwife said it was common for an expectant mother to fumble things."

Elizabeth frowned at him. "I did not 'fumble' anything. It went flying across the room."

Darcy raised a brow at her. "Do you have a better explanation?"

She opened her mouth to retort but found she had

no alternative theory to offer. The inkling of one tickling her brain would be dismissed outright as preposterous, and fairly so. "I believe I ought to return to our rooms, for I do not imagine Lady Catherine will wish to see me again this evening. I shall make a point of apologising to her tomorrow."

***

Stupid, clumsy girl! Lady Catherine was beside herself with fury as she thrust open the double doors of her chambers, sending them flying into the walls behind them. The plaster would be cracked, but she hardly cared; it was already in disrepair from similar strikes. *Why would she not simply* drink *it? Then we might all be rid of her!*

She went immediately to her dressing room, where her lady's maid had the good sense to already be present. Renfield trembled as she undressed and re-dressed her mistress.

When Lady Catherine re-emerged, it was to unwelcome news. Mrs Knight stood with hands folded primly at her waist. "Your guests have sent their regrets for dinner, my lady, and will be taking trays in their rooms."

"What, all of them?"

"Yes, ma'am."

Lady Catherine banished her housekeeper from her sight without so much as a thank you, furious at this turn of events. There would be no further opportunities that evening to press Miss Bennet into taking the tonic. *Curse that wily chit! And my nephew for hovering so diligently.*

She lowered herself into a chair by the fire. "I shall

simply have to invite my new niece to a private tea tomorrow, just the two of us, where Darcy cannot intervene."

Elsewhere in the house, those accursed bells began ringing again. Lady Catherine shouted to no one in particular, "Cease that infernal chiming!"

Against her express wishes, the bells continued their defiant tune, assailing her ears relentlessly. None of the servants she called up could determine the source, though they flitted about the place searching for one. In the end, the ringing ceased as abruptly as it had started, the perpetrator undiscovered.

CHAPTER SIXTEEN

Elizabeth woke to the clear, resonating sound of a bell. She was uncertain how it had roused her at all, being so sweet and quiet, but it vibrated on the air as she sat up in bed. Beside her, Darcy slumbered on, apparently unconscious of any out-of-place sounds.

The fire crackled lazily in the hearth, bathing the bedchamber in an ambient glow. Even so, the room was chilly, and Elizabeth rubbed the goose-skin rising on her arms. It never felt so cold at Pemberley, not even in the winter.

Presuming that she had been roused by the tolling of the hour, Elizabeth dragged the covers up to her neck and edged closer to Darcy's warmth. As she was beginning to recline, the bell chimed again from somewhere behind her.

Her spine stiffened, and she sat up rigidly straight, unaccountably fearful of what she would find when she turned round. Her pulse beat erratically at the thought, but she knew she must. The anticipation of the unknown was equally as frightening, if not more so, as facing whatever lurked in the shadows beyond her vision. Slowly, tentatively, she inclined her head until she was looking over her right shoulder.

The door to the hall stood wide open. Elizabeth knew very well that it had been closed before she and Darcy had gone to bed. The servants used the dressing room to enter and leave the chamber, so she doubted that either her maid or his valet were the culprits. Were they being spied upon by persons unknown?

Elizabeth jostled Darcy's shoulder to wake him. He grumbled incoherently but did not otherwise stir.

"Fitzwilliam," she hissed, glancing over her shoulder at the open door. A shadow appeared on the wall in the corridor, alternately stretching and contracting as it drew closer. She could hear footsteps now.

Elizabeth's sense of alarm rose to new heights, and she whipped back round to her husband, redoubling her efforts to rouse him. "Wake up. Please, please wake up!" Still, Darcy remained deeply asleep.

Creak.

Petrified, Elizabeth held perfectly still, her only movement her heaving chest as she struggled to breathe.

Ding.

She swallowed, gathered her beleaguered courage, and turned to face the doorway.

Therein stood a small, willowy figure cloaked in brilliant white. She wore what appeared to be a nightgown, with her long, alabaster hair falling lank about her shoulders. She glowed brightly yet held no candle to account for her radiance, so Elizabeth knew that she must be in the presence of someone no longer living.

This notion was confirmed when she realised that she recognised the pale lady. She gasped out her unearthly visitor's name. "Miss de Bourgh!"

Anne de Bourgh, save for her nighttime attire and unbound hair, appeared just as she had in life when Elizabeth had made her acquaintance the previous spring. Then, as now, she was so colourless as to be nearly translucent, with her milky pallor, white-blonde hair, and faint grey eyes. She was thin and small, almost childlike in stature, and generally withered in appearance.

Even as Elizabeth took in the wraith that was once Darcy's dear cousin, her horror dwindled. Anne was no longer among the living, it was true, but there was no sense of danger about her either. She stood there placidly on the other side of the threshold, patiently waiting for Elizabeth to acknowledge her. She did not lunge, nor did she make any effort to frighten; she merely waited. As if she wanted something.

"Do-do you wish to speak to your cousin?" Elizabeth ventured, indicating the slumbering Darcy with a trembling hand.

Anne opened her mouth as if to reply, but no words were forthcoming. Her brow furrowed in consternation, and she tried again to no better success. At length, she resorted to a simple shake of the head—*No*.

Inhaling a deep breath through her nose, Elizabeth released it shakily. "Do you require something?"

Again, she moved her mouth as if intending to speak,

but no sound emerged. She drew her lips into a thin line, visibly frustrated, then nodded—*Yes*.

It seemed that Anne, even if she had managed to pierce the veil and re-enter the living world, could not easily communicate. With this in mind, Elizabeth would have to compose her queries carefully to ensure that a simple yes or no would suffice.

Just to be certain of Anne's purpose, Elizabeth asked again, "Are you here to speak to Mr Darcy?"

No.

"Do you wish to speak to me?"

Yes.

Elizabeth was taken aback. Although she had been acquainted with Anne prior to her death, no one would have ever accused them of a deeper connexion than that. It occurred to her with a start that perhaps this haunting was a consequence of her marriage. Was Anne restless in her grave because Elizabeth had ostensibly snatched Darcy away from her?

"Are you angry with me for marrying Mr Darcy?"

Anne seemed to laugh, though it was silent, and shook her head—*No.*

"So you are not here to punish me for stealing him from you?"

No.

Elizabeth breathed a sigh of relief. "Thank goodness. Do you wish me to pass on some sort of message?"

Anne stood there for a moment, face scrunched in thought, before offering a faltering nod—*Yes.*

"You did not wish to speak to Mr Darcy, so…Colonel Fitzwilliam?"

No.

"Lady Catherine?"

The light that set Anne aglow intensified, making her difficult to look at directly. Elizabeth shielded her eyes until her otherworldly visitor dimmed again. Once she had, she delivered an emphatic shake of the head—*No!*

"Is the message for your uncle? Or the viscount?" Elizabeth proceeded to list off all their common acquaintances, including the Collinses, but received a negative response for each. It was not long before she had exhausted all the possibilities and could conjure up no more. "Perhaps if I knew what the message was, I would know whom to deliver it to. Can you tell me what it is?"

Again, Anne made the effort to speak with no success.

"I forgot you cannot talk. Forgive me. Can you write it down?"

Anne slumped her shoulders, shaking her head in apparent defeat. Then she straightened and turned as if to leave, beckoning Elizabeth.

"You wish for me to follow you?"

Yes.

Elizabeth bit her lip, unsure whether she was willing to leave the relative safety of her bed and husband. Anne continued to linger patiently in the doorway, deciding Elizabeth in favour of going. The poor girl was watching her with palpable longing and not a trace of menace about her countenance; she seemed desperate for aid.

With one last glance at Darcy—as well as a quiet apology for doing something she knew he would disapprove of—Elizabeth climbed out of bed, slipped on her dressing gown, and approached Anne, who rapidly disappeared down the hall and out of sight. Elizabeth paused at the threshold, her heart fluttering wildly in her chest, and hesitated to follow. Recalling Anne's pleading entreaty, she stepped out into the hall.

※

Elizabeth awoke with a start, her heart hammering within her chest and the babe in her belly fluttering wildly. Beside her, Darcy snorted and roused himself, crying out, "What is the matter?"

At first, Elizabeth did not answer him, for she was unsure of the truth. After he urgently prodded her to respond, she managed a raspy, "I-I believe I was dreaming."

"Are you well?" Darcy asked, more urgently still.

"I—yes, I am well." She placed her hand upon the protrusion of her midsection and felt the child calm beneath her fingertips. "It was only a dream."

It had been an intensely vivid one, rife with intricate detail, but still only a dream. Anne de Bourgh had not escaped her tomb to visit in the darkness, nor was she attempting to convey any sort of message to the living. *It was only a dream.*

Beneath her fright, she found herself oddly disappointed, as if she had read a story to the end only for it to falter on the last page. As if the monster stalking the protagonist had turned out to be a man after all, one who merely sought to steal her dowry and not her living soul. A kinder conclusion but deeply unsatisfying.

Darcy drew her closer and pulled her head to his chest where she could hear his heart thudding stridently against his ribcage. He pressed a kiss to her temple and breathed out a relieved, "Thank God."

They lay back, tangled together, and Darcy's breathing evened out a short time later; he had fallen back to sleep. Elizabeth lay awake picturing the ghostly visage of Anne lurking just out of sight and jumping at every ringing stroke of the hour.

CHAPTER SEVENTEEN

When Elizabeth woke again, it was to an empty bed. She squinted against the harsh sunlight streaming in through the bowed window, groggy and confused. *Where am I?* A handful of blinking seconds more and her recollections crystallised into sharp reality. *I am at Rosings Park. Anne's funeral was three days ago. Where is Fitzwilliam?*

A glance at the clock nearest her bedside explained both her solitude and the harsh quality of the morning—it was nearly nine, well past her usual time to rise and begin her day. Her husband, no doubt, was already up and about; he could never manage to sleep much past the cockerel's crow.

She stretched out her aching back, and her spine crackled and popped in protest. To the empty room, she complained, "How wretchedly exhausted I am."

Between her wriggling babe—who seemed inclined to dance a merry jig every time Elizabeth lay down to rest—and that disconcerting dream featuring Anne, it was no wonder she had slept so ill. After waking from it, she had not returned to sleep until…she did not actually know, but she recalled lying awake for a long while, incapable of repose. Each time she managed to sink into a doze, the chiming of the hall clock roused her; there was something quite ominous in the ringing of a bell in the darkness of night.

A folded sheet of hot-pressed paper lay upon Darcy's otherwise vacant pillow. She plucked it up and read:

My dearest, loveliest Elizabeth,
As you did not sleep well last night, I could not bear to wake you this morning. I advise you to remain where you are for the rest of the day and allow me to make your excuses to Lady Catherine, as well as your apologies for last night.
If you should require my attendance, send a servant to find me in the study, where I shall be for much of the day. I shall come and see you around midday, and we may eat together. I have high hopes that you can be tempted by plainer fare and have already ordered the kitchen to procure broth, toast, and such.

Yours &c,
F

PS – If my aunt sends up more of that horrid tea, I beg you to refuse it.

There was no question of either accepting or rejecting it, for she intended to be far away from the house if and when it arrived. "A walk will be just the thing to clear my head this morning. Fitzwilliam will simply have to accept that I shall not lie abed for nonsensical reasons."

Elizabeth kicked off her covers and rang the bell for her maid—though she winced at the echoing chime rising up from the depths of the house. She banished the irrational spike of alarm at the sound and moved to sit at the dressing table, where she began to unwind her plait.

After dressing and eating a quick breakfast from a tray in her room, she all but scampered downstairs. Darcy was already shut up in the study, and Lady Catherine was known to sleep until at least eleven, so there was little danger in passing the Throne Room at this hour. She would have to be cautious upon re-entering the manor to avoid detection, but for now she was free to roam about the grounds without fear of being detained.

Once out of doors, Elizabeth breathed in the cool, fresh air before releasing a satisfied sigh. *There is nothing like a brisk walk to set one to rights.*

She skipped down the front steps and proceeded directly to the kennels, where Freddy greeted her with a happy bark. Fondly scratching the dog's ears, she cooed, "There's my girl! Are you ready for a nice walk?"

"Good morning, Cousin."

Suppressing her vexation at being caught, Elizabeth turned to see the colonel standing nearby with a cheerful grin spread across his face. Her smile in return, she knew, was weak. *I forgot about him. Why is he not poring over papers with my husband?*

She offered him a reluctant greeting. "Good morning."

There was a glint of laughter in the officer's eye as he said, "Do not look so happy to see me, else your husband will grow jealous. I have only just managed to talk Darcy out of fighting my brother—do not waste my efforts by making me his next target."

Freddy abandoned her to bound up to the new arrival, and the colonel happily obliged her bid for attention. As he vigorously fondled her ears, he asked, "Are you off for one of your walks?"

"I am."

"Do you mind if I invite myself to accompany you? I survey the park every year, as you know, and your charming company would be greatly appreciated as I do so."

She lifted a sceptical brow, imagining she was peering at him over a pair of spectacles. "And you just so happened to come across me for this purpose?"

"Indeed. I am a man given to taking opportunities when they are presented."

Weary of maintaining her veneer of cold politeness, to which her disposition was not suited, Elizabeth's shoulders slumped. "My husband put you up to this. Is he to follow me about by proxy now?"

Chuckling, her companion shook his head. "Darcy is unaware of my movements, I assure you. Last I saw of him, he was holed up in the study writing to my father, who demands frequent intelligence on our search for Anne's will. Not that there is much to report, as yet. In any case, it does not require the pair of us to pen a letter, so I allowed the pleasant weather to lure me out."

"A most convenient story."

"Believe what you will, but it is the truth."

Elizabeth narrowed her eyes, searching for any hint of chicanery in the colonel. He allowed her inspection without complaint, waiting for her to finish with his smile firmly in place. "My husband truly did not send you to follow me about?"

"I cannot say that he would not have done, had the thought occurred to him, but, as far as I am aware, he thinks you are still abed. I am here entirely of my own volition and desire, though I feel increasingly unwanted."

Elizabeth's stance eased, at last convinced of the man's innocence. "I apologise. I have been made wary by his protectiveness of late."

He offered Elizabeth his arm, which she accepted. They began strolling away from the kennels towards the woodland, following the path that would split off into many smaller ones beneath the verdant canopy. Freddy scampered alongside them, nose to the ground and following the zig-zagging trail of some fascinating scent. "It is Darcy's way to take care of others. He has always done so. Even as a lad he was constantly admonishing his friends to take more care in their exploits and abstain from doing anything outrageously foolish. I cannot express to you how irritating it was. And you should have seen him with Anne! He hovered every bit as much as Mrs Jenkinson when she first fell ill, until she at last convinced him to stop."

Elizabeth looked to the colonel with palpable interest. "How? Perhaps I should employ the same method."

Smiling devilishly, he replied, "She cast up her accounts on him after he insisted upon carrying her from one room to another. I cannot say that she did so on purpose, of course, but she did make a point of complaining that his jostling upset her stomach."

She grimaced. "How revolting."

"Yet effective. After that, he was more willing to listen to her when she objected to his ministrations."

"How do I force him to listen to *my* objections?"

"Appealing to Darcy's sense of reason is the only way to deal with him. Make sure to be specific about your demands—otherwise he will continue to do whatever he believes to be best and endure your charming scowls."

"*Colonel.*"

"Apologies. It is in my nature to be sporting at the worst possible times." More seriously, he asked, "I assume you know why Darcy is so fretful over your pregnancy? Aside from his usual inclination to coddle everyone, I mean."

"No, I cannot say that I do."

There was a pause of poignant silence from the colonel, during which he became yet more solemn. "Do you recall how his mother died?"

Elizabeth halted in place, her eyes growing wide. One of her hands rose up to cup her mouth, and she emitted a breathless, "Oh."

Her companion stopped walking likewise and, with a tender expression of recollected pain, said, "I see it did not occur to you before now, but Darcy is absolutely terrified—*terrified*, I tell you—that you will meet the same fate as Lady Anne in childbed. He was nearly twelve, you know, when she died giving birth to Georgiana, and it has stuck with him, as it would any child. After her death, he witnessed his father slide further and further into grief, blaming himself for what happened, and I think that had as much effect on my cousin as the death itself. To his mind, you are in danger, and he is the one to have put you there."

"Childbearing is a natural consequence of marriage—he must know that."

"Of course he does, in a rational sense, but his love for you makes him entirely *ir*rational at times. Were he to lose you…well, I do not like to think of that. He would never be the same man again, just as he is not the same as he was before his mother died. Only worse, because now he has fewer people remaining to comfort him."

Elizabeth was powerfully ashamed of herself for not making the connexion between Lady Anne's demise and Darcy's overbearing worry. Georgiana had mentioned to her previously that their mother had succumbed after giving birth to her, but Elizabeth had thought little of it since. She was not unsympathetic to Darcy's loss—certainly not!—but, having never suffered the death of a parent herself, she had not considered the influence such an event might have upon him. Of course he would be nervous for her after seeing the way his mother's life had ended; it was only natural.

Tears, which had been her good friends of late, sprung to her lashes, and she fought to blink them away, but they fell regardless. "I am such a fool for not seeing this sooner. A terrible wife!"

A large handkerchief appeared in her line of vision, and she accepted it, burying her sodden face within its folds. "You are not a terrible wife. I have never seen my cousin so happy as he has been since your marriage, and that is entirely due to you."

Elizabeth could feel Freddy pawing at her leg, whining helplessly. *Dear, sweet creature. I do not deserve your comfort.* "I cannot help but to cry. And I *am* a terrible wife! How could I be so insensible to his pain?"

She felt a large hand awkwardly patting her back. "Do not let Darcy catch you saying so, or he will be more overbearing than ever. If you think he is difficult now, just wait until he thinks you require more of his devotion—you will never shake him."

Elizabeth could not help it: she giggled. It came out as something of a gurgle, but her mood was instantly lightened. She emerged from the depths of the handkerchief, sniffling but managing a tremulous smile. "Oh dear, he really would begin carrying me about, would he not?"

"There can be no doubt of that. I can picture it now!" cried the colonel, waving his hand before him as if attempting to conjure the image in the air. "He will have one of those grand palanquins built for you, all done up with fine draperies and an abundance of pillows. He will hire four—no, *eight*—footmen to cart you about, and he will lead the procession like the ringmaster at Astley's. You will be the talk of the *ton,* and all the other ladies will insist on having their own palanquins. It will be a new fashion. Really, you must cheer up and think well of yourself, else you will be endangering the backs of every male servant from here to Newcastle."

By the time he had finished describing his scene, Elizabeth was again dabbing at her eyes with the handkerchief, but only because they were leaking with mirth. "My goodness, but you do paint a picture. Very well, for the sake of others, I shall make an effort to think better of myself."

The colonel swept the hat from his head and bowed to her with a flourish. "The servant class of our great kingdom thanks you, madam."

Upon rising from his ridiculous bow and replacing his beaver, he held out his arm for her to take again. Elizabeth did so, and they resumed their perambulation at an easy pace. Save for a few sniffles and dampness upon her cheeks, the only sign of her troubles was a lingering gravity that she could not entirely banish.

"I shall speak to my husband when we return to the house, per your suggestion," she said, full of purpose. "Hopefully, with it all out in the open, we can come to some sort of compromise while also quieting his concerns. I thank you, sir, for your excellent advice."

"I am no Lady Catherine, but I do my best."

She laughed wanly at this jest, shaking her head at him, and they settled into a comfortable silence as they strolled down the lane. Freddy remained close, occasionally bumping against her mistress's leg or licking her gloved palm. *She truly is the sweetest thing.*

The day was, if anything, more pleasant than the one before, with less wind and chill. Along the roadside, various flowers were in bloom, dotting the grass with an assortment of colours. There were sweet violets, crocuses, daffodils, and various others, but the greatest preponderance was wood anemone. The soft white and pink blooms created a carpet upon the woodland floor, leading deeper into the trees. Elizabeth noted that they seemed especially thick upon the short path that led to Anne's tower as they passed it.

"So, ah...how does your sister do?" the colonel asked, breaking the quiet.

Elizabeth turned her face up to his but found him pointing it studiously ahead of them. There was a light flush of pink high on his cheekbones, only slightly disguised by the shade of his hat.

"You mean Jane?" She thought she understood him to be asking after Kitty—whom he had rescued from the clutches of the dastardly Wickham the previous summer—but chose to be coy in her answer. Her second youngest sister had been reticent about the colonel, but there had been a bashful look about her when he was mentioned at Pemberley on the eve before Elizabeth's wedding to Darcy. She had believed it to be an adolescent romantic whimsy without reciprocation, but the colonel was telling in his awkward questioning. "She and Mr Bingley are settling well into their new house in town. They are greatly anticipating the forthcoming Season."

If she were not mistaken, her companion winced slightly. "I meant your other sister."

Elizabeth could not help a wry smirk and felt that her jocular cousin was not the only one inclined to be sportive at inappropriate times. "I have three other sisters besides Jane. You must be more specific, sir."

"Miss Kitty, I am asking after the welfare of Miss Kitty, as I am sure you are well aware. Take pity and spare me your japes, if you please."

"You have caught me out. I was teasing you. Kitty is well—or as well as can be after her ordeal."

Lowering his head to fix Elizabeth with a serious expression, his jaw tight, the colonel asked, "Is she truly so miserable over Wickham? I explained to her that he was a scoundrel, but that mangy cur has a way with young ladies that sticks with them. I do hope she is not still enamoured of him."

"Oh! No, that is not my meaning," Elizabeth hurried to say. "I do not believe Kitty was ever really enamoured of Mr Wickham, merely taken in by his flattery for a short period. She has always been weak to a compliment." *Likely because she does not receive enough of them at home.*

His shoulders sagged, and Elizabeth had the sense that he was relieved. "I am glad to hear it."

"What I meant was that her sense of personal safety, her trust in people—especially men—has been shaken. She attempted to back out of the elopement at the last moment, did you know?"

"I did. It was then that I intervened."

Pressing his forearm, Elizabeth silently conveyed her gratitude. "And my entire family is thankful for it. In any case, Wickham's refusal to accept her reversal, and how roughly he treated her, must have been quite frightening. She has flinched away from almost every man since."

"I am sorry to hear it. I would not wish for her experience with Wickham to colour her opinion of my sex unduly. She ought to be allowed to find her own happiness one day."

"One day, she will meet a gentleman, or perhaps renew an acquaintance with an old, reliable friend"—Elizabeth slid her gaze to Colonel Fitzwilliam, but his expression betrayed no consciousness—"and feel comfortable enough to consider him. Until then, there is no rush, for she only recently turned eighteen."

"If that should happen," he replied, his voice low and somewhat melancholy, "I shall wish her joy. She is a sweet girl deserving of every good thing."

"She is."

They said no more for a good length of time until the colonel offered a non-sequitur. "Did my cousin ever explain to you how Freddy got her name?"

Freddy grinned up at them and wagged as if in anticipation of an amusing story and pleased about her part in it. Elizabeth smiled. "Do tell."

"In point of fact, she is named after my brother."

Elizabeth snorted, a consequence of attempting to stifle her amusement. "How did that come about?"

The colonel's mouth spread into a grin that could only be described as wicked. "It will not entirely surprise you to learn that my brother can sometimes be a right bit— Ahem, *boor,* and I thought it an appropriate tribute to name one of Darcy's female pups after him. Marbury did not especially care for it, of course, and Darcy attempted to change it to no avail. I do own some regret over the business, however." Here, he sighed with gusto, making a great show of his feigned penitence. "I feel I have grievously wronged my canine friend, for now she is stuck with an unpleasant association to a fat-witted coxcomb. She deserves better, I think."

Elizabeth swatted his arm, though it was done with more playfulness than censure. "You are incorrigible!"

CHAPTER EIGHTEEN

After walking a mile or two, Elizabeth was ready to admit fatigue and turn back. They returned Freddy to the kennels and continued on towards the manor.

They found Darcy in the entrance hall, struggling to don a glove while barking at a footman to make haste in fetching his hat. His head lifted when the door closed behind them, abandoning the recalcitrant article to the side table as he rushed over, demanding, "Where have you been?"

The colonel leant in Elizabeth's direction and spoke in a whisper that echoed off the marble lining the hall. "See? I told you he did not send me to follow you."

Darcy fixed a glare upon Elizabeth. "I went upstairs to see you, only to find you absent. Blake told me that you had gone walking again, expressly against my wishes."

Instead of feeling that familiar upsurge of irritation with him, Elizabeth experienced only the softness of pity for the young boy who had lost his mother too soon and the man who feared his beloved wife would leave him the same way. She relinquished her companion's arm and went to her husband, taking both his hands in hers. From the periphery of her vision, she saw the colonel silently slip away, leaving them to themselves. "Forgive me, my love, I ought to have been more considerate."

Darcy eyed her suspiciously. "You regret walking out? Does this mean you are feeling unwell? I can call for the apothecary if need be, or take you back to London to see my own physician—"

Shaking her head, Elizabeth calmly interrupted his brewing distress. "I am perfectly well, I assure you. What I meant was that I should not have been so dismissive of your feelings, that is all."

"So you will refrain from overtaxing yourself from now on? Stay where I can watch over you?"

Elizabeth's heart constricted at the pained hopefulness in Darcy's voice. She squeezed his hands, a silent communication of understanding. "Let us adjourn to greater privacy"—she nodded at the space around them, which bustled with the activity of a grand house—"and discuss this further. I am certain we can reach a compromise."

The wariness lingered on her husband's features, but he nodded his agreement. "Very well. Then let us do so in our chambers. I would like you to rest."

Elizabeth's lips quirked with amusement at her husband's expense. "I shall submit, but only if you promise to listen to what I have to say. I shall likewise promise to listen to you in return."

Just as Darcy was leading them to the staircase—"Are

you certain you do not wish for me to carry you?"—a strident voice abruptly imposed itself upon their notice. "Darcy, is that you? Attend to me at once."

Elizabeth sagged with frustration. "Is it too late to pretend we did not hear?"

Darcy urged her closer to the stairs with his hand upon her lower back. "Go on up. I shall make your excuses."

"No, no, I shall come with you, else you will have no reason to leave her for hours. Besides, I owe her an apology for the incident with the tea. What say I begin to yawn in ten minutes? Then we may both escape upstairs for our conversation."

Darcy kissed the backs of her fingers. "Very well, but only because I am determined to see you to our chambers myself. You might slip away again if I turn my back."

Hugging his arm to her—the greatest display of affection she could show in a public space—Elizabeth assured him, "I promise I shall not. I swear to stay with you always."

As Collins droned on about the same tedious topics he covered daily—her condescension, his gratitude, grief over Anne, and so on ad nauseum—Lady Catherine listened with only half an ear. Her parson never said anything of interest to anyone; his greatest value was in following her commands without the inconvenience of questioning them.

She might have interrupted him or sent him away,

but the headache throbbing behind her eyes meant it was far easier to let him carry on with his endless condolences while she stared blankly at nothing and sipped her willow bark tea. She had not slept well of late, finding herself frequently jarred from repose by odd noises: creaking doors, soft footsteps, muffled sobbing, the incessant jangling of a bell—all of them issuing from her daughter's room. This would have caused her no concern save for the fact that Anne was *dead*.

The first few times it had occurred, Lady Catherine had risen from her bed and stalked into Anne's former bedchamber only to find no one present. She had, naturally, believed the perpetrator to be hiding and demanded that they show themselves, but no one would come forwards. Even a search of the room turned up no sign of anyone besides herself.

Dreams, that is all, she had concluded after several interrupted nights. *Though why I should conjure fancies of trespassers in Anne's rooms, I have no earthly idea.*

"It was devastation! That horrible beast dug up half my flowers and nearly all of my—"

"Where have you been?"

Lady Catherine settled her teacup into its saucer with an inelegant clatter as Darcy's shout overpowered Collins's monotonous diatribe about his garden. It was followed by the softer murmur of other voices, one of which was the lighter feminine tone of that lowborn wife of his. She could not make out what they were saying with any clarity.

"I say, that was—"

"Quiet!" Lady Catherine barked, silencing Collins

and straining to listen. The dolt shrank back in his chair as if she had physically struck him into compliance.

"...went upstairs...to find you gone...expressly against my wishes."

Darcy seemed to have gained control of himself, for Lady Catherine could discern nothing more than reverberating murmurs after that. She had heard enough to understand the gist of their conversation, however, and a gleeful smile crept across her lips. *It seems my nephew is regretting his choice already. I need to see this for myself.*

"Darcy, is that you?" she called. "Attend to me at once."

There was no direct response, merely more incoherent muttering, and she was on the point of sending Collins to fetch them when the door opened and Darcy strolled in with Miss Bennet on his arm. Her nephew did not look best pleased to be there, but then that was his usual way; he had sported that grim expression in her presence since he was a boy.

As for Miss Bennet, she blithely walked into the room as if she belonged there, as if she were not present on Lady Catherine's sufferance. She smiled in that coy, teasing way that had always characterised her expressions, and Lady Catherine had no doubt that she was mightily pleased with herself for having ensnared Darcy and elevated herself to a sphere in which she did not belong. *I would cast her out but for the sweetness I anticipate from my revenge.*

"There you are. It has been an age since I have seen either of you."

"Apologies, Aunt," said Darcy as he gently settled Miss Bennet on the sofa nearest to her. He then took the seat next to his so-called wife. "Mrs Darcy has required more rest of late. It was not our intention to neglect you."

"If Miss Bennet is so unwell, you really ought to try the tonic I recommended last evening." The same tonic that had ended up in her lap; her lip curled at the recollection. "Of course, one must actually *drink* it for it to be effective."

The clock struck one, and Lady Catherine frowned at it. The hands read a quarter past midday; it must still be broken even though she distinctly recalled ordering its repair.

Miss Bennet cleared her throat. "I owe you an apology for upsetting my tea into your lap. I have no notion of how it happened, but I must have been clumsy and incautious. I do hope you can forgive me."

Never. "If you are truly repentant, you will partake now. Collins, ring the bell and order a fresh pot of tea."

"Of course, my lady! Right away. I have always lauded the benefits of a good cup of tea and—"

"*Now.*"

Collins stumbled to his feet and scurried across the room.

"Given that your tonic provokes Mrs Darcy's stomach—"

"I have always much admired this room," Miss Bennet said, interrupting her husband. He glowered at her, but she continued without paying him any mind. "The theme is fascinating. Sir Lewis was knighted, was he not?"

Lady Catherine nodded. "Yes, it was a great source of pride to him and his father. They renovated Rosings Park in honour of his title. Arthur de Bourgh did not live to see it finished, of course, but they undertook most of the project together." *And nearly bankrupted the estate trying to fashion it after a medieval castle. Imbeciles.*

Miss Bennet's lips twitched. "Arthur de Bourgh? What a happy coincidence."

Impertinent chit. "Quite."

Sir Lewis had been a silly nincompoop of the same ilk as Collins, lacking the dignity of his station or the wit to manage an estate without running it into the ground. Of course, had he not done so, he would not have required Lady Catherine's dowry and contracted their marriage, so she supposed that she must be glad of his idiocy to a point. Even if Sir Lewis had been an oaf so enamoured of fairy stories that he had wasted the bulk of his fortune, he had at least left her Rosings. Well, he had left Rosings to *Anne*, but that amounted to the same thing—until Anne had reached her majority. After that, stewardship of the estate had become more…complicated, but Lady Catherine had managed. She was confident that Rosings Park would devolve to her in the end; it was hers by divine right.

While Rosings had been grand at one time, it was sadly beginning to show its wear. Lady Catherine made a point of covering up the most egregious cracks and stains with tapestries and the like, but without more extensive repairs it would continue to wilt in the same fashion as the daffodils Collins had brought her. Her refined taste and keen eye for furnishings could only go so far. *Curse that artful girl. Were it not for her, Darcy would have married my daughter and funded all the necessary improve-*

ments. *Because of her, I am forced to resort to patching and covering blemishes like a painted whore.*

The maid arrived with a fresh pot of tea, forestalling any further conversation on the subject. The tray was piled high with various edibles as well, which Darcy foisted upon his wife as if she had not eaten in a week. Instead of issuing him the same sort of irritated glower she had sported during their recent encounters, Miss Bennet smiled sweetly and made no protest as he filled her plate. There was no way the girl would ever eat even half so much, but she seemed content to allow him his peculiarities. Lady Catherine wondered what had changed her position on Darcy's overbearing manner.

As it did not matter and she did not especially care, she turned her attention to pouring the tea. Into Miss Bennet's cup she added a large dollop of the tonic and a heaping teaspoon of sugar to disguise the taste, then stirred the concoction until it was perfectly blended. She passed it to the trollop, who accepted it with a murmur of thanks. The blasted clock chimed again, this time thrice, and she glared at it; she would enquire of Mrs Knight which of the servants merited dismissal for disregarding her explicit command. She would not stand for such egregious laziness. "My lady!"

Lady Catherine was afforded no more warning than this before Collins abruptly flung himself upon her person and wrestled her to the floor. She shrieked in protest, but it was barely audible above the deafening crash that coincided with it. A subsequent crisp tearing sound, like fabric being violently rent, followed, then a crunch, a crash, and finally comparative silence.

"Get off me!" Lady Catherine snarled, thrusting

Collins's meaty body from her own. He smelt abhorrent. *Does the man never bathe?*

Collins tumbled onto the floor and curled on his side, groaning in pain. "F-Forgive me, your ladyship," he wheezed, his face contorting with every slight movement. He then collapsed into an insensible heap, having fainted.

She raised herself upon the point of her elbow and found herself bemused by the bits of rubble that tumbled about her. She inclined her head to where she had been seated and discovered that her beloved chair lay in pieces beneath an enormous painting. The portrait of King Arthur—previously suspended above the mantelpiece—had fallen from its prominent position and been ripped to shreds on the jagged remains of her ruined throne. The tea table had also collapsed, crushed beneath the debris that had so unceremoniously fallen upon it. Her tea service had not survived the ordeal either.

It occurred to her that Collins had perhaps just saved her life. *I suppose I must reward him for this.*

"Aunt, are you injured?"

Lady Catherine turned towards her nephew's voice and found him several yards distant, separated from her by the deluge of destruction that had destroyed half the room. His arms were wrapped tightly about his wife, cradling her to his chest with one hand clutching at her hip and the other pressing her head into the crook of his shoulder. The chit clung to him likewise, eyes squeezed shut and coughing at the plaster dust, which settled over them like a London fog. She turned more deeply into him, protecting her mouth and nose, while

Darcy bundled her yet closer. He looked pale and vaguely ill.

Behind them, nearly to the far wall, the sofa they had been seated upon was overturned as if they had jumped back and out of calamity's way with a great deal of force. How it had landed quite so far from its original position was a mystery, but her nephew's innate strength must have been supplemented by his panic.

Darcy called to her again, though he did not yet relinquish his hold on Miss Bennet's trembling form. "Aunt? Are you harmed?"

Lady Catherine took stock of herself but could find nothing amiss other than a touch of soreness where Collins and his bulk had collapsed upon her and pinned her to the floor. She was about to answer him and insist that he set aside that ninny he called a wife to aid her when the door burst open and Fitzwilliam darted in just ahead of a contingent of servants. "What happened?"

"There has been an accident," replied Darcy, nodding to the pile of detritus that used to be her sitting room. "See to Lady Catherine and Collins."

Fitzwilliam was already in motion again, picking his way through the clutter in his aunt's direction. He held out his hands to her and lifted her off the floor, depositing her into a lesser chair before seeing to Collins. A quick press of his fingers to the parson's neck later, he assured the room, "He lives. I think he has merely fainted. We ought to call for the doctor."

The servants drew nearer, all of them looking about them in horrified wonder at the scene.

"The plaster has cracked," commented Percy, peering up at the empty place where the painting once hung. A fissure split the wall like a bolt of lightning, spreading nearly to the ceiling, where it was blocked by the fan vaulting.

Mrs Knight peered up at the damage with bafflement. "How in the world...?"

"It was bound to happen sooner or later. Have you seen the water damage behind that tapestry of Guinevere?"

During the confusion, Lady Catherine caught a glimpse of Darcy scooping his wife into his arms and making for the door. "I am going to take Mrs Darcy upstairs and out of harm's way. I shall return once I am assured she is well."

"Stay with your wife, Darcy, I can handle this."

At that, Darcy swept out of the door without another look back.

Fitzwilliam then directed the servants to stop gaping at the wall and get to work cleaning up the debris, which they immediately did. He sent one of the footmen to seek out Nichols, then set about attempting to rouse Collins himself. The parson grumbled his way into consciousness, then hissed in pain while Fitzwilliam assisted him into a sitting position.

At least I am spared the search for a new clergyman.

Lady Catherine did not move from the chair Fitzwilliam had planted her in until her lady's maid arrived to lead her upstairs. As she quitted the room, that stupid broken clock chimed again, its sound a tinny ring of triumph to her ears.

CHAPTER NINETEEN

Darcy carted Elizabeth over the threshold of their bedchamber as if she were still his new bride, nestled in his arms and pressed to his thudding heart. He deposited her gently on the bed while ordering Blake to fetch the local apothecary. No matter how Lady Catherine swore by his methods, Darcy would never put his wife in the care of Nichols; he surely had done Anne no good.

Elizabeth, who had admirably maintained her patience throughout his insistence upon sweeping her up and whisking her away from danger, grasped hold of both sides of his face and forced him to look at her. "I am not injured in the slightest, and there is no need to call anyone to attend me." Over his shoulder, she repeated this instruction to the maid.

Blake replied in an uncertain tone. "If you say so, madam. Do you require anything? I can fetch you some calming tea or prepare your nightgown."

"I thank you, no. Go downstairs and see whether

they require additional hands to clear up the throne—that is, the drawing room."

"Very well, if you insist, but do ring if you need me. I shall come directly."

A door closed behind Darcy, and Elizabeth returned her attention to his face. Her eyes were large and soft, full of concern. "I promise you that I am well. I was nowhere near the portrait when it fell."

"It crushed the tea table, Elizabeth!" Darcy could hear the shrill note in his voice but could not stifle it. "Had we not leapt back in time—" His conjecture was cut off by the constriction of his throat. What if he had *not* been in time?

Elizabeth hushed him. "But we did. We are not harmed in any way—barely even dusty."

He slumped down onto the bed beside her, suddenly aware how difficult it was to remain upright. Elizabeth drew him into her embrace, cradling his head to her bosom while she stroked his hair and cooed endearments in his ear. "There now, all is well. All is well."

They remained in that position for some time, though Darcy could not say how long. At length, his trembling subsided, and he was able to relieve Elizabeth of his weight—which must have been considerable to her—but his arms remained looped about her waist. "Forgive me, my love. I do not know what came over me."

Elizabeth stroked his face with the backs of her fingers, her blue-green eyes searching his for further signs of distress. "There is no need to apologise. You suffered a fright."

"*You* were the one to have a fright, not I." He

squeezed his eyes shut as another shudder assailed him. "I can still picture you reaching for your cup, just before…"

"And thanks to your quick thinking, we were both moved out of harm's way."

He could not consciously recall doing so, but his body had apparently acted of its own accord and placed them well out of range of danger. The experience had been unnerving, to say the least, and abjectly terrifying when he considered how close he had come to losing his beloved wife to the capricious whims of ugly furnishings. "That is just it—I did not think at all. We were across the room before I realised what was happening."

"Then I must thank your instincts. Regardless, you gallantly preserved me from injury. I am far more concerned about you." She paused before tentatively asking, "Ought I to call for the apothecary on *your* behalf?"

"For something to soothe my tattered nerves?" Darcy bristled. "I am not your mother, Elizabeth. You need not coddle me with draughts and smelling salts."

Elizabeth sighed, and Darcy thought her patience with him might be waning. "I only wished to help. I suppose we are alike in that respect."

"What do you mean?"

"I think you know." She sent him an expressive look, but he still did not understand. She became more explicit. "You have been treating me as if I am fragile ever since learning of my pregnancy. It is wholly unnecessary as I am as healthy as I have ever been."

"I suppose you are now going to scold me for being overbearing, but I am not sorry for it. You *are* fragile, and it is my duty to care for you, even when you do not like it. I could never live with myself if I allowed you to come to harm through my neglect."

To his surprise, Elizabeth did not stubbornly defend herself but rather took his hand within her own and fixed him with a sympathetic expression. "I am not going to scold you, dearest. In fact, it is I who owe you contrition. I have not been as considerate of your feelings as I ought, thinking merely of my own affront."

Now Darcy was utterly bemused. What could have caused this miraculous reversal of opinion? "What do you mean?"

"The colonel joined me on my walk today, and—"

"I ought to wring his neck for that." Darcy would certainly be having words with his cousin later, and if that devolved into fisticuffs, so be it. Fitzwilliam needed to learn a lesson about disobliging a man as regards his wife. "He knows my feelings on the matter of you walking out and ought to have escorted you back to the house immediately."

"As I was saying," she continued, a touch of asperity in her tone, "the colonel joined me on my walk today and enlightened me as to why you have been less than joyful regarding my pregnancy. No, do not deny it"—she held up her hand as he had, indeed, opened his mouth to protest; he snapped it closed at her silent command—"for I needed to hear it. I am ashamed to admit that I did not consider what your mother's death in childbed must mean to you.

"You were old enough to understand the import of her loss but not necessarily the means. You knew that your sister's entrance into the world meant your mother's departure from it, so those ideas have been inextricably linked in your mind. However, you must learn to accept that our circumstances are different."

"You cannot deny that childbirth is a dangerous business. Women and babies die all the time in the endeavour, and that is a fact."

"It is," she acknowledged with more calmness than he could muster, "but remember that my mother brought five healthy daughters into the world and lives on today in robust health."

"You are not your mother, Elizabeth."

She clasped his hand tightly. "Nor am I yours."

This struck Darcy powerfully. If it was unfair to compare Elizabeth to Mrs Bennet, then it was equally—if not more—unfair to compare her to Lady Anne. His fear had blinded him to this rational conclusion.

"So far," Elizabeth continued, "I have had few complaints as regards my own pregnancy. I shall also remind you that I have been with child for around five months now, and you were blissfully unaware until a week ago. If I had been suffering, do you believe you would have been ignorant of it?"

Darcy's concession was slow in coming. "I suppose not, but I was not mindful to look for any signs until you informed me of your condition."

"Exactly my point. You did not see any suffering until you looked for it, and then you largely imagined it. Aside from a few minor symptoms, which the midwife assured us both are common, I have been as well as can be expected."

"You cannot ask me to stop worrying about you, for I shall not. It is impossible."

"I would never demand such an unreasonable thing, but I shall insist that you cease to treat me like a piece of fine china. I know my own strength and am not liable to break."

He swallowed thickly. "But what if you do? I...I am afraid. Afraid of what I know—and of what I do not. I cannot help myself."

"You are not the only one who is afraid."

Darcy sought to meet her gaze at this quiet admission, but she evaded him. "What do you fear?"

"I worry that I am not prepared for motherhood," she confessed, her tone subdued. "I fear that I shall fail our child after he or she is born. Look at the example I have at home."

"You are not your mother, Elizabeth," Darcy reminded her gently but with pointed emphasis.

She laughed softly. "How ungentlemanly of you to use my own argument against me. Even if I am not, I still fret that I am not responsible enough to be a good mother."

Darcy winced, recalling his execrable behaviour of the previous day. There was nary a tremble to Elizabeth's voice, but her expressive eyes showed him that he had cut her deeply with his thoughtless remarks. "I should never have intimated that you were irresponsible. I was speaking from my own pique in the moment and not the rational truth. I think you will make an *exquisite* mother, and there is no one else I should ever trust to raise our children but you."

Elizabeth leant towards him, touching her forehead to his. "And there is no one else I should ever wish to be the father of my children."

They basked in this tender moment for some time before Elizabeth sat back and gave him a look that was both fierce and determined. Their gazes were perfectly aligned as she said solemnly, "My own concerns aside, I hope to at least somewhat assuage yours. I cannot promise you that nothing will happen to me, no one can, but you must begin to regard my condition with more optimism. Think on everything we stand to gain rather than what you might lose. Remember, I am carrying your child within me at this very moment. Is that not incredible?"

"It is," Darcy conceded, warily eyeing her stomach. A slight protrusion was visible due to the angle at which she reclined.

Elizabeth brought his hand to the convex curve of her belly. Her eyes fluttered closed. "Feel."

Beneath his hand, Darcy felt the tiniest possible nudge and snatched his hand back, leaning away from her. "Was that…?"

Laughing, Elizabeth recaptured his wrist and tugged it towards her, replacing his hand upon her abdomen. "That was your son or daughter. Is it not—oh! There it was again. Did you feel it?"

Darcy could not honestly say that he had, but—there! Another slight flutter. He blinked rapidly as he felt tears begin to form.

Elizabeth's wonder escaped her on a sibilant breath. "Is it not marvellous?"

Darcy replied in a hoarse whisper. "It is."

They were both silent for several minutes as Darcy continued to marvel at the sensation of his child moving within his wife. It felt like tiny footsteps against his palm, or perhaps little pebbles bouncing harmlessly off his skin. At length, the child settled, and the movement ceased, but Darcy kept his hand in the same place he had last perceived it.

"I believe he or she has decided to take a nap," Elizabeth commented. She was curled up against his side, her head resting upon his shoulder.

"You must be right." Darcy rubbed her stomach gently, but the baby did not stir for him. "It is incredible, the idea that our child is growing within you at this very moment. That one day he or she will be born and…" This reminder of childbirth stilled Darcy's tongue, for he was not yet entirely inured to the worry and fear he associated with it. Even now, it rose up like bile in his throat, threatening to make him sick.

Elizabeth placed her own hand upon his, settling its motion. "And all will be well."

"I still cannot banish my fears entirely. What if you…?"

"I shall not." She said so on a purring note, one which instantly distracted him from his exasperation. Or perhaps it was the dainty hand inching its way up the inside of his leg that had done the mischief.

His voice emerged as a rasp. "What are you doing?"

"Reassuring you."

He swallowed as her fingers tickled their way up his inner thigh, though it was the lesser of responses his body experienced. He swiftly grasped hold of her hand, pressing it in place before it could roam farther. "I am not sure this is a good idea."

Elizabeth slid closer to him across the bedclothes, using her free hand to skate up his chest, over his shoulder, and into his hair. Her lips were a hair's breadth from his as she whispered, "The midwife assured me that there is no harm in lying together. Let me comfort you."

Darcy opened his mouth to pointlessly protest, but any words were converted into a groan when she captured it in a sensuous kiss. He was powerless to resist the lure of her seduction from that point on.

CHAPTER TWENTY

Ding.

Elizabeth's eyes flew open instantly, as if she were awaiting a signal to wake. She sat up in her bed, the sheets sliding free of her shoulders and pooling about her hips. Darcy grumbled a protest in his sleep, but she had no attention to spare for him. Her gaze went immediately to the open doorway, where a visitor loomed.

Her breath fogged in the chill air as she welcomed her otherworldly guest. "Good evening."

The pale wraith smiled and nodded in return greeting. As before, Anne was garbed in a simple nightgown, her hair cascading down her back, and her incandescence chased away the darkest shadows. She might have been a candle in the night, or perhaps a waxing moon.

"I suppose you have come to pass on your message?"

Yes.

"Are you yet able to speak? Or write?"

A frown. *No.*

Elizabeth could feel frustration radiating from Anne every bit as much as the eerie glow she cast. She pitied the poor woman, taken so soon and beset by unfinished business. She felt entirely helpless. "I should like to help you, but I do not know how."

Anne turned as if to leave but paused at the threshold. She lifted her hand and beckoned Elizabeth with a crooked finger.

"You wish me to come with you?"

Yes.

Her last dream had cut itself abruptly short when she had attempted to follow Anne from the room, but perhaps tonight would be different. If not, she was willing to try again and again until they met with success, so dearly did she wish to aid this wandering spirit and to sate her curiosity. Regardless of her motives, Elizabeth again sensed no danger in the escapade—and even if there was, it was naught but a dream, and she would necessarily wake, unharmed.

Sliding free of the sheets and Darcy's clinging arm, Elizabeth donned her robe. Anne smiled softly before turning and gliding from the room and into the corridor. Swallowing down her trepidation—*'tis only a dream*—Elizabeth followed in her wake.

The corridor looked almost exactly as it was meant to, with red walls, numerous white doors, and a coterie of knights standing guard in their alcoves. The only difference Elizabeth could discern was that these knights had taken a more aggressive stance, with their swords pointed up and out, forming an arch of gleaming metal over the hall. She rather hoped that they would not be required to go that way.

Anne hovered to her immediate left, stationed in front of the double doors that concealed Lady Catherine's chambers. On either side of them was a tall pair of elaborately wrought vases, painted red and spider-webbed with golden cracks. They were overflowing with daffodils, which practically throbbed with light, almost to the pattern of a steady heartbeat.

At first, Elizabeth thought Anne meant to lead her into her mother's rooms, but she turned instead to a single door immediately across the hall from where they stood. Anne floated towards it, and the door sprung open under some invisible persuasion; she disappeared inside, her hair rippling behind her like a ribbon tumbling in the wind. Elizabeth stole one final glance over her shoulder at where Darcy still slept, apparently unconscious of her doings, before taking a steadying breath and crossing the threshold herself.

She could not guess what she would behold in this strange world of ghosts and pulsating flowers, but there was nothing so terrifying inside. It was a large bedroom done up in soft pinks and whites, the domain of a young lady. The bed coverings were all ivory, the hangings a dusky rose, and the window bench—a mirror image of the one in the chamber she shared with Darcy—was upholstered in the same fabrics. On the table beside the bed was a small pile of books and a silver bell with a handle; Elizabeth imagined it was intended to call forth a servant without getting up. The fireplace, also familiar in structure, was a pale castle set into one wall. It boasted its own pair of knights standing to either side, bearing banners with a familiar image of a chalice overflowing with white and pink flowers.

Belatedly, Elizabeth realised where they were. "Is this your bedchamber?"

Yes.

Anne crossed the room and made directly for the window. She raised both hands and, like the hall door, it swung open under the inducement of some mysterious force. Anne climbed upon the bench and waved Elizabeth closer, indicating with the point of her finger that they were to decamp through there.

Elizabeth swallowed uneasily. "You mean to jump from the window?"

Yes.

"I am liable to fall and become injured."

No.

"Yes, I assure you that will be the case should I leap from this height."

Anne shook her head, irritated, then proceeded to climb through the window. She dropped from sight like a stone.

Elizabeth raced to the opening, not entirely certain what she expected to see through it, and leant against the casing to peer out. She was taken aback to find the last scene she had expected. Rather than finding a crumpled body at the base of the decaying courtyard fountain, Anne waited patiently in the centre of the circular room at the top of her woodland tower, surrounded by dusty furnishings and dappled by colourful petals of moonlight. She beckoned Elizabeth forwards with a knowing smile.

"Of course, this is a dream," Elizabeth said, eyes

darting about to take in the scene. "I had nearly forgotten. Forgive me for doubting you."

Anne smiled and beckoned again, encouraging her to climb through the window into the unfathomable setting she now inhabited.

Her hesitation banished, Elizabeth clambered onto the bench. Bracing herself against the casement, she leapt through it and landed with nary a thud on the plush circular carpet inside the tower.

She looked behind her and found the window to Anne's bedchamber transformed into the large round one unique to the tower. Elizabeth approached it and peered out but could see no sign of the room she had come from. In fact, the manor house of Rosings was not visible—all she could discern were trees and the thick carpet of blooming anemone on the woodland floor.

"Simply marvellous," she said, exhaling it on a breath infused with wonder.

Ding.

Elizabeth's attention was recalled to Anne at the chiming toll, though she could not say from whence it came. She did not worry about such trifles after all she had already experienced this night.

Anne stood—hovered?—beside her rosewood desk, the delicate tips of her fingers resting upon its surface. She stared at Elizabeth with intent.

"You wish for me to look in the desk?"

Anne's eyes gleamed a potent silver, and the desk drawer slid open of its own accord.

Elizabeth strode forwards eagerly. Whatever Anne was presenting to her notice must be the key to why she had sought aid, the answer to the mystery of why she had strayed from the grave. What could it be? A letter? A lost token? Her misplaced will? If the latter, Darcy would be so pleased.

Before she could so much as peek inside, the tower room broke apart and scattered like flower petals on the wind.

CHAPTER TWENTY-ONE

Elizabeth startled awake with a gasp. As with her previous dream of Anne, the experience had been so vivid as to seem entirely corporeal, despite its fantastic qualities. Returning to reality was rather like being dunked into an icy cold bath; it stole one's breath and incited a great deal of shuddering.

The baby apparently shared her feelings. Elizabeth pressed her hand to her swelled abdomen and absently soothed her unborn child. Against all probability, it settled into a lazier fluttering.

"Elizabeth?" Beside her, Darcy struggled to prop himself up on his elbow. The covers slipped from his bare shoulders, favouring her with an enticing view. His form was especially tantalising in the contrast provided by early morning light, each muscle more deeply defined by dusky shadows. "What is the matter?"

"Nothing, my love. Merely another dream." She shivered involuntarily.

"Get back under the covers to tell me about it. You

must be freezing." Darcy reached for her and tugged her closer.

Recalling her own nudity, Elizabeth willingly submitted to her husband's urging. She laid back and curled up to his chest, resting her head within the comforting shelter provided by the crook of his shoulder. She supposed they ought to rise soon and begin the day, but she was not yet inclined to do so. They had been secreted away in their own private haven since yesterday afternoon, following the harrowing incident in Lady Catherine's Throne Room, at first to redress a few problems between them, then to…reestablish their marital connexion. Thoroughly.

After several hours of indulging themselves, Darcy had ventured out to meet with Fitzwilliam, who had been left in charge of setting the drawing room to rights and seeing to the needs of those affected. Nichols had been called upon for his services and, after declaring Mr Collins 'well enough' to proceed home in the pony cart where his wife could tend to him, he had provided laudanum for the overwrought Lady Catherine. As their hostess had been sedated and Fitzwilliam did not require any assistance, Darcy had then returned to Elizabeth with the news.

Once she was resettled, Elizabeth said, "I am sorry for waking you. I know you did not sleep well."

A snicker rumbled beneath her ear. "I did not sleep for long, it is true, but the repose I had was deep and restful. I dearly wish you could say the same. Will you tell me of your dream?"

"I would not want to upset you."

Beneath her, Darcy stiffened. "Why should your dream upset me?"

"I dreamt of…your cousin."

"Fitzwilliam?"

"Anne."

"Anne?" He sounded startled.

"Yes. I suppose coming here, witnessing your grief over her death, has put her in mind. I have dreamt of her the last two nights."

"And these dreams were…frightening? I can imagine how they might be, given recent events. After seeing her laid out, then attending her burial, I have been assaulted by a few troubling fancies myself. It is entirely common, but you must dismiss them from your mind. Even in life, Anne meant no harm to anyone."

Elizabeth shook her head. "No, you mistake me. The dreams are not frightening, per se. It is only a little disturbing to see someone so recently deceased—someone I hardly knew—visiting me in that manner. I almost feel as if…"

"As if?"

"It is too ridiculous. Forget I said anything."

"I could never find you ridiculous." At the poignant rise of her brow, Darcy laughed and amended, "I could never find your *concerns* ridiculous. Allow me to share your burden."

Breathing deeply, Elizabeth confessed, "I feel as if Anne is attempting to tell me something, though of course I have no notion what."

Darcy merely stared at her, blinking slowly as if suddenly awoken from a heavy slumber.

"There! See? I knew you would think me ridiculous. I should never have told you."

Keeping the counterpane securely pressed to her upper half, Elizabeth wriggled out of her husband's embrace, only to be forestalled by a strong forearm looped about her waist. He allowed her to squirm ineffectually and abuse him with empty threats for several moments before pinning her to the bed and swooping in for a kiss. Thoroughly distracted, Elizabeth allowed him to continue, and the familiar stirring of passion that arose from their playful combat consumed her.

It was some time later that they both collapsed against the sheets again, sweaty and breathless from their exertions. Darcy elevated himself upon the point of his elbow, rested his chin against the prop of his hand, and looked down at her with a silly grin. "Have I eased your troubles, my love?"

Elizabeth giggled. "You have, indeed. I applaud your methods, sir, for they are most effectual."

Darcy pressed his smiling mouth to hers in another sweeping kiss, one more tender than ardent, and drew her closer. Upon breaking the kiss, Elizabeth resumed her position against his shoulder, sighing contentedly. "We never did finish our conversation yesterday."

"I disagree. I thought it concluded quite well."

Slapping playfully at his chest, Elizabeth corrected herself. "I meant that we never discussed how we mean to go on. I understand your anxieties, but you cannot continue to treat me like a delicate china teacup that is liable to break with every slight touch. You will drive me mad and have to visit me and our child in Bedlam."

"Nonsense, I can easily afford a private nurse."

Another light slap induced him to become more serious. "Obviously, I would not wish to risk inducing your insanity, but you must acknowledge that greater care ought to be taken while you carry our child."

"You take your protectiveness too far. I am pregnant, not ill, and can do much of what I have always done—walking, for instance. The midwife encouraged me to keep at it for my health and the health of the baby. She says it will give me strength when it comes time to deliver."

Darcy's hand, which had been caressing her, stilled at the mention of childbirth but resumed its sweet ministrations after only a short pause. The baby nudged lightly at his fingers, and he smiled. "If you say that you are hale enough to continue with your daily constitutionals, then I suppose I must believe you. And yet, you are always so fatigued in the evenings that I assume you require more rest than you did before."

"I do, but I am always full of energy early in the morning—that much has not changed about my habits. If I flag towards the end of the day, it does not necessarily follow that I must lie abed at the beginning of it. Truly, I shall expire of tedium if you continue to keep me cooped up in our bedchamber."

Darcy allowed himself a smirk before sobering. "You have always been a strong walker, and I know it brings you much pleasure, so I shall trust your judgment of your own exhaustion. However, it is less the exercise that concerns me and more the chance that you might meet with some calamity. I would greatly prefer it if you do not walk out alone."

She cuddled closer with a light sigh. "I suppose I can

accommodate you there. Might you be willing to be my walking partner?"

"As often as I am able," he agreed with a kiss to her forehead. "That will not always be the case, but I shall rearrange my obligations to accommodate your needs as much as possible. When I am not free, I ask that you take a servant with you—a footman, even a maid, would provide the oversight I am seeking. Should you face any sort of danger, they can assist you back to safety and fetch help."

"For you, I shall endure it, even though I prefer solitude on my walks. Will you also stop pushing me to eat more?"

"You require proper nourishment, Elizabeth. I only mean to help."

Elizabeth cupped his chin within her palm, her eyes softening. "I know you do. Allow me to partake of what I can and in the amounts I can stand. I have found over the last few months that I am at my best when I eat several smaller meals rather than one large."

"I suppose that is a fair concession. You are the best arbiter of your own needs, and I shall do my best to respect that." Darcy turned his face to press a kiss into her palm. "That said, should you ever require a greater degree of cosseting, do let me know, and I shall happily indulge you."

"I shall remember that when my feet begin to swell."

"I am, as ever, at your service."

Eventually, Elizabeth and Darcy conceded to the necessity of greeting the day. They met Fitzwilliam in the breakfast room, though Lady Catherine was still nowhere in evidence.

After settling Elizabeth in a chair and procuring her delicacies from the buffet—after first ensuring he was selecting the items she desired and in the proper amounts—Darcy sat down next to her with his own plate. "How fares our aunt this morning?"

"I cannot say, for I have not heard a peep from her yet," replied Fitzwilliam, refilling his cup. "Then again, laudanum is potent stuff. It would not surprise me if we do not hear from her until the afternoon."

Darcy unfolded his napkin and draped it over his knee as he said, "I suppose it would do her good to rest. In the meantime, what shall we entertain ourselves with?"

"I should like to go walking, if you are inclined to escort me," said Elizabeth, her mouth turning up coyly.

Darcy snickered at her. "I suppose I ought to have anticipated as much. After breakfast?"

"That should suit. I am anxious to call at the parsonage. I cannot imagine that Mr Collins is a forbearing patient, and I should like to offer Charlotte any services she requires for his care. He was injured at Rosings, after all, and it is our duty to see that he is made as comfortable as possible in his recovery—and to ensure that he does not drive his wife to Bedlam during his convalescence."

Fitzwilliam joined Darcy in laughing at the picture she painted of the long-suffering Mrs Collins and her insufferable charge. "You are a compassionate woman, Mrs Darcy. My cousin does not deserve you."

"I shall not quibble with you there, for you are perfectly right," Darcy conceded with a smirk. "However, she is stuck with me now, for better or worse, so I must do what I can to earn my place."

Elizabeth shook her head at the pair of them before picking up her fork and resuming her breakfast.

From her bedchamber window, Lady Catherine narrowed her eyes at the retreating figures of her nephew and his artful wife as they strolled away from the manor hand in hand. It was disgusting how the girl continued to play the coquette with Darcy even after they were married. *She is already carrying his child—she ought not to try so hard. It is pathetic.*

Somewhere along the hall, Lady Catherine heard that blasted bell jangle again. It did so at least thrice, and she turned to glower at the closed double doors that separated her chambers from the corridor, contemplating whether she ought to investigate the source of the infernal ringing. It had done her no good before; she was always led into Anne's chamber only to find it conspicuously empty.

Deciding that she was still too fatigued from the laudanum Nichols had prescribed her the prior evening, she sniffed and crossed to her dressing table where a small wooden chest sat beside a tall vase of daffodils. She stroked the lid fondly. "I shall take care of that upstart soon enough. Even if I cannot see Anne wed to

Darcy, there is no reason I must allow an unworthy chit to usurp her place. It is the least I can do."

That annoying bell rang again, more tenaciously, and Lady Catherine turned to glare at the doors. She would not achieve a moment's peace until she determined the source of that racket; not knowing was absolutely maddening.

Her pursuit of the mystery was forestalled by the stool tucked beneath her dressing table. Seemingly of its own accord—though she must have caught it with her foot without realising—it slid into her path and tripped her up. She squawked and flapped in an undignified fashion but found herself unable to arrest her fall; down she went, straight to the unforgiving hardwood floor with an audible crunch. When she attempted to right herself, a searing pain shot up her leg, and she cried out.

All the while, the mysterious bells jingled a merry tune.

CHAPTER TWENTY-TWO

"I do hope Mr Collins makes a speedy recovery."

No sooner had this statement passed Elizabeth's lips than she winced at the agonising howl that followed them out. She nodded at the maid who had escorted them to the door, a silent permission to return to her mistress, and proceeded down the garden path on her husband's arm as the door slammed shut behind them.

Mr Collins's bravery of the previous afternoon had resulted in a bump to his crown and a twisted knee, but no worse. The apothecary had been called in for a more thorough opinion than Dr Nichols could be bothered to provide prior to expelling the parson from Rosings to his own residence. This was well, for none but Lady Catherine put any stock in the physician's advice. Mr Julius, a jolly old sort, had declared his patient on the mend but had reasonably adjured him from moving about too much lest he test his luck and more seriously harm himself.

Alas, Mr Collins had attempted another feat of nonsensical gallantry that very morning. Upon being informed of the Darcys' visit, he had become greatly alarmed by the supposition that they were there to bring tragic news of Lady Catherine. In his garment-rending hysteria, he had insisted on going to her and tripped—calamity had thus ensued.

The small party gathered in the sitting room had become aware of Mr Collins's escape only when he tumbled down the stairs and landed in a blubbering heap. Darcy had assisted the poor man to a chair, assured him that his patroness was well, and then they had speedily adjourned to allow the household to see to its master.

Darcy's expression was pained as he opened the gate and guided her through it. "I cannot help but feel responsible for his misfortune."

Elizabeth patted his hand sympathetically. "No one could have anticipated that he would respond to our visit in such a way."

"Regardless, someone ought to have sent word to the parsonage of Lady Catherine's continued good health. It is no secret how devoted he is to her."

"I am certain that someone did, for Charlotte made only polite enquiries after her. I dare say the blow to his head—and possibly the draughts Mr Julius prescribed—have addled my cousin's mind. As you are well aware, Mr Collins is not the most perceptive man, even at his best."

Darcy sighed as they entered the wood, a breeze swaying the treetops. "I think what distresses him the most is being denied the opportunity to dote on Lady

Catherine. Were he convalescing at Rosings, perhaps he might be more complacent and would not have attempted such a rash action."

Elizabeth shook her head at the absurdity of it all. "You may be right, but then there is no knowing with a man such as Mr Collins. He might have fallen down the grand staircase at Rosings instead and not lived to realise his own mistake."

They strolled along the footpath for a few silent minutes until they reached the overgrown turning that led to Anne's tower. Elizabeth paused there, searching for the concealed point of entry.

"What is it?" queried Darcy, halting likewise.

"I should like to visit the tower again."

"Again?" Darcy's left brow rose in interest—or perhaps suspicion. "I had no notion that you had discovered Anne's tower, yet you say you have been to it before?"

"Once." *Or twice, if one were to count my dream from last night.* Darcy's expression crumpled into one that heralded a scolding, so Elizabeth hurried to elaborate. "Freddy and I stumbled across it when we last called upon the parsonage. It was the same day she made merry in the gardens there."

His premeditated lecture apparently thwarted by mortification, Darcy's scowl shifted into a grimace. "Another reparation we owe Mr Collins. I wonder what she so disliked about your cousin's daffodils."

Poor Freddy had been left behind with her friends at the kennels for this particular sojourn. It would have been unfeeling to take her back to the parsonage during Mr Collins's convalescence, and regardless of how lowly she regarded his intelligence, Elizabeth was not of a mind to finish him off. No doubt hearing of Freddy loose in his garden again would induce apoplexy.

"It is difficult to say, but she was quite thorough in their ruination. Now, help me find the—there!" She tugged on his arm, leading him to the spot where the greenery parted just enough to allow easement.

Darcy followed, though not without protest. "Elizabeth, you cannot go lumbering into the woods. Remember your promise."

"I promised I would take no unnecessary risks and would bring an escort—a bargain that I have fulfilled. Come now, hold this sapling out of my way." She pushed the spindly young tree into Darcy's hand and ducked under it to where the rutted path became more prominent. Her husband sighed in defeat before following suit.

Roughly twenty yards into the trees, the wood gave way to the clearing containing the ruins they were searching for. Elizabeth found herself equally awed as she had been upon first discovering it. The church bells ringing in the background only added to its grandeur.

"Your uncle had a singular sense of style."

"He did," Darcy agreed, neck craned back to take in the entirety of the structure. "He had a fascination with King Arthur and his knights, as I am sure must be obvious."

"Was it due to his own knighthood?"

"You would think so, but no. I believe the interest originated in his father—who was named Arthur, you might recall—and the knighthood came much later. Sir Lewis used to regale my father with tales of how he assiduously courted the favour of the king in order to receive the honour. It would not have been difficult for him—a friendlier man you could not hope to meet."

Elizabeth smiled fondly at the notion of Sir Lewis making himself agreeable to King George. "I cannot help but think of Sir William Lucas when you speak of him so."

"I had not considered it before, but there is a remarkable resemblance between them."

"I would not draw such a comparison before your aunt! Can you imagine her outrage?"

Darcy made a pretence of shuddering, and Elizabeth laughed.

They reached the steps that led up to the whitewashed door, and Elizabeth reached out for the brass ring, but Darcy forestalled her. "Allow me to go first and ensure that the structure within is sound."

Elizabeth rolled her eyes at him, but there was no true exasperation in the motion. She stepped out of the way, jestingly presenting the closed door with a sweeping wave of her arms, and haughtily entreated him, "By all means, after you."

Darcy shook his head at her and took up the brass ring himself. With a hardy tug, the door swung free on its hinges, and he leant forwards to peek inside before crossing the threshold for a more thorough inspection.

After listening to him shuffle about and knock on various surfaces for an interminable period, Elizabeth called to him, "I have already been inside and suffered no mishap."

"It is an old building and could have many hidden dangers."

"It is not nearly as old as Rosings."

At last, Darcy emerged, dusting the grime from his hands with his handkerchief. "Perhaps not, but it is not as well maintained out here in the woods."

Elizabeth raised a brow at her husband. "Did we, or did we not, just pay a call to a man who was injured by a falling painting in your aunt's withdrawing room? I have visited Rosings enough times to say with authority that it was an inevitability. I suspect the place has not been renovated since Sir Lewis's time, and it is in dire need of repairs."

Darcy shook his head, visibly exasperated. "So I have told her for years, but there is little money for the endeavour. But enough about Rosings—shall we go upstairs?"

"We shall."

CHAPTER TWENTY-THREE

As they ascended, Elizabeth felt an odd sort of tingle shiver through her body, from the tips of her toes to the roots of her hair. Somehow, it brought to mind her dream from the night before, a soft recollection of her nighttime wanderings, though she could not articulate precisely why that should be. *I suppose it is more the setting than the sensation.*

The staircase was too narrow for a pair of fully grown adults to walk abreast, so Darcy led the way to the room at the top. After pushing open the trapdoor and climbing through, he turned back to assist Elizabeth, then closed it behind them. "One can never be too safe. I recall Fitzwilliam falling through once when he was not minding his feet."

"Oh dear. Was he terribly injured?"

Darcy shrugged. "Only his head—no great loss."

Elizabeth laughed. "I take it you and your cousins spent a great deal of time here once?"

Darcy was standing in the direct centre of the room,

spinning in a slow circle as he took in the scene. When he replied, his voice was somewhat distant, as if speaking from another time. "Yes, we used to come here to play at every annual visit while the adults talked up at the house. Anne was our damsel in distress, and we—Fitzwilliam and I—her daring knights. I cannot tell you how many times we defended her honour from dragons and trolls, only to return to Rosings for dinner and look on helplessly while her own mother relentlessly badgered her."

Elizabeth went to him and wrapped her arms about his waist, resting her cheek against his shoulder. "I wish I had taken the time to know her better when I visited before. I feel as if I have missed out."

Darcy's arms came up, and he returned the embrace, pressing a kiss to her bonneted head. "Anne was delightful but also very shy, much like Georgiana. Worse, she was often quite ill and not up to conversation even if she wished to make the effort. When you knew her, she was almost as bad as I had ever seen her—though that did not prevent Lady Catherine from redoubling her efforts to see us engaged."

"Poor girl."

After another kiss, this time a soft peck to Elizabeth's lips, Darcy stepped back from her and began to more thoroughly examine the room. Following his example, Elizabeth wandered in the opposite direction to allow him the time he required to regain equanimity; it had been her experience that her husband sometimes needed a moment to himself to achieve this endeavour.

While Darcy bent to inspect one of the bookcases, Elizabeth wandered aimlessly, searching without particular purpose. She could understand why Anne would have loved this place; it was light, bright, and sparkling in a way that Rosings Park was not. The entire room was bathed in a warm pink glow and shimmered with the stained-glass pattern cast upon the floor. No doubt she had spent as much time here as her health allowed, out from under Lady Catherine's imperious eye.

A glimmer of movement caught Elizabeth's attention, and she turned. There, next to the desk, she thought she saw—but no, it could not be. A trick of the flickering light had made her believe for a moment that Anne was there with them in the tower. She was again assailed by a spontaneous quiver, though perhaps this time the cause was not so mysterious. *You are beginning to see things, Lizzy.*

"Elizabeth?"

Shaken, she turned to her husband, who was peering at her with a queer expression. Realising that she must have gasped or otherwise betrayed her amazement, Elizabeth was quick to reassure him. "Dust caught in my throat. I am well."

"Do you wish to go back down?"

"It is only dust. I dare say I can struggle on."

With a playful roll of his eyes, Darcy returned to perusing the book—a tome about the Holy Grail, she noted—splayed open in his hands.

Trepidation and irrepressible interest warred within her as she roamed the tower room, touching and observing everything except that desk. It had featured prominently in her dream, which was perhaps why it cast a siren's lure upon her now, teasing and taunting her with glimmering visions. Yet, no matter how she rationalised, her eyes frequently strayed to it, tempted by it or perhaps oddly hoping to catch a glimpse of some ethereal figure. She did not really believe in ghosts—*Or do I?*—yet she half expected to see a young woman in a long white nightgown appear there at any moment, beckoning her nearer.

At length, curiosity won out over caution, and she tentatively approached the desk. It was placed directly below the stained-glass window and, as a result, was dappled in multicoloured light that shimmered like sunshine on Pemberley's lake. There, in the lower right-hand corner, were Anne's initials; Elizabeth traced them with the tips of her fingers.

The surface of the desk was clear, save for Anne's quills and ink pot—long dried up—patiently awaiting the return of their owner. Was there anything concealed within? Her skin prickled as she reached for the drawer set into the centre and slid it open. She peered inside, her pulse beating at a quickened pace as her anticipation mounted.

Therein lay an innocuous tome, bound in white leather with a length of pink ribbon marking a page somewhere in the final third of the volume. It had no title stamped across the front or any other distinguishing marks to suggest its contents. Doing her best to temper her expectations—*a favourite novel, surely*—Elizabeth picked it up and opened it to the inside cover.

January 1, 1812

The new year begins dreary and cold, as I suppose one must expect in the winter months. Mother has complained ceaselessly about the rain, though even she must acknowledge that the weather means her no personal affront. Regardless, she drones on endlessly about it as if it is the fault of some unknown person who seeks to undermine her authority on the proper amount of rain one might reasonably expect this time of year. Mrs Jenkinson says...

As recognition of what she held in her hands arose, Elizabeth trailed her fingertips down the handwritten text, full of astonished wonder. She could not help but consider, however impossible the notion, the likelihood that she had been somehow led to this discovery by unseen forces. *Miss de Bourgh?*

The baby jumped inside her womb, startling Elizabeth from her reading. She cried out—more of a soft 'oof' than anything—drawing forth Darcy, who was at her shoulder in moments. "Is something the matter?"

"No, I was merely surprised by a sudden kick." She rubbed her belly for emphasis. Mindful of worrying her husband, she dispelled any ghostly ruminations for the present; she might ponder at leisure when she was less likely to alarm Darcy with her distraction. "Look here. I believe I have discovered our cousin's diary."

Darcy took the journal from her hands and leafed through a few of the pages, nodding. "I believe you have. I had no notion that Anne kept a diary."

"It seems she stored it here rather than at Rosings. I found it inside the desk."

Closing it, Darcy regarded the pale cover thoughtfully. "I wonder whether she kept others. If so, there might be mention of her will in one of them, possibly even a clue as to its location."

"You do not think it would be in this one?"

Darcy opened it up to the first entry and tapped at the date at the top—January 1812. "Given when it was penned, I suspect this is her most recent one. I cannot see why she would discuss her will in it unless she expected to die. As we know, her death came rather suddenly."

Elizabeth took the diary from his hands and blindly perused the page. Anne had a fair, if unsteady, hand as she described the tedium of Rosings Park in the winter. "I suppose not, but perhaps someone ought to read it just in case?"

"It could not hurt, though I doubt it will provide much assistance, and I would rather not..." His words faded, his countenance overspread with sadness.

Tucking the journal against her chest, Elizabeth used her free hand to rub his back. "Of course it would cause you pain, and presumably the colonel as well. Why not let me read it? And any older ones we might find."

"If you are certain..."

"Quite certain."

Ding-dong, ding-dong.

The church bells rang the hour, and Darcy proclaimed that it was time to depart. Elizabeth's stomach was beginning to grumble riotously, so she was not inclined to object. With Anne's diary tucked beneath her arm, she allowed her husband to assist her through the trapdoor and down the stairs.

CHAPTER TWENTY-FOUR

When they arrived back at the manor house, the Darcys found the place in uproar.

"What is going on?" Darcy demanded to no one in particular, but he was disregarded by the various servants crossing to and fro through the hall. From upstairs, he could hear his aunt screeching, but her words were unintelligible and informed him of nothing. She could be on her deathbed or irritable over some imagined slight; he could not know without context.

Fortunately, Fitzwilliam appeared on the top landing just then to provide it. He rapidly descended the staircase, looking harried. "Darcy, the next catastrophe is yours to manage, for I have done my fair share."

"What happened?" Elizabeth asked, her eyes fixed upon the upper hall from whence Lady Catherine's strident tones issued.

"Our dear aunt tripped over something in her room —a footstool, or some such—and has badly twisted her ankle. Nichols is with her now, but I suspect he wishes he were anywhere else."

"Goodness, Lady Catherine has suffered a great deal of mishaps lately," observed Elizabeth with a frown.

Fitzwilliam laughed and shook his head. "Teacups flying about, pictures falling upon her head, tripping over footstools... If I believed in such things, I would think she was cursed."

Elizabeth appeared struck by this notion, her face paling a shade.

"Curses, indeed," Darcy grumbled as he carefully observed his wife. She had complained of hunger on the way back, so perhaps that was to blame for her waning colour. When she showed no signs of immediate faintness, he asked his cousin, "Is there aught you need from me?"

"No, it is all well in hand, though I am certain Lady Catherine will be expecting a visit to her sick room at some point—she is not to leave it for at least a week or two. If I were you, I would wait for Nichols to administer the laudanum before paying your call." He issued this suggestion with a wink.

After refreshing himself and dutifully paying a sickroom visit to Lady Catherine—who had at last been silenced by the anticipated dose of laudanum—Darcy sat down to eat a simple meal of cold meats, cheese, and bread in one of the lesser dining rooms with Elizabeth and Fitzwilliam. It was smaller and more modestly decorated than the one his aunt insisted upon using, enabling their party to converse at an easy distance rather than from yards away from one another.

"Elizabeth discovered something interesting in Anne's tower."

After swallowing down his bite of ham, Fitzwilliam replied, "Oh?"

"Our cousin kept a diary," said Darcy, setting his napkin atop his empty plate. "She found only the most recent volume, but there is a decent chance that there are others."

"Were they not stored in the tower with the one you found?"

"I am afraid not. I perused the bookshelf and discovered naught but Anne's favourite novels and poetry—mostly the ones she kept hidden from her mother."

Fitzwilliam laughed. "I recall bringing her a copy of one of Mrs Radcliffe's novels once and going to extraordinary lengths to prevent Lady Catherine from seeing it. I resorted to dropping it out of the window into the shrubbery when she walked in upon my presenting it to Anne."

"That would explain the stains."

"I thought we were safe! Lady Catherine never goes into the library. I dare say I have not seen her in there either before or since—it was just ill luck. Had you been distracting her properly—"

"Oh no, do not lay the blame at my feet," Darcy objected with a hearty guffaw. "I am not responsible for your lack of foresight."

Elizabeth's gaze moved between Darcy and Fitzwilliam as if she were watching a tennis match, allowing them their banter as she steadily ate her meal. To Darcy's satisfaction, she had nearly cleared her plate, even though she had not piled it as high as he might have wished. He would make sure that she took more refreshment in an hour or two.

"In any case, I thought we might search Anne's room for more journals. If they exist, they might aid us in locating her will."

"If *that* even exists. I am beginning to believe it conjecture."

After ensuring that Elizabeth had eaten her fill, the trio travelled upstairs and into the family wing to where Anne's former chambers resided. They were situated directly across the hall from Darcy's usual guest suite—a contrivance Lady Catherine had once hoped might lead to a speedy engagement. It had not occurred to her, apparently, that the sounds of Anne retching into her chamber pot throughout the night were not much of an enticement.

When Darcy opened the door and tried to wave Elizabeth through, she stopped just short of crossing the threshold, an expression of consternation on her face. "Is something wrong?"

She shook herself and presented him with an easy smile. "Not at all. I just oddly feel as if I have been here before."

With a hand to the small of her back, Darcy guided her inside and shut the door behind them. Fitzwilliam was already within and looking about. "It is so similar to our own chambers that it is little wonder that you should feel so."

It was true. Save for the colour scheme—Anne preferred pinks to blues—and a view of the courtyard, the rooms were nearly identical. There was a turreted fireplace against one wall guarded by a pair of knights, a cosy window seat from which one could enjoy the babbling cadence of the fountain—not that it had been functional in years—and the furniture was of the same heavy, old-fashioned variety.

"That must be it," Elizabeth agreed absently, her eyes wandering slowly about the space as if in a dreamlike state. Darcy touched her elbow, and she startled back to herself. "Forgive me, I was wool gathering. Let us divide and conquer."

They separated to search different parts of the room, with Elizabeth going directly to the table beside Anne's bed and Darcy to the set of low bookshelves on one side of the door. Fitzwilliam had disappeared into the dressing room. They were all quiet save for the shuffling of fabric and the sliding of drawers.

Darcy perused the whitewashed bookshelves and found more of the same as he had encountered at the tower, albeit nothing that would provoke Lady Catherine's ire. There were some slim volumes of poetry, a handful of unobjectionable novels, historical texts, and one particularly thick tome of Arthurian legend. The nameplate inside read 'Sir Lewis', making him smile. Otherwise, the shelves were relatively empty, especially near the top where several books lay haphazardly on their sides. He leant closer and found a subtle void in the dust where a line of folios might have once rested, but he could not be sure. All he knew for certain was that Anne was a great reader, having little strength to take pleasure in much else, and the bareness of her shelves bothered him.

Fitzwilliam emerged from the dressing room, declaring, "Nothing but gowns and some empty bottles of tonic. Any luck out here?"

Elizabeth sat on the edge of Anne's bed, cradling a silver bell in her cupped hands as she stared solemnly at it. Her reply was soft and absentminded. "No, nothing."

"I think they might have once resided here," Darcy said, lightly tapping the bookshelf with his index finger, "but they are certainly not there now."

Fitzwilliam turned his gaze to the fireplace, narrowing his eyes with suspicion. He strode towards it, picked up the poker from its stand, and began prodding at the ashes in the grate. "I think someone has been burning something here."

Darcy walked over, resting his hand against one of the turrets as he bent to inspect Fitzwilliam's findings. "Anne has been dead for nearly a fortnight now. Why would it still be this dirty?" The fireplace was absolutely filled with ash and blackened detritus; it had obviously not been swept clean after its last use.

Fitzwilliam's jabbing with the poker unearthed a piece of leather, which might have once been white, curled in on itself like a shrivelled flower. A bit more sifting uncovered a few bits of singed paper. He picked one up and brought it closer to his face. "I think we might have found the journals."

"What?" Darcy held out his hand for the scrap, and Fitzwilliam carefully laid it upon his palm. There was not much left of the page, but a single word—'Mother'—in Anne's hand was scrawled across it. "Why on earth would anyone burn Anne's journals?"

Fitzwilliam stood, dusting ash from his hands. "Perhaps to protect our cousin's privacy? It is not unknown for a loving relative or devoted servant to burn letters after someone has died, and journals would certainly fall into the same category."

Shaking his head, Darcy said, "Mrs Jenkinson was let go well before Anne died."

"Then her maid, or Lady Catherine herself. In fact, given the state of the hearth"—Fitzwilliam waved his blackened hand at the unclean fireplace—"I should say our aunt is the most likely culprit. Why she did not order someone to tidy up after her, I cannot say."

Darcy nodded along; it sounded plausible to him. "That is unfortunate."

"We at least have her most recent journal," Elizabeth said. "It is just across the hall in our chamber. I can begin reading it today, if you like."

Taking her nearest hand into his possession, Darcy lifted it to his lips and pressed a kiss to the back of it. "No hurry, but I thank you for your earnest desire to help. Read it at your leisure and let us know what you find."

Elizabeth's eyes were drooping again, and she fought to prop them back open. Perhaps it had not been the best idea to begin Anne's diary before bed, but the rest of the day had been consumed with assisting Darcy and Colonel Fitzwilliam in the search for the missing will.

After promising that she would not lift anything heavier than their lamp or wander off on her own, the gentlemen had allowed her to accompany them to the attic to explore the possibilities therein. They had sifted through a great deal of old furniture—much of which was somehow older and uglier than that adorning the public rooms downstairs; the de Bourghs could not, as a whole, be described as arbiters of good taste—and various knickknacks before discovering a wealth of old documents in a far corner. Many of them were dated well before Anne's lifetime, but a few crates would require further scrutiny. Darcy had ordered them all carted down to the library, where he and the colonel might sort through them in greater comfort on the morrow.

By the time this task was completed, dinner was imminent, and they had all gone down to change out of their dusty clothes before partaking in a light meal in the same small dining room they had utilised at midday. After that, Elizabeth's fatigue overcame her, and she excused herself to bed, leaving the gentlemen to their port.

Now exhaustion was creeping in, and she felt she could not continue reading. After one too many nods that she jerked herself awake from, Elizabeth conceded defeat, marked her page with the provided pink ribbon, and set the diary aside for the night. Within minutes, she was deeply asleep.

Elizabeth stirred and sat up, blinking about at the curved stone walls and decorative windows of Anne's tower. She was reclined upon the ivory sofa in her nightgown and bare feet as if she had intentionally fallen asleep there. Unlike previously, she was fully aware that she was dreaming, having expected it after the previous nights of fantastical jaunts.

As if to confirm her suspicions, there was Anne, standing beside the desk across the room, glimmering in the faceted moonlight streaming through the window behind her. The shards of coloured light seemed to pierce her form, which did not seem entirely solid, providing no barrier to the pattern casting itself upon the floor. She smiled at Elizabeth, but it was wan and tired.

"Good evening. We discovered your diary today. Did you...mean for me to find it?"

Yes.

Elizabeth felt a thrill at having guessed correctly. Her next words came with eager rapidity. "I hope you do not mind that I have perused it a little. Your cousins are hunting for your will and hope the journal might contain some clue as to its whereabouts."

Anne nodded, though whether in assent or simple understanding Elizabeth could not say.

Given that her older volumes had been reduced to ash, perhaps at Anne's instruction, Elizabeth felt it imperative to declare, "I promise to keep your secrets. You need have no fear of my sharing any of its contents. I shall even destroy it after reading it, if that is your wish."

A hasty, urgent shake of the head—*No!*

"You do not want me to read it?"

No—a bemused pause—*Yes.*

"If you are unsure..."

More emphatic shaking. *No, no, no.*

Elizabeth was still not entirely clear what Anne

wished for her to do. It must have shown on her face, for the incorporeal lady waved her hand over the rosewood desk, and the diary appeared upon its surface. She tapped it emphatically with one finger.

"The diary is important..." Elizabeth surmised aloud. "You wish me to read it?"

Yes!

"And then...give it to your mother?"

Anne clutched at her lifeless heart, horror writ plain upon her pale face.

Frustrated, Elizabeth asked plainly, with a touch of a whine to her tone, "What do you want me to do?"

Anne swallowed deeply and opened her mouth, but no sound emerged. She shook her fist, then calmed, apparently ready to try again. She closed her eyes and appeared to turn her meditation inwards. Elizabeth watched, fascinated, as a soft light began to emanate from her form. It was most concentrated at a singular point in her throat.

When her mouth opened again, a single, echoing word issued forth: *"Tell."*

CHAPTER TWENTY-FIVE

The following morning, Elizabeth woke bleary and muddle-headed, a proper reflection of the weather, which had turned overnight for the worse. It was not quite raining, but the sky was woolly and overcast, perhaps foretelling a storm rolling in. The baby wriggled as if unsettled by this forbidding change, and she stroked her stomach to quell its discomfort, though she herself felt little solace.

Her attention was distracted from the window by the entrance of Darcy, who emerged from the dressing room tugging at his cuffs. He slowed to a stop upon seeing her sitting up in bed. "I hope I did not disturb you."

Although Elizabeth could not shake her irrational sense of gloom, she forced a smile for his sake. *He already worries so much.* "Not at all, I only just awoke. Are you on your way down to breakfast?"

"No, Fitzwilliam and I agreed to meet in the library first thing this morning to tackle that mountain of papers we unearthed yesterday. If you require me, that is where I shall invariably be until dinner."

"Is it really necessary to hole yourselves up for an entire day?"

Seemingly aware of her dismay, which must have been apparent in her tone, Darcy's air became conciliatory. He sat beside her on the edge of the mattress and took up one of her hands. "If we hope to conquer the pile before we leave on Saturday, yes. Otherwise, I cannot see how we might accomplish it."

"Very well, but at least promise me you will take a few breaks to walk about. I would not have you exhaust yourself."

He pressed a firm kiss to her forehead. "I promise you I shall. Fitzwilliam is impossible to deal with unless one exercises him properly. Worse than Freddy, even." He snickered at his own jest.

Elizabeth gave him another weak smile. "Is he as awful an object as you when you have nothing to do?"

"Have I been an awful object since marrying you?" Darcy's good cheer dimmed as his eyes roved Elizabeth's face. "If you require me to remain with you, I shall."

She cupped his cheek and touched her lips to his. Upon withdrawing, she forced herself to be rational. "I thank you, but no. Finish your business so that I may have you all to myself without distraction later."

"Are you certain?"

"Entirely." A weary sigh escaped her. "I dare say I am affected by the weather. I had hoped to go walking again, perhaps with Freddy, but such seems improbable now."

She nodded at the bowed window and the sombre grey sky visible through it.

"Perhaps you would care to join me and Fitzwilliam in the study?"

Elizabeth wrinkled her nose as she recalled the great deal of sneezing she had endured the day before in the attic. "I think not. With the pair of you up to your necks in dusty old documents, I do not think I could bear it. I believe I shall remain in our rooms and read Anne's diary by the fire."

"An excellent notion. I shall order your breakfast when I do so for myself." With another kiss to her forehead, he was gone.

As soon as Darcy left, Elizabeth rang for Blake to help her dress. Her breakfast arrived in a timely manner, just as Darcy had promised, and she settled herself at the table by the fire to partake of it.

After finishing, Elizabeth found herself too warm to continue sitting by the hearth and adjourned to the window seat with Anne's diary. The rain had begun in earnest now, fat droplets sliding down the panes in haphazard patterns while a creeping fog rolled across the grounds. It encircled the base of the house like a moat, discouraging anyone from either entering or escaping. She dearly wished she had been able to walk to the tower—just visible above the trees in the near distance—but instead she was trapped within Rosings.

Nothing for it. I shall have to make the best of where I am. She wrapped herself up in her favourite shawl—a soft green cashmere that had ably seen her through a Derbyshire winter—and opened the volume at the last page she had marked. Setting the pink ribbon aside, she began to read.

March 29, 1812, Easter Sunday

Mr Collins' sermon might have been interminable if not for what I observed amongst the congregation. Darcy has been behaving oddly since his arrival, but until I witnessed him in the company of Miss Bennet I could not put my finger upon the cause. Now I believe I have figured him out: <u>he is in love</u>!

This sounds absurd even as I pen it here, but I have never seen Darcy so attentive to any lady, not even his sister. I might have chalked his interest up to mere ennui—Mr Collins does not inspire rapt attention in his congregation—except his eyes continued to follow Miss Bennet about the drawing room when she and the Collinses arrived after dinner. He even moved closer to hear her play!

Even if the symptoms of his attachment are clear to me, his cousin who has known him most of his life, I do not think Miss Bennet is aware. Neither is Richard, if his flirtations are any indication—I imagine it is now equally painful to Darcy as it is to me to watch him make himself agreeable to our pretty visitor. Let us hope that Mother continues to see only that which she wishes to; I should hate to see her wrath unleashed upon poor Miss Bennet, who knows not what she does to inspire it.

In any case, Miss Bennet shows no sign of returning Darcy's affections, or even recognition of them. He really ought to make more of an effort to show his feelings, else his reticence will leave her entirely in ignorance. Mrs Collins joined with me in this opinion when I slyly mentioned it to her.

A wry curl lifted one end of Elizabeth's mouth as she read this passage, knowledge of what came after it rendering the contents darkly amusing. She found Anne to be an exacting observer with a keen understanding of those around her; far better than she herself had been at the time. *She was entirely correct—I was blind to his affections.*

She turned to the next page with a sigh and read on through several months' worth of daily minutiae of life at Rosings Park. She smiled fondly at Anne's witticisms and observations, rolled her eyes at each reference to Mr Collins, and gritted her teeth at every report of Lady Catherine's thoughtless cruelty. It seemed to Elizabeth that, while her ladyship certainly took a great deal of interest in her daughter's doings, rarely did she express it with any tenderness.

At length, she reached the entry that detailed the state of affairs at Rosings Park after word of her marriage to Darcy had arrived. Elizabeth could not help wincing but did not lift her eyes from the page. She was morbidly curious to know how Lady Catherine had responded to the news.

September 10, 1812

As I sit to write this, it is with a trembling pen, for a report has reached Rosings that my cousin Darcy has lately married Miss Elizabeth Bennet, and we are all in uproar. Or rather, Mother is in uproar, and that amounts to the same thing.

Dear Lord, I have never seen her so undone. It was a fearsome thing to behold. I have not words to adequately describe the expression on her countenance, nor the horrible sound she made after reading Darcy's letter. At first, I thought she was having some sort of terrible fit and asked Mrs Jenkinson to fetch her some of my tonic, but Mother dashed it out of her hand and screeched such invectives that we did not dare attempt to calm her again. Even now I can still hear her unholy howls of rage. They must be echoes in my mind, for I made haste to abandon the manor for my tower once I understood what had upset her so. I think Mrs Jenkinson and I shall shelter here for the night.

Despite Mother's response, I must say here, even if I shall not be able to do so anywhere else, that I am happy for my cousin and Miss Bennet—or <u>Mrs Darcy</u>, rather. I do not regret refusing his hand all those years ago, even for an instant; had I accepted him, I would have deprived him of the happiness which must now flow from so perfect a union. Miss Bennet, from what I know of her, is his ideal match: clever, bold, fearless, and kind. I say so from my own paltry observations and also the recommendation of Mrs Collins, who has been a good friend to me since coming to Kent. (I cannot say that marrying Mr Collins was the wisest thing she has ever done, but as it has benefited her—and myself— greatly, there is no cause to repine.) I had hoped that Darcy might speak to Miss Bennet of his feelings some months ago, when they were both still here at Rosings, but I suppose the timing was not right or he feared Mother's wrath—given what I have seen of it, he was right to do so.

I sincerely wish them both every happiness in the world. God willing, I shall live long enough to see them again and offer my best wishes in person. As I write this, however, I suspect that I hope in vain, because Mother can nurse a grudge like no other, and it is not at all certain that I shall outlive her.

A month's worth of entries followed this one, each of them along the same vein. It seemed that Lady Catherine had not taken the news well at all, and Elizabeth found herself consumed with guilt that Anne had been forced to endure such histrionics. Not for the first time, Elizabeth felt a great swell of pity for poor Anne.

October 15, 1812

More than a month after learning of my cousin Darcy's marriage, Mother continues to rage. Sometimes at Darcy himself, more frequently at Mrs Darcy—whom she still stubbornly refers to as 'Miss Bennet', though that has not been her name for many weeks now—and lately her ire has turned to me. 'Why did you not capture him when you had the chance, Anne? Now we shall never restore Rosings to its former glory', and 'Just look at you! This is why Darcy married that lowborn strumpet', and 'Had you only listened to me, you would be Pemberley's mistress by now', etc. Only the last one gives me pause, but not for the reasons she thinks. I merely wish I were anywhere but Rosings of late. Some days I really wish it <u>would</u> fall down around my ears.

I admit to being stung by her words, but no more than that; I have already endured a lifetime of cruel remarks, vicious pinches, and vituperative lectures so cannot be unduly wounded by her tantrums now. I am inured. Even so, I keep as much out of her way as possible lest her cane strike me when she is least in control. There are times that I think I even see some ill intent gleaming in her eye, though Mrs Jenkinson says I am imagining it. I shall keep to my tower, regardless.

At least Darcy need not endure Mother's temper. I have successfully preserved him from it and count it as a great achievement.

CHAPTER TWENTY-SIX

Subsequent entries—more than a month's worth of them—detailed Lady Catherine's vindictive campaign to belittle her daughter at every opportunity. The words that wretched, awful woman had used to denigrate Anne! Elizabeth would never have spoken so against the dastardly Mr Wickham, much less her own child. The paper was splotched with the evidence of Anne's understandable distress as she described each verbal assault.

Swiping a tear from her own cheek, Elizabeth turned another page.

November 30, 1812

It has been a full se'nnight since I last put pen to paper, and I have greatly missed doing so. Such is the risk I run by keeping my diary hidden in my tower, as my frailties are liable to render me bedridden at any time. Still, 'tis far better than leaving my private thoughts where Mother can read them for herself; I learnt that lesson in the year eleven and shall not make the mistake of allowing her access again. I still wince at the memory of the beating I endured when she discovered my true feelings for my cousin...I am amazed she did not hobble me. Just in case, I burnt the volume from 1807 lest she uncover the secrets therein. No doubt her punishment would be even more severe were she to learn that I could have accepted Darcy then and thus prevented his marriage.

I have been horribly ill since my last entry in this volume. It began as a simple cold; we attempted to quell the symptoms with Mother's special tonic—horrid, smelly stuff that clings to my nose hairs and is as yellow as the bile I cast up—but then my stomach became unsettled, and I could not keep it down for anything. Mrs Jenkinson was beside herself when we used up the last of it, but thankfully I began to improve shortly thereafter. Dr Nichols is presently brewing up a new batch, but until then I shall have to do without my daily dose.

Elizabeth, recalling exactly the horrid smell Anne described, found it incredible that she was ever able to keep it down at all. Her own stomach rebelled at only the slightest whiff.

Her thoughts on Lady Catherine were growing increasingly dark at every report of her hatefulness. Georgiana was right to fear her, if this was how she treated Anne, and Elizabeth vowed never to subject her child to her ladyship's company. When Darcy saw the contents of this journal, he would surely agree; never would he have allowed his aunt to carry on in such a fashion had he been aware of it at the time.

Perhaps a schism is unavoidable, after all.

December 8, 1812

I must say that, aside from some persistent weakness, I have not felt this well in years. As a child I was always beset by some malady or another, but it was not until sometime after Father died that Mother began to worry that I would follow him to an early grave. He reportedly displayed all the same symptoms that I presently do—nausea, stomach pains, every sort of vile thing you can think of—and died within the year. Dr Nichols says that these things are often found in families, thus explaining how and why I am the last remaining de Bourgh, but swears that medical science has advanced enough to keep me alive. He was too late to save Father, but the hope is that he will succeed with me.

That said, I am beginning to experience some doubts regarding his prowess. I have not taken Mother's tonic—which Dr Nichols lauds to the skies as a miraculous cure—since I was in the throes of my last bout of illness, and I feel perfectly well. Better, even, than I did before the sickness beset me in November. Is this mere coincidence? Or have I been unintentionally weakened by the tonic? I have asked Mrs Jenkinson her opinion, and she is as lacking in answers as I. We have determined to abstain from the tonic a little longer and see what results.

Most of the entries following this one were entirely

uneventful, and Elizabeth was glad of it, for Anne's sake. The dear lady had partaken of more frequent excursions—driving out in her phaeton, calling upon Charlotte, visiting her tower, et cetera—while managing to avoid Lady Catherine save for at mealtimes.

Unfortunately, it seemed that Anne was not meant to enjoy good health and tranquillity for any great length of time. Near the end of December, she recorded an alarming report.

December 21, 1812

I have not witnessed Mother so enraged since learning of Darcy's marriage. Then, she boiled over with it, but now she is all cold menace. I am ashamed to admit that I quailed under her glare when she confronted me, certain I was about to be met with violence. I was not, but the clenching of her fists upon her cane made the danger seem imminent. I think the presence of Dr Nichols was the only thing that prevented it.

My sin: I confessed that I have been abstaining from my tonic.

I had genuinely thought she would be pleased to learn that I was strong enough to forgo it, but I was badly mistaken. Dr Nichols came to the house to examine me, as he does the third Monday of every month, and his report was favourable. So favourable that he asked whether I had been doing aught differently to effect such a positive change in my health. I informed him that the only change was the cessation of my tonic, at which point Mother's mood shifted for the worse.

Mrs Jenkinson attempted to defend me from Mother's chastisement by explaining that I had been better off without the tonic, but she would hear nothing of it. She lambasted my dear companion, accusing her of putting my life in danger by withholding my medicine. It was only after much pleading that I convinced Mother not to turn my dear Jenkinson out of the house.

When Mrs Jenkinson shared her observation that the tonic made me violently sick, Dr Nichols countered that it was meant to; according to him, purgatives are known to have healthful benefits for those beset by troublesome humours. By his reasoning, one needs to expel a sickness from the body lest it spread and overwhelm a person. Someone with a chronic condition such as my own requires this treatment frequently to keep the worst symptoms at bay. Dr Nichols credits Mother, a self-proclaimed herbalist, for the creation of the tonic in question. He has even been prescribing it to his other patients, thus accounting for his shortage back in November.

(By the bye, I have never been so horrified by my mother's knack for collecting weak-willed pawns to do her bidding. Mr Collins might be a dolt, but he has caused no real harm as far as I know—though that, perhaps, is due to the intervention of his sensible wife. Dr Nichols might well be sickening half the village to please his patroness.)

I begin to harbour grave doubts regarding my treatment. Both Mother and Dr Nichols appear absolutely convinced that my wellbeing depends upon my routine consumption of the tonic, despite the evidence that suggests the contrary to be true. I know they mean well, but is not the road to Hell paved with good intentions?

December 25, 1812, Christmas Day

I wish I could say that today was a merry occasion, but that would be a lie. Far from experiencing the joy of the season, I begin to grow afraid that my previous assumptions regarding Mother's good intentions are false. I begin to believe she means me harm.

Even as I write this, I doubt myself. What sort of mother would seek to hurt their own child? Accidents occur, certainly, but I cannot fathom the sort of monster who would injure their progeny by design. It seems impossible—and it ought to be! However…

I began taking the tonic again and fell immediately ill. So ill that I collapsed and had to be carried to my room, where I remained in the utmost agony for hours. When it came time to take another dose, I begged Mrs Jenkinson not to give it to me, but Mother stood over her and made sure her will was done. I was up for the rest of the night, writhing in pain and sure that I was going to die. Mrs Jenkinson stayed with me throughout, and I caught her sobbing over me more than once.

In the morning, Mother again prompted Mrs Jenkinson to feed me the tonic—which I now regard as nothing less than poison—despite every tearful objection. How could anyone witness such misery and still persist in the belief that they were helping?

I was wondering that very thing as Mrs Jenkinson prepared my cup, her hands shaking as she poured it out. I kept my eyes trained on Mother, beseeching her as much with my expression as with my words to cease this torment, but she remained unmoved. Indeed, she stared at me in utter silence, observing me minutely. When Mrs Jenkinson brought the tea to my lips—I was too weak to lift it myself—Mother gave me the queerest smile. I shall never forget it as long as I live, and I shudder to think of it now.

When the tea washed over my tongue, I knew that Mrs Jenkinson, at least, could no longer bear my suffering. It tasted only of chamomile, my favourite, and had neither that awful acrid taste nor yellowish tint to it which would suggest she had included the tonic. There was an unspoken understanding between us to say nothing of its absence.

That was three days ago, and I am only now strong enough to leave my rooms. Mother has never been fond of the sickroom and so left my care to Mrs Jenkinson once she was satisfied that the tonic regimen had been resumed. I played along, pretending to be sicker than I was to convince her.

Mrs Jenkinson, who can never bear to believe ill of anyone, remains convinced that Mother is merely misguided and that her intentions are good. I, however, am growing increasingly certain that she means to kill me. I cannot say why or for how long Mother has harboured this ill intent, but I fear that it is only a matter of time before she achieves her ultimate ends.

Elizabeth turned to the next page so quickly that she nearly tore it, her heart racing and aching for some reasonable explanation that would dispel the awful suspicions growing there.

What she found was the final entry.

January 1, 1813

Although it has been my habit since I was thirteen to begin a fresh journal at the start of each new year, I suspect that this will be my last entry—in this volume or any other. Mrs Jenkinson, my dear companion and last remaining protector, has been dismissed from her position and banished from Rosings Park. And it is all my fault.

This afternoon while Mrs Jenkinson prepared my tea, Mother became aware that I am again forgoing her wretched tonic. She confronted Mrs Jenkinson, ordering her to add it to my beverage as instructed, and the dear woman was brave enough to refuse, though she trembled visibly. She did her best to convince Mother that the tonic was harmful, but Mother refused to hear her. When it at last came to the point, Mrs Jenkinson would not be induced to knowingly injure me. She was dismissed on the spot and thrown from the house without even affording me a chance to bid her farewell.

I do not blame Mrs Jenkinson for my sorry state, for she did everything she could to protect me. The sweet creature did not understand, until the very end, what sort of danger I was in; or what sort of danger she found herself in—oh, Mother's threats were horrible! A bolder person than my dear Jenkinson would have crumbled under their weight, and she was as courageous as she knew how to be.

Whosoever should read this diary, I beseech you, please tell Mrs Jenkinson that she was more mother to me than my own. She looked after me, taught me, loved me as only a mother would, and I loved her as if I were her child in truth. The privilege I was born into cannot compare to the affection so freely given by my dear Jenkinson.

I write the next passage in the hopes that someone will eventually discover this diary where I have hidden it in my tower, safe from my mother's control. She never visits this place, has all but forgotten its existence, and I pray that it remains so. Should it not, every last scrap of evidence of her misdeeds, her despicable sins, will be erased, and I shall never see justice done.

One might wonder why I do not reach out for aid. With Dr Nichols as her conspirator, the Collinses blind to her malfeasance, and the servants fearful of her wrath, Mother has seen to it that there are none close by to render it. As for my family, the de Bourgh line is now defunct—or it will be in short order; I have no illusions that I have much longer to live—and the Fitzwilliams are loyal to Mother. Who would believe me? I hardly believe it myself, though there is little room left for doubt. I could count on Richard or Darcy to ride in on their white steeds and rescue me, but I fear my missive would reach them too late—if even I could send a letter to them without my mother being aware of it.

My final will and testament resides at the offices of a Mr Harold Stephens, local solicitor to Hunsford village. Should the document conveniently go missing, or should Mr Stephens bow to my mother's demands and disavow any knowledge of it, know that Mrs Jenkinson has been entrusted with a copy as well. Knowing for many years that Mother would be displeased by the contents of my will, for I altered it without her knowledge, I made certain that at least one record of it existed beyond her sphere of influence. I sent it off to London with Mrs Jenkinson during one of her visits to her sister, and she dutifully deposited it at a bank per my direction.

In case this diary falls into the wrong hands, I shall not say which one, but Mrs Jenkinson will know. I have instructed her to send word to my cousin Darcy once she hears of my death, and I have every confidence that he will see my final wishes executed to the letter. You will likely find my former companion on Edward Street, residing with her sister. Even if not, Mrs Younge will surely know how to reach her after the exchange of a few coins.

I can hear searchers calling my name from the woods, so I must close here before they discover the tower. I am not likely to possess the freedom or the strength to return, and so, to whomsoever this may concern, I bid you adieu.

Anne de Bourgh

CHAPTER TWENTY-SEVEN

The journal fell from Elizabeth's slackened grip into her lap, landing against her folded knees with a soft thump. She stared blindly at the page where Anne's last words were scrawled in trembling lettering, unable to fully comprehend what she had just read. Somewhere along the hall, a bell was chiming in rhythm with her thudding heartbeat.

Anne murdered.

Her own mother the culprit.

The tonic.

Dazed by shock, Elizabeth turned to behold the tea tray that had come in with her breakfast, placed innocuously on the low table before the hearth. She jumped up as if it had scalded her from across the room, inelegantly scrambling farther away from it and onto the bed.

Dear God, I drank nearly half the pot, was her initial dismayed thought. Her hands flew immediately to her abdomen, willing her child to move and assuage her worst fears. As active as the baby was in the middle of the night, it did not oblige her now, and her alarm swelled into panic.

Ding.

Suddenly, the baby jumped and began to wriggle as if prodded awake by the errant chiming of the unseen bell. One of Elizabeth's hands moved from her midsection to cup her mouth as a relieved sob tumbled from it. *All is well, all is well…*

It was several minutes before she could quell her tears and steady her nerves enough to think rationally. *Calm yourself, Lizzy. There is no reason to think Lady Catherine meddled with the tea. She has been in her rooms since Tuesday and has had nothing to do with the refreshments since then.*

Had not Lady Catherine been exceptionally persistent about Elizabeth drinking her dreadful tonic? It had not seemed strange until after reading Anne's accounting; her ladyship was always pestering someone to do something that she swore would be to their benefit, even when it was more often to their detriment. Elizabeth had never thought that Lady Catherine would attempt to *intentionally* harm her, however.

With shaking hands, she searched through Anne's diary, looking for the portion where she described the tonic—*yes, here it is*—and the question was resolved once and for all. The colour, the acrid smell…and Lady Catherine herself had once said that her daughter had taken it prior to her death. Horrible as the recounting was, it at least further reassured Elizabeth that her own tea had not been altered.

Perhaps it was some sort of mistake? Mrs Jenkinson might have been right all along in that her mistress was unaware of the tonic's toxicity and had given it to Anne with the aim of improving her health. Who would wish to murder their own child? Or—Elizabeth's hand curled protectively over her abdomen—someone else's?

Elizabeth again referred to the diary, leafing through the pages with one fumbling hand while the other remained pressed to her stomach.

> ...Mrs Jenkinson prepared my cup, her hands shaking as she poured it out. I kept my eyes trained on Mother, beseeching her as much with my expression as with my words to cease this torment, but she remained unmoved. Indeed, she stared at me in utter silence, observing me minutely. When Mrs Jenkinson brought the tea to my lips—I was too weak to lift it myself—Mother gave me the queerest smile. I shall never forget it as long as I live, and I shudder to think of it now.

There was no mistake. It was decidedly the same substance, and there was no mystery about what it would do to anyone who drank it. Anne was quite clear on that point—*Lady Catherine had known what she was doing.*

Sinking back into her pillows, Elizabeth allowed the diary to lie splayed open along its spine as she stared across the room at the tea tray. It sat there so innocently, a commonplace vision of hospitality, hiding its sinister secrets in plain sight. Or at least, it might have had Lady Catherine been at hand to serve her. She shuddered.

What should she do next? Anne herself had not been able to affect her own rescue; by the time she had realised what was happening, she had been too weak and helpless to reach out for aid. And Mrs Jenkinson, her single ally, had been banished from Rosings and threatened with dreadful consequences to keep any illicit knowledge to herself—not that there was any proof that she could offer.

Tell.

Anne's single utterance rang in Elizabeth's ears, and she knew instantly what needed to be done. "I must find Darcy."

Elizabeth scrambled off the bed. With the diary tucked securely against her chest, she raced for the door and flung herself out into the hall. She was only a few steps down the corridor, on her way to the stairs, when she was arrested in place by a voice that sent a shiver up her spine.

"Miss Bennet, there you are. Do come in for a spot of tea."

Unable to endure the stuffiness of her rooms any longer, or the ennui that beset her while separated from the rest of the household, Lady Catherine had ordered the double doors to the hall propped open. She had watched numerous individuals come and go from her armchair, foot elevated on a matching stool, though none of them had stayed long to entertain her, and she was ready to expire from the tedium. Darcy, who could usually be counted upon to do his familial duty—even though he never came to the point with Anne—had offered her some vague excuse about Fitzwilliam waiting for him in the study before scampering off. *Go on, then. Tear the house apart for Anne's will—you will never find it.*

Aside from her ungrateful nephew, she had been forced to contend with the scuttling of servants. Not even Collins, that noghead, could be bothered to call. She did not especially favour his company, but he would at least be an improvement over maids and footmen who had nothing to say aside from 'yes, your ladyship'. Lady Catherine had dismissed the lot of *them* ages ago because she could no longer stand their nervous fidgeting.

She sat at greater attention when the door next to hers opened with greater than usual force, and that strumpet her nephew had married came dashing out. Her dress was rumpled, and her hair was a fright, yet she seemed eager to make her way downstairs in that state by the way she all but ran down the carpeted corridor.

This was too good an opportunity to allow to pass.

"Miss Bennet, there you are. Do come in for a spot of tea."

The girl stopped dead in the centre of the hall, apparently petrified in place. It took her a good deal longer to turn round than it ought to, and once she had, Lady Catherine could see that her face had gone a milky white. Was the girl in such a rush because she was ill?

Perfect. "Come on, girl, do not stand there staring at me—come in, come in."

Miss Bennet's throat worked as she visibly swallowed. "Actually, I was just on my way to find my husband. I have an errand that will permit no delay."

"Nonsense, whatever it is can wait until after you have taken some refreshment."

The girl took a few mincing steps backwards, clutching a nondescript book tightly to her chest. Her knuckles were turning white from strain. "I really must speak to Mr Darcy—"

"Come in and *sit down*," Lady Catherine barked in her most commanding tone. "I have been exceedingly dull, and I insist that you come in and entertain me. Ring the bell as you enter."

Miss Bennet at last drew closer, though she acted as if she were approaching the gallows. She did indeed tug on the bellpull as she moved past it, wincing as it jingled out of sight. She took a seat upon the chaise, perched on the very edge of the cushion as if poised to flee at a moment's notice. The book she was holding remained tightly within her clutches.

"What is that you are reading?"

Miss Bennet swiftly removed the pale leather tome from her lap and stuffed it beneath her leg. "Just an old novel."

"I suppose it is full of ridiculous murder plots and villainous witches and the like? I have never cared for such nonsense."

Miss Bennet's eyes widened. "I suppose it is."

A maid entered just then, bringing the stuttering conversation to a halt. Tea was ordered, and Miss Bennet attempted to demure, but Lady Catherine remained firm in her purpose; she might not have another opportunity to feed the chit her special tonic if she did not do so now. Sir Lewis and Anne had been easy enough, for where had they to go but Rosings Park? Darcy meant to leave on Saturday and take his wife with him, so time was short to accomplish her ends.

With that in mind, Lady Catherine flicked her fingers

at the wooden chest sitting upon her dressing table. "Bring that to me."

Miss Bennet appeared to hesitate but then rose to do as bidden. Oddly, she took the book with her, resulting in her balancing it and the chest when she came back. She set the box on the tea table and resettled herself on the chaise.

"Open it."

She did so and unaccountably flinched, staring in what Lady Catherine believed to be horror. *What has she to be so anxious about? She cannot know what it will do to her.*

"My special tonic. You do not appear at all well today, so I must insist that you take some. Carrying a child is a taxing endeavour, and you must keep your strength up."

The girl seemed, for once, at a loss for words. She merely stared at the rows of yellow tonic in their glass phials as if she could hardly comprehend them.

It ought to be impossible, but…does she suspect?

"My mother was quite the horticulturalist," Lady Catherine commented, observing Miss Bennet closely. The girl's foot bounced beneath her skirts as if she could not will it into stillness. "As was my sister. I am sure you have seen her rose garden at Pemberley."

Miss Bennet nodded.

"I, too, enjoy an English garden, though of course I do not condescend to till the land myself. I leave that to rougher hands than mine, such as your cousin's. You must have noted how well he keeps me supplied with flowers.

"My mother not only passed down an appreciation of gardening but also her vast knowledge of herbs and tinctures. She did not dabble in the stillroom, of course, but she was fascinated by the cultivation of plants for the purpose of remedies, ointments, and the like. I have frequently studied her notes and adapted her methods myself. You see how Collins's garden thrives under my direction, to say nothing of the plants here.

"This tonic," Lady Catherine waved her jewelled hand at the open chest of phials, "is distilled from daffodils grown right here at Rosings Park. Dr Nichols has begun to use it for his other patients, and it has done wonders for them."

Miss Bennet, whose gaze had travelled to the case of tonic, snapped her attention back to Lady Catherine. She wavered where she sat, as if on the verge of fainting, and her chest was beginning to rise and fall with alarming rapidity.

"It did not help my poor Anne, unfortunately," lamented Lady Catherine, an irrepressible grin stretching across her face, "but then I suppose it cannot mend a disappointed heart. She took a turn for the worse after Darcy married."

Whatever colour remained in Miss Bennet's countenance instantly fled, leaving her a ghostly, chalky white. She was clutching at the cushion beneath her as if for dear life. "Lady Catherine, I...I-I must return to my rooms. I fear I am about to be ill."

She knows.

"My tonic will put you to rights. Stay for a cup of tea before you go."

Clang, clang, clang!

Lady Catherine was distracted by the loud resonance of bells. They rang at a furious clip, creating such a racket that conversation became all but impossible. The noise was so deafening that she was forced to press her hands over her ears.

Tearing her gaze away from her intended prey, Lady Catherine glared into the hall, where a maid was swiftly approaching with the tea service. She bent to set it down on the table as Lady Catherine demanded, "What is making that infernal noise?"

Clang, clang, clang!

The maid leant in closer, the tray still suspended between her hands. Her face was scrunched in concentration as she shouted, "I beg your pardon, my lady?"

"What is making that noise?"

"Eh?"

"The bells, you stupid girl! Where is that ringing coming from?"

The clanging was suddenly overshadowed by a loud crash issuing from a much closer proximity. The maid had lost her grip on the tea tray, and it had dropped to the table, crushing the box of tonic beneath its weight even as the china shattered into various pieces. A yellow trickle bled from the mangled chest, dripping onto the carpet below.

"Look what you have done!" Lady Catherine screeched at the maid, who shrank back several paces in the face of her mistress's rage. If she had her cane to hand, she would have given the worthless chit something to cower about.

"My goodness, how unfortunate!" Miss Bennet cried, her voice shrill and frantic. It was barely audible over that blasted clanging. "Do let us call for some help, hm?"

Miss Bennet was on her feet the next instant and

bustling the clumsy maid away the one after. She paused only long enough to retrieve her book, and they escaped over the threshold before Lady Catherine could issue so much as a single order to the contrary.

Clang, clang, CLANG!

Not that they would have heard me over this ghastly noise!

She might have gone after them, but she had already made the attempt to leave her chambers earlier in the day, and her ankle had collapsed under her weight. Even if she were willing to endure the pain, she could not possibly overtake them when she was hobbled. All that was left to her was glowering at their retreating forms as they abandoned her to the horrid knelling of the inexplicable bells.

The moment Miss Bennet's skirt vanished from sight, so too did the bells cease their assault upon her ears. Lady Catherine tentatively lowered her hands but heard not so much as a jingle. She was left alone in the ringing silence.

CHAPTER TWENTY-EIGHT

Fitzwilliam tossed a sheaf of papers onto his discard stack, then turned away coughing at the cloud of dust he had stirred up. "It is like searching for a needle in a haystack. Why do we not just let Lady Catherine have the old pile and be done with it?"

Darcy picked up another bundle of age-yellowed documents yet to be eliminated from their search. He did not lift his gaze from the page he was skimming as he replied, "Because that is not how inheritance works. We must do our due diligence and ensure the proper heir is identified."

"Who else would she have left it to?"

A frenzied scrambling on the other side of the wall adjoining the library distracted Darcy from answering. He looked up from his page—which turned out to be a laundry bill—and frowned at the panelling. Fitzwilliam stopped to do the same. "Do you hear something?"

The scratching and clamouring continued, now

accompanied by muffled grumbling. "Which one was it...*The Lady of the Lake*...? No..."

"Is that Elizabeth?" Curious, Darcy dropped the papers onto the desk and moved to the wall sconce that operated the hidden door. The concealed panel popped free and listed inwards. He grasped the edge and pulled it fully open before stepping out into the library beyond.

There was his wife, her trembling fingers pulling book after book from the shelves to his left, apparently searching for the one that would grant her access to the study. She was far from discovering it; *Le Morte d'Arthur* was to his right and on a lower shelf.

"Elizabeth?"

She jerked upright and scurried back a few paces, apparently frightened by his sudden appearance. When she turned to face him, Darcy was immediately alarmed by her countenance; her eyes were wide and bulging, her pallor was ghastly, and she seemed to be breathing too hard for her exertions. She froze when she saw him, then cried out and threw herself into his arms. Darcy stumbled back a step as he caught her.

The colonel appeared at Darcy's shoulder, his typically jovial face contorted with concern. "What is going on?"

"Anne!" Elizabeth said on a gasp. "The tonic! *Lady Catherine.*"

Darcy had never seen his wife so overwrought. He led her to the nearest armchair and urged her to sit. When she would not release him, clinging to his coat as if for dear life, he sank onto the cushion himself and pulled her into his lap. She acquiesced to this new position willingly, twining her arms about his neck and burying her head under his chin.

Darcy was at a loss as to what to do. He looked to Fitzwilliam, who appeared equally baffled.

It was some minutes before Elizabeth was able to collect herself into any semblance of composure, but she managed it with several steadying breaths and Darcy's stalwart presence. At length, she calmed, though she remained pale and visibly distressed. "Forgive me, I have suffered something of a fright."

"There is nothing to forgive. Can you tell me what has you so upset?"

"I have just finished reading Anne's diary—oh! The diary, where is it?"

Elizabeth moved to stand, but Darcy held fast to her hips. "Anne's diary? What has that to do with anything? Did you read something that disturbed you?"

"Before I tell you, we must find the diary! It is the only evidence."

"Evidence?" Darcy's brow folded in consternation. "Of what?"

"Here it is," Fitzwilliam announced, standing from where he had bent to retrieve the volume from the floor. "You must have dropped it in your search for the hidden door."

Elizabeth breathed a heavy sigh of evident relief. "Thank goodness. I do not know how I possibly could have explained without it."

Fitzwilliam crossed the room to where they were seated and took up a chair opposite them. He placed the diary on the low table between them before settling more comfortably, legs crossed and fingers steepled as if he were anticipating a long story. "Perhaps you ought to do so and relieve us of the anticipation. What has you in such a dither?"

Elizabeth sucked in a deep breath then released it. "I do not know whether you will believe me, but…"

She went on to relate the most fantastical tale Darcy had ever heard, or close to it. Anne's diary was, by Elizabeth's description, full of outrageous theories and accusations against Lady Catherine, which, if true, were monstrous. What sort of mother would harm her own child? Even an accidental poisoning was terrible to contemplate, but premeditated murder? No, it could not be so.

Yet Elizabeth seemed convinced that Lady Catherine was guilty. Not only did she hold Anne's diary as evidence, but also a recent encounter she had only just escaped in the mistress's chambers. Whatever Lady Catherine had said or done must have unintentionally coincided with what Anne had written.

"…so I ran from there as fast as I could and sought you out here. I hardly know how I managed it. I was so confused and frightened."

When she concluded her story on a quavering note, they were all silent for some time, digesting this new and outlandish information. Darcy could not speak for either his wife or his cousin, but he was admittedly sceptical of Elizabeth's findings. Anne had been sickly for many years, and her death, while sudden, had not been entirely unexpected. Further, it was entirely possible that her illness had addled her mind, making her believe in preposterous things; what if her accounting were nothing more than delusion?

Fitzwilliam was the one to break the silence by the clearing of his throat. "What you have brought us is... extraordinary. How can you be so certain it is true?"

"If it is not true, then not only was Anne out of her mind, but I am as well. You did not see how Lady Catherine looked at me—that horrid smile." Elizabeth shivered, inducing Darcy to rub at the goose-skin erupting along her arms. "And she all but confessed to having the necessary knowledge to poison someone. Did you know she makes the tonic herself?"

Fitzwilliam nodded. "She has mentioned it is her recipe, yes. Though I believe Nichols is the one to actually brew the concoction for her."

"She told me she has it distilled from *daffodils*." She said this in a tone implying that Lady Catherine had shown her hand, but Darcy was perplexed. Botany had never been amongst his interests beyond the practical aspects of plotting out a harvest, and Fitzwilliam—whose countenance betrayed his own bewilderment—had not even that much expertise. Testily, Elizabeth continued, "Daffodils are exceptionally toxic to anyone who eats them. I am no expert, but I have worked with my mother and sisters in the stillroom, and we were warned to never use daffodils in our tinctures. A small dose is enough to make someone violently ill."

"What sort of ill?" Darcy asked.

"Nausea, vomiting, stomach cramps...it is awful. One of our pigs escaped into the garden once and ate up the flowerbed. The poor thing did not make it."

A faint prickle of unease assailed Darcy, for Elizabeth described Anne's symptoms perfectly. Of course, many different ailments resulted in stomach upset, but if Lady

Catherine was truly making her tonic from a toxic plant...

"Perhaps it was an accidental poisoning?" Darcy suggested hopefully. "As we all know, my aunt purports to be an authority on many things, yet she often overestimates her prowess."

Elizabeth shook her head. "I thought that myself at first, as did Anne and Mrs Jenkinson, but when she stopped taking the tonic, Lady Catherine insisted that she resume. Mrs Jenkinson explained frankly that it was making Anne ill and that she should not take it, but Lady Catherine would not hear her. When Mrs Jenkinson persisted, sure that a mother would never wish to harm her child, she was dismissed and threatened to hold her tongue."

"What if Anne was out of her wits?" asked Fitzwilliam. Darcy, who had reasoned the same, nodded.

"Anne's accounting is entirely lucid, I assure you. You must read it for yourself if you do not believe me."

"It is not that we disbelieve you, dearest," Darcy soothed, rubbing her back, "it is only that what you have brought to our attention is..."

"Ludicrous."

Darcy glared at his cousin, who offered a chagrined smile in return. "I was going to say incredible. Anne might have believed her mother meant to harm her, but is it not more plausible that she misunderstood? She was weak and dying when she wrote that diary. Furthermore, Lady Catherine would have no motive to do what you are implying."

"Aside from wishing to punish Anne for refusing to

indulge her most cherished wish?" Elizabeth looked to Darcy with palpable meaning.

Fitzwilliam remained unconvinced, his brow lifted in a sceptical arch. "Lady Catherine has always hoped to tie Rosings to Pemberley, it is true, but I cannot see her descending to such depravity when Anne failed to marry Darcy. It is nonsensical. No one could possibly be that petty."

"I assure you that this diary"—Elizabeth laid her hand upon its cover, her fine eyes ablaze with conviction—"is absolutely full of examples of your aunt's wanton viciousness towards Anne. She treated her own daughter worse than a stray dog in the street, sniping and striking her whenever her mood grew foul. I admit that I did not think it possible at first, but further reflection has convinced me that Lady Catherine is capable of many despicable things."

Elizabeth's accusations sat heavily in Darcy's gut. "I saw no sign of injury when we visited. Are you certain?"

"Most of the abuse was inflicted by Lady Catherine's tongue, but there were occasional beatings. I think the tonic was her primary weapon—first for control, then to dole out retribution."

Darcy looked to Fitzwilliam, who appeared as unnerved as he felt by Elizabeth's reasoning. It was well known that Lady Catherine was a captious ogre—they themselves used to flee from her shadow as boys—but this was something far worse than hurt feelings. *Could it be possible?*

"Do not take my word for it," declared Elizabeth, lifting Anne's diary from where it sat innocently on the table. She placed it in Darcy's hands. "See for yourself."

Hours later, after Fitzwilliam had retreated to his rooms for the night, Darcy reclined on the library sofa lost in the labyrinth of his thoughts. Elizabeth slumbered fitfully against his thigh while he stroked her hair absently and stared into the fire, contemplating what he had read in Anne's diary.

It could not be true, and yet...all the pieces fitted. The timing of events all aligned with his understanding of them; there was the missing will, the spontaneously dismissed Mrs Jenkinson, and the suddenness of Anne's death. And the spite so uniformly visited upon her by Lady Catherine—Darcy had seen some small signs of it in the past yet never realised how horrendous it truly was. Why had she not sought help? Did she believe it was merely the way of things to be mistreated by one's parent? *I ought to have protected her.*

Further, much as Darcy strained to find some recollection to refute his suspicions, he could not recall observing any particular instance of grief in Lady Catherine since arriving at Rosings Park. She had donned her mourning clothes, but little else suggested she had recently lost her only daughter. She was as cantankerous and domineering as always but not despondent. The greatest show of feeling she had displayed in his presence was anger—and that had been primarily directed at Elizabeth.

Then there was her forceful insistence that Elizabeth take her dreadful tonic. Lady Catherine was stubborn, but she could generally be managed if one were firm with her, and yet she had not yielded in the slightest after repeated refusals. One would think that, after Anne had died, she might have at least doubted the efficacy of her brew, but she had persisted against all indication that the tonic was unhelpful.

A quick perusal of a botany guide had confirmed Elizabeth's assertion that daffodils—from the genus *Narcissus*—were poisonous, which was supposedly common knowledge amongst those who dealt frequently with plants. Elizabeth had known it, her sisters likely did as well, and Lady Catherine herself was a professed herbalist; surely, she would have been aware of their toxicity?

On the one hand, the totality of information proved that his aunt had, at the very least, behaved irresponsibly in regard to Anne's health. It was not entirely out of character for Lady Catherine to become caught up in her own greatness or to dismiss the opinions of others when they contradicted her own. It was just like her to be heedless of the harm she caused others.

On the other, a good deal of it suggested something more sinister afoot. She *must* have known that daffodils were not a healthful component, and yet she had distilled a 'remedy' from them. Then there was her apparently great anger that Darcy had married Elizabeth, which, by Anne's report, had been terrible to behold. Having failed to secure the match her mother wanted, had Anne outlived her usefulness?

Darcy's mind revolved round and round, the known facts tumbling about in his head like leaves in the wind, but he still could come to no firm conclusions. Was his aunt guilty of the worst crimes imaginable? Or was she merely ignorant and stubborn? Was she resentful enough of Elizabeth to do her harm? Or was the encounter above stairs merely a grave misunderstanding on his wife's part?

He was distracted from his whirling thoughts by Elizabeth shifting in his lap. Darcy might not have all the answers to this dilemma, but one thing he knew for certain: he would protect his wife and their child at any cost.

CHAPTER TWENTY-NINE

As thunder grumbled overhead and rain lashed at the windows, Darcy felt a considerable sense of foreboding. The more sizeable storm was in his mind as he grappled with what he knew and what he thought he knew—his aunt, a murderess? Anne, her victim? Elizabeth, her next target? He would have bustled his wife into their carriage that moment and retreated to London had it been safe enough for travel, but the weather made the roads muddy and slick, hazardous even for those not in a delicate condition. He could not take the risk to Elizabeth's—or the baby's—health, not without knowing where the greater danger truly lay.

His gaze wandered from the wet scene outside to where his wife sat in a chair by the library fireplace, bundled in her favourite green shawl with a book propped open against her knees even as her eyes drooped slowly closed. Poor Elizabeth, beset by dreams all night long, had not slept peaceably, and the dark circles under her eyes were a testament to that.

Freddy lay curled up on the hearth rug at her feet, watchful for any slight movement from her mistress. The dog had popped up repeatedly to examine Elizabeth at any time she so much as yawned and would not lie back down until assured with scratches and soothing words that she was well. Percy had vehemently protested against admitting Freddy to the house, given Lady Catherine's edicts that dogs belonged in the kennels, but Darcy was glad he had held firm on the matter. Freddy not only provided a good deal of comfort to his dear wife but would serve as an admirable guard if it ever came to…no, he could not think of it without feeling sick.

The door to the hall swung open, and Darcy, equally as vigilant as Freddy, stood immediately to attention. His stance eased somewhat when he recognised the figure of his cousin. "What news?"

The colonel had set out for Hunsford village that morning to gather as much information as he could about the fire that had destroyed the solicitor's office there. Per Lady Catherine's information, it had occurred several months prior to his cousin's death, yet it was not mentioned in her diary. Such an omission was odd for Anne, who would have necessarily been aware of such a catastrophic event; not only did she frequently drive her phaeton through the village, but all the locals would have been gossiping about it. Either it was a gross oversight on Anne's part or something else was afoot. Fitzwilliam had volunteered to venture out and discover the truth of the matter.

His cousin hastily shut the door behind him and traversed the room to the seating area, where Darcy met him. Elizabeth, instantly cured of her malaise by the colonel's entrance, sat up straighter in her chair and looked to him with anticipation writ across her features.

Fitzwilliam's coppery hair was somewhat damp from his trip to the village, but he had obviously changed his clothes, which were pristine. "No one can tell me *how* the fire began," he said without preamble, "but it is the assumption that Mr Stephens must have left a candle burning and it tipped over sometime in the night, sending the place up. I imagine a business like that, full of dry old documents, would burn like a tinder box. It is a miracle they were able to contain the blaze before it spread to the next building. More importantly, I have ascertained *when* it occurred—February the twenty-eighth."

Darcy frowned. "Did not Anne die on the twenty-sixth?"

Fitzwilliam's eyes darted between them with meaning. "She did indeed. Thus explaining the omission in her diary. However, our aunt led my father to believe it had occurred well prior to Anne's death. It is not definitive proof of anything, of course, but the timing is dubious. After all, why should Lady Catherine lie about something like that unless there was a reason to misdirect us?"

Elizabeth was quick to answer. "She could not have your father looking more deeply into the incident and so thought to make it appear unrelated. If the fire occurred prior to Anne's demise, there would be little reason to suspect there is foul play afoot."

"Exactly." Fitzwilliam tipped his chin to Elizabeth, his aspect grim. "I admit that I have been sceptical about Anne's reasoning, assuming that her mind must have been addled near the end, but I have to say my doubt is diminishing. There is no one thing that convinces me, but rather the totality of the evidence is suggestive. Anne's documentation of her illness, Mrs Jenkinson's sudden dismissal, the timing of the fire at Mr Stephens's office, Lady Catherine's shading of the facts...threads that, when woven together, create a disturbing tapestry."

Nodding along with the colonel's recitation, Darcy could not help reaching the same conclusion. "Agreed. The question now is how to proceed. We cannot merely confront Lady Catherine with our findings because she will never admit to any sort of wrongdoing. Even were the evidence indisputable—and it is a far cry from that—she would resolutely maintain her innocence until the end."

"The only missing piece is the will," said Fitzwilliam. "If we were to actually lay our hands upon it, it would go a long way to proving our conjectures. Even if it does not necessarily prove murder, it at least suggests fraud on her part, and my father could intervene. If nothing else, she will not be allowed to profit from her malfeasance. Of course," he concluded with a wry grimace, "inheriting this place might be more curse than blessing."

Elizabeth's titter at Fitzwilliam's jest died away quickly. "I should like to see justice done on Anne's behalf, if possible. She wants...that is, I am sure she would wish the truth to come out."

Fitzwilliam exchanged a look with Darcy that was at

once baffled and incredulous. "You speak as if you have conferred with my late cousin about this."

The way Elizabeth's gaze dropped to her lap and she fiddled with her fingers told Darcy that she possibly had—or thought so, at any rate. He recalled then that Elizabeth had mentioned dreaming of Anne previously and wondered whether that was the source.

"You will not believe this," she said quietly, still staring at her knees, "but Anne has been visiting me. It was she who led me to the diary in the first place, in fact, and the origins of our new knowledge."

The library was silent save for the crackling fire, lashing rain, and the unobtrusive jingle of a bell somewhere in the house. Neither gentleman seemed to know quite what to say to this revelation, incredible as it was.

Darcy's first instinct was to disbelieve what his wife was telling them, having never been inclined to a superstitious bent previously. However, their mutual experience of the past summer gave him pause; no matter how he had rationalised the strange teasing lights, the inexplicably locked doors, and marvellous coincidences of that time, a part of him could not explain how all of it had coalesced into his happily ever after with Elizabeth. He had thought it due to Fate, but was that any less preposterous than meddling spirits? Elizabeth finding the tower—the existence of which she had previously been in ignorance—and Anne's diary hidden therein defied rational explanation every bit as much as their accidental meeting in a gallery at midnight. Perhaps they *were* being guided by unseen forces.

By the plain expression of dubiety on Fitzwilliam's face, his cousin had reached the opposite conclusion.

"Well, that is…ahem, forgive me, but what you say is incredible. It is difficult to believe that Anne's spirit—ghost, or what have you—revealed this mystery to you."

Elizabeth straightened her spine and squared her jaw. "I assure you it is true. No matter how 'incredible' it may sound, I would never have found Anne's diary without her showing me the way."

Darcy approached his wife and laid a hand upon her shoulder, drawing her attention. Softly, he assured her, "I believe you."

She appeared nonplussed, with her mouth gaping open and her lashes fluttering in fitful spasms. "You do?"

"I do," he replied, all earnestness. "I admit that I have been sceptical in the past, but after last summer I am more inclined to accept that there is much in the world that I do not fully comprehend. What was it that Shakespeare said?"

Her gaze softened as she quoted, "'There are more things in heaven and earth, Horatio, than are dreamt of in your philosophy.'"

"Exactly so." He stroked her cheek, and she leant into the caress, eyes shining.

"Pardon me," interjected Fitzwilliam, a dry quality to his tone, "but I require more convincing. I mean no offence."

He directed the last to Elizabeth, who waved his apology away. "It does not particularly matter whether you believe me, for there are plenty of concrete facts to arouse suspicion regardless of how we discovered them. Anne's diary is perhaps our strongest piece of evidence, but it requires further corroboration. We need the testimony of Mrs Jenkinson."

"You are correct, of course." Fitzwilliam bowed to her in concession. "It ought to be our first matter of business. Whether she seconds Anne's accusations or refutes them, Mrs Jenkinson is the person we must apply to for answers."

Darcy picked the diary up from the tea table where it had been innocuously sitting since that morning when they had surreptitiously escaped their chambers. It had not been out of his possession since Elizabeth had brought it to them the previous day. He turned to Anne's final entry, skimmed it, and tapped the paragraph of interest. "Right here, it says that Mrs Jenkinson most likely went to her sister in Edward Street—Dear Lord."

Fitzwilliam's mirroring grimace told Darcy that he understood the problem, but Elizabeth looked between them in puzzlement. "What is the matter?"

"I had all but forgotten that Mrs Jenkinson is related to Mrs Younge," Darcy explained, though he despised the necessity of speaking *that woman's* name. It tasted rancid on his tongue. "Her elder sister, in fact. That was how Lady Catherine came to recommend her to me as Georgiana's companion two years ago."

Comprehension arising, Elizabeth's nose wrinkled. "Goodness. I never would have thought that the pair of them would be sisters."

"They are entirely different creatures, I assure you. Mrs Jenkinson's devotion to Anne was genuine, while Mrs Younge's to Georgiana was...well. It is an unpleasant business but one we must undertake. We shall leave for London as soon as this ghastly rain lets up."

Elizabeth gripped his sleeve. "We cannot leave without seeing this to the end. What of Anne and the justice she is owed?"

Clasping the hand she clutched him with, Darcy replied, "If our suspicions are true, we cannot stay here, dearest. I dare not risk your safety, especially if you truly are her next target."

"But all the tonic was destroyed," she argued. "Unless she means to harangue me to death, I do not see how she can harm me. Besides, what if Anne needs to communicate again? So far, I am the only person she has reached out to—unless you count what I presume are assaults upon Lady Catherine."

Elizabeth's conjecture provided a new perspective on the overturned teacups, falling paintings, obliterated thrones, misplaced footstools, and destruction of her tonic but did not provide Darcy any real sense of ease. "If nothing else, I need to seek out Mrs Jenkinson and see my uncle about our suspicions. We cannot stay, Elizabeth."

"I will not leave," she replied, all stubbornness. She withdrew her hand from his and stood, ready to do battle. "You cannot force me unless you intend to throw me over your shoulder and make off with me in the carriage like a common highwayman. Anne requires my aid, and I intend to provide it."

"Elizabeth—" He cut himself off, full of exasperation, and pinched his nose with his thumb and forefinger. "You are being unreasonable."

"No, I am being *responsible*. I cannot, nor will I, allow a murderess to go free and do nothing about it. My place is here where I can communicate with Anne and fulfil her final wishes."

Their argument might have persisted for longer if Fitzwilliam had not interrupted. "Let us compromise. Darcy, why do you not stay here with your wife while I go to London? Both of us are not required on the errand, and frankly it will go much faster if I am the one to conduct it. If I leave now, I can be there and back by tomorrow. Further, with the rain and Elizabeth in her condition, it is not at all safe for her to travel. She is better served staying here under your guard, even if she must share a roof with Lady Catherine."

Darcy threw up his hands, frustrated. "Very well! Since you are both against me, it will be as you say, but I need you to promise me"—he said this to Elizabeth, fixing her with his most weighty stare—"that you will not spend any time with my aunt, alone or even supervised. You will stay at my side at all times, or barred in our rooms if I should ever be required to step away from you. Above all, do not eat or drink anything without my approval—I shall task Blake and Bailey with overseeing our meals whilst we remain in residence to ensure that Lady Catherine has not enlisted someone to doctor your tea. We cannot be entirely certain that none of the tonic survives. I know you do not care for my coddling, but I require this of you in order to keep you and our child safe. Are we in agreement?"

Elizabeth nodded along throughout his diatribe. "Yes, of course. I have had quite enough of your aunt's company to last me a lifetime, I assure you. What you ask is entirely reasonable, under the circumstances."

"Good." He turned to the colonel and held the diary out to him. "Godspeed."

CHAPTER THIRTY

The couple had largely managed to avoid Lady Catherine's company for the remainder of Friday, save for one unavoidable instance. Darcy had been called to her chamber to defend Fitzwilliam's sudden departure and listen to her vociferous complaints on the matter. Apparently, the colonel's excuse of 'pressing business for my unit' had not satisfied her, though likely nothing would have. Darcy had escaped her clutches by fabricating a need to attend Elizabeth, whom her ladyship was told was bedridden. Every offer of succour from tea to calling upon the services of Dr Nichols had been firmly rebuffed, leaving their hostess more irritable than ever.

At length, Darcy had managed to extricate himself and return to a fretful Elizabeth, whom he had safely ensconced in their shared chambers with Blake and Freddy standing guard. Their personal servants had not been apprised of the full scope of their suspicions—it was far too soon to risk such exposure of Lady Catherine's character; what if they were wrong?—but were told enough to understand that no one besides themselves were to be trusted with Mrs Darcy's care. Darcy had given them some twaddle about her stomach being too sensitive for the food of Rosings Park, but he had been so severe on the subject that it left no room for countermand. It was clear from Blake's minute attention to Elizabeth's every sniffle and Bailey's reported row with the chef that they were taking his admonitions seriously.

Freddy had remained at Elizabeth's side, despite the continued protestations of Percy, for Darcy would not countenance any comfort being revoked from his beloved wife. Freddy had been a stalwart companion and soothing influence on her fraying nerves. Though often wilfully playful, the dog had seemed to sense that her mistress required steadiness, and she provided it ably.

As safe as she felt surrounded by Darcy, Freddy, and their servants, Elizabeth found herself frequently anxious about the babe. She had discovered that they would become active immediately after she ate, so she kept a plate of biscuits—whose baking Blake had carefully managed herself—at hand to nibble on whenever she required the reassurance of feeling her child move.

Elizabeth had dreamt of Anne again the previous night and informed her of the colonel's jaunt to London to seek out Mrs Jenkinson. Anne had nodded as if already aware of this, which Elizabeth supposed she must be; it had become apparent of late that Anne was watching over them all like a guardian angel.

Since Elizabeth had woken with a headache and it continued to rain, albeit at more of a drizzle than a deluge, it had been agreed that the Darcys would remain in their chambers for the day rather than going down to the library. They had snoozed away the early morning, then pursued quiet activities to keep their minds active while their bodies remained stationary. Both of them frequently peered out of the window in hopes of seeing a carriage rolling up the drive.

Darcy stood from the desk where he had been languorously attending to his correspondence, groaning and stretching out his back. After a particularly loud pop, he lamented, "I am growing too old to sit for so long."

Freddy unfurled herself and hopped from the bed. She went to Darcy and began pawing at his leg, whining.

"I believe she requires a walk," Elizabeth commented around a yawn. "I could use one as well, lest I fall asleep, but I suppose I ought to remain here." She nodded to the window, which was bespeckled with rain droplets.

Darcy ruffled Freddy's ears indulgently. "Agreed. I shall take her myself. I would enjoy stretching my legs, even if I must get a little damp in the pursuit. Let me call for Blake so she can sit with you while I am gone."

"No, leave Blake to her duties. She ought to be bringing a tray up soon and even now is likely overseeing its creation."

Frowning, Darcy protested, "You cannot be in here alone."

"Nonsense, I am perfectly safe in our rooms with the doors locked. You will return shortly, I am sure, and Blake will undoubtedly be here before you. If I am alone for more than five minutes I shall be greatly surprised."

Darcy's eyes darted between her and an increasingly agitated Freddy, who was dancing on her paws in that particular way that meant she was on the verge of soiling the carpet. He sighed resignedly. "Very well, but be sure to lock the door after I leave, and do not open it to anyone besides me. Promise me."

She yawned again, delaying her reply. "I promise."

"Very good." Darcy planted a kiss to her forehead, then left with Freddy trotting after him.

Elizabeth remained reclined in her window seat for a few dozing minutes, disinclined to move due to her weighty fatigue. When her chin dipped to her chest and she startled back to full wakefulness, an errant thought reminded her that she had not locked the door after Darcy's departure. With a stretch and a groan, she roused herself and shuffled across the room.

She had just reached for the key when a heavy knock sounded from the other side. Assuming it was her husband, chased back indoors by the pelting rain, she grasped the latch and pulled the door open, prepared to favour him with a teasing jest.

It withered on her tongue an instant later as she realised her error. She moved to close the door again but found it blocked by the blunt, silver-tipped end of a cane, which shoved against the wood with enough force to cause her to lose her footing. This was enough to grant entry to Lady Catherine.

"I see you are up and about again, Miss Bennet," observed the lady as she pushed her way inside, her steps uneven on her injured ankle. She nudged the door closed behind her with the cane. "You might have improved faster had you drunk my tonic when you had the chance."

Elizabeth, still unsteady on her feet thanks to her

shock, staggered backwards and away from the intruder. She regained her balance against one of the bedposts, placing it between her and Lady Catherine like a sentinel. "I rather doubt that."

Lady Catherine leant heavily on her cane in her pursuit. "What do you know, impertinent chit that you are?"

Standing straight and steady, Elizabeth declared, "I know everything."

※

Almost the moment he and Freddy had stepped out of doors, the anxiously awaited carriage containing Fitzwilliam and Lord Matlock pulled up in the drive. His cousin sprang out of it the instant that it halted, his uncle scrambling after him, and they raced up the steps and into the front hall without awaiting assistance from the bevy of footmen and their umbrellas.

Darcy was hard upon their heels, eager for news. He was so impatient for it that he blithely disregarded Percy's cry of dismay when Freddy shook herself dry all over his livery. "Well?"

Fitzwilliam swept his hat from his head, then slicked his damp, ruddy hair away from his face. His countenance was grim. "It is all true."

"All of it?" Although he had rationally expected this conclusion, Darcy was aghast all the same. "Mrs Jenkinson corroborated Anne's testimony?"

"She did, indeed," said Lord Matlock, answering for his son. Although the earl could never be accurately described as a cheerful sort of man, rarely did he carry the sort of gravity that seemed to weigh upon his shoulders at present. "Spoke to her myself, after Richard brought her to me. He showed me the diary as well. My sister has much to answer for."

"Where is Mrs Jenkinson?"

Lord Matlock grunted as he shrugged out of his damp greatcoat. "In London, under my protection, as is the will she concealed on Anne's behalf. It, as well as the diary, are in the safekeeping of my solicitor."

"And who—"

A loud crash sounded from above, inducing all three gentlemen to angle their heads back and stare at the ceiling, mouths gaping open. Freddy's ears lay flat upon her head, and the hair on her neck stood to attention as she growled in the wake of the commotion.

"What the devil was that?" demanded Lord Matlock.

Clang, clang, clang!

An icy feeling of deepest dread filled Darcy's gut. "Elizabeth!"

He was darting up the stairs without being conscious of taking flight. Freddy was ahead of him by several paces, while Fitzwilliam and Lord Matlock hurried along behind, all of them desperate to thwart whatever calamity was now occurring.

CHAPTER THIRTY-ONE

Ding. Ding. Ding.

Really, is every clock in Kent broken? That ringing is insufferable!

Forcing her aggravation aside, Lady Catherine responded to Miss Bennet's assertion with a scoff. "You know 'everything', do you? That is just like you, always believing yourself the quickest wit, the cleverest person in the room. You know *nothing*, child."

The impudent chit glared at Lady Catherine even as she cowered behind the bedpost. "I know you poisoned your own daughter—murdered her, in fact. I have proof."

At this, Lady Catherine threw her head back and laughed. "What sort of proof could you possibly have against me? Anne died of an acute attack of illness. Nichols will attest to it."

"I have your daughter's testimony, written in her own hand, that accuses you of slowly sapping the life from her with your vile tonic. And all for what? Because she outlived her usefulness?"

"Because she would not obey!" Lady Catherine spat, then realised her error. More collectedly, she continued, "You know nothing of a mother's duty to her child. Anything that I did for Anne was done for the best."

"For the best? You *killed* her with your horrid potions. Your own child! What kind of mother are you?"

"A far better one than you will ever make! I know what is owed to my family, my name, my position in life—you are nothing but a thieving interloper who stole my daughter's future out from under her. Were she here now, she would spit upon you with contempt."

Ding. Ding. Ding!

"I think not. Anne never wanted to marry Darcy, nor he her. He asked her once, did you know?"

Lady Catherine could feel heat rising in her face. It bubbled beneath the surface of her skin, ready to erupt. "You lie! If Darcy had proposed, she would not have dared to disobey my wishes."

Miss Bennet laughed without humour. "Except that she did. My husband explained to me that he once offered for Anne in the hopes of getting her out from under your thumb. She refused him because she did not wish him beholden to this failing estate or your unreasonable demands. Had either of them realised what you were actually about, that you were more *monster* than mother, perhaps it would have turned out differently, but instead one of them is dead and the other plagued with regrets."

"You have always been an artful creature, exerting your wiles upon every man in the vicinity. You used them on Collins, Fitzwilliam, Darcy—and probably untold others. You are a loathsome, devious harlot with no concept of the truth of matters."

"Then why do you not explain them to me?" the chit challenged, chin lifted as if she were some noble defender of Anne. Beyond her, the standard held aloft by one of those stupid knights waved slightly in an unfelt draught. "From where I stand, your only motive appears to be greed and petty revenge."

"You could not possibly understand," Lady Catherine snarled. "When—or I should say *if*—that child is born, you will come to learn that discipline is a necessary element of child rearing. If you do not provide a firm guiding hand, children will ruin themselves. Just look at Anne! Had she obeyed and captured Darcy, she would still be alive today, settled in her proper place as the mistress of Pemberley. Instead, *you* have lured him away and thwarted my plans, leaving me no recourse but to punish my daughter harshly. I never meant for it to go so far, but she had to learn her lesson."

Miss Bennet gasped. "That is preposterous! I had no hand in your treating her so dishonourably and neither did my husband. He was free to marry where he chose and was encouraged in that pursuit by Anne herself. Do not blame others for your misdeeds. Besides, it is starkly apparent that greed was your incentive. Why else try to force your daughter into a union she did not want and then punish her for not achieving it?"

"The youth today! None of you have any concept of duty. You are provided with every possible thing you could require, assiduously tended and educated from infancy, all so you can go your own way in the end. Such selfishness is disgusting."

"One does not raise children simply to…to do one's bidding. They are people with their own thoughts and feelings."

Lady Catherine could not help a cackling laugh. "You are painfully naïve."

"*You* are evil." The accusation emerged from Miss Bennet as a hiss, full of contempt. "Tell me, because I have been wondering, did Anne's will play a role in your decision to be rid of her? Was this her final 'betrayal'?"

"I did not know Anne had cut me from her will until after she was dead. Mr Stephens brought it to my attention the next day, so you cannot accuse me of acting for pecuniary advantage."

"And yet you set fire to his offices to preserve Rosings for yourself, killing him in the process."

She waved away this objection just as easily. "I could not let the estate devolve into unworthy hands, could I? After everything I have done to keep it solvent? It was a practical matter."

"Murdering an innocent man is a practical matter?"

"In this, as in everything, you are woefully unschooled. This is exactly why you ought never to have quit the sphere in which you were brought up, for you have only brought suffering into mine."

The girl had the temerity to point an accusing finger at Lady Catherine as she loudly declared, "The suffering is all on your head!"

"It is soon to be on yours."

Lady Catherine took up her cane and lunged forwards, swinging it in Miss Bennet's direction. The girl cried out and stumbled back, just out of range of the silver-tipped end of the makeshift cudgel. Lady Catherine pursued her, issuing another swipe, which she ducked, and pressed her closer to the fireplace. *If she will not hold still and take her punishment, I shall corner her!*

Clang! Clang! Clang!

Those blasted bells began again, knelling in warning. Lady Catherine disregarded them, and when Miss Bennet moved for the door to the hall, she blocked her path. The chit had no choice but to stumble backwards against one of those ridiculous knights Sir Lewis had insisted upon installing all over the house.

The knight teetered, providing the perfect distraction for her to pounce. While Miss Bennet struggled to prevent the thing from collapsing atop her, Lady Catherine executed another lunge with her cane.

This movement resulted in a shooting pain from her ankle, and she stumbled, crying out. Miss Bennet used this to her advantage and dodged out of the way just in time to avoid receiving the pummelling she so richly deserved. The cane instead struck the knight and—

There was a deafening crash, a shriek of the utmost rage, and the bells fell silent.

CHAPTER THIRTY-TWO

Elizabeth lay splayed on the ground, both arms cradling her abdomen in a protective stance, and groaned. Her shoulder hurt, as did the knee and hip she had landed upon, but the pain did not feel like the lingering sort. More importantly—

She breathed a shuddering sigh of relief when the baby moved, wriggling about in what felt like an anxious panic. Elizabeth squeezed her eyes shut a moment, tears wetting her lashes, and willed her own terror to subside.

Another groan from a short distance away reminded Elizabeth of her precarious position, and she scrambled upright, scuttling away from the prone form of Lady Catherine where she lay crumpled upon the hearth beneath the bulk of a pair of gleaming knights. She had struck one with her cane in her vicious pursuit of Elizabeth, causing it to topple over into the other and both of them to land atop herself. Most of her body was concealed by the pile of armour, save for a single twitching hand and the volume of her skirts. A trickle of blood seeped from the mound, puddling into a gruesome lake of glistening crimson.

Less than a minute after Lady Catherine had met her fate, and well before Elizabeth could adequately comprehend what had happened, the door to the hall was flung open, and Freddy burst into the room just ahead of Darcy. "Elizabeth—dear God, are you well?"

Her courage of the last quarter of an hour dissolved at the entrance of her husband, and tears poured forth. She clumsily rose to her feet just in time to throw herself into Darcy's arms and bury her face in his cravat, sobbing his name.

Darcy set her away from him, eyes wild and breathing heavily. "You must tell me now, are you hurt? The babe?"

Elizabeth shook her head emphatically. "No more than a bruise or two, I promise, and I believe the child is well. It is moving even now." She drew Darcy's hand to her belly and witnessed the relief on his face at the flutter beneath his palm. *How differently he acts towards the baby now that he has felt it move.*

She turned to the heap of metal and twitching limbs upon the hearth. "But Lady Catherine…"

The colonel was crouched over his aunt's prone form, working to dig her out from the dismantled armour. Lord Matlock stood at his son's shoulder, frozen in apparent shock. Between his waxen pallor and white-blond hair, he looked as much a ghost as Anne.

Darcy used his finger to gently tip Elizabeth's face back in his direction. "What happened?"

Falteringly, Elizabeth described how Lady Catherine had arrived at the door shortly after Darcy had left—her ladyship must have been watching for his departure, she belatedly presumed—and forced her way inside. "I was so stupid! I never meant to go against your wishes, I swear it. I thought it was you come back from your walk and…and…"

Darcy hushed her with soothing words and gentle circles upon her back. "There now, it is over, my love. Do not berate yourself so harshly."

Once she had collected herself, Elizabeth proceeded with her explanation of how Lady Catherine had attacked her, resulting in a merry chase about the room until she had struck one of the knights and…well, the rest was fairly obvious.

"I had always known her to be intractable and difficult, but she is entirely mad. What could she have been thinking?" mused Lord Matlock from where he stood out of the way, observing as his son directed the servants to carry his sister to her own rooms. So far, she was still breathing, but she had not stirred, nor was she responding to any attempts to rouse her.

Darcy gathered Elizabeth to his chest and pressed a kiss to her crown. "Some things defy rational explanation."

<hr>

Although he would have preferred to tuck Elizabeth into bed, Darcy did not wish to expose her further to the calamity in their chambers. Thus did they adjourn to the library, where she would be most comfortable.

They were still there an hour later, Elizabeth curled up in his lap while Darcy stroked her back and whispered endearments into her hair, when Fitzwilliam and Lord Matlock appeared. Freddy, more on guard than was her usual wont, stood and growled at the newcomers until Darcy told her to stand down. She did but kept a suspicious eye on Lord Matlock as he collapsed into an armchair; Fitzwilliam she allowed to pet her without complaint.

"She yet lives," Lord Matlock said wearily, rubbing his eyes with his thumb and forefinger. When he dropped his hand into his lap, he continued, "For now, at least. The apothecary—Jules?"

"Julius," corrected Fitzwilliam, equally as jaded as his father.

"Yes, him. Mr Julius says it could go either way, but he cautions us to expect the worst."

Fitzwilliam snorted, and Darcy was tempted to do the same. The 'worst' case would be to have Lady Catherine survive and make another attempt on Elizabeth's life. Not that they would remain at Rosings long enough for her to try; tomorrow, rain or no rain, he would be returning his wife to the comparative safety of London. There, she could be properly looked after with no lethal tonics or bludgeon-wielding maniacs in sight.

"Her housekeeper wanted to call in Nichols for a second opinion, but I have already sent the magistrate after *that* lout. He is the law's problem now. Ours is to decide what to do with Catherine, should she wake from her coma."

Fitzwilliam slammed his fist against the arm of his own chair. "We ought to hand her over to the magistrate along with her quack! She should hang for what she did to Anne, and potentially to Sir Lewis as well. Do you recall how sudden his death was?"

"To say nothing of poor Mr Stephens," said Elizabeth, speaking for the first time since their relations entered the room. When Lord Matlock regarded her with a blank expression, she reminded him, "The local solicitor. The one whose offices burnt down with him inside. Lady Catherine all but confessed to me that she had ordered it set aflame. We are fortunate that only one person was killed and additional damage to the village was prevented."

The earl grimaced. "Even if she is guilty of all this and more, it does not alter the fact that society does not look kindly upon the kin of murderers. We shall all be ruined if her transgressions are widely known."

Objections were immediately—and loudly—raised by both Darcy and Fitzwilliam, but Lord Matlock quieted them with a barking order. "Enough of that! I am not saying that Catherine ought not to be punished, only that we do so discreetly. She has obviously gone mad, so ensconcing her in some decrepit little cottage where she can be properly supervised is not so outrageous."

"You only mean to protect your precious reputation," spat Fitzwilliam.

Lord Matlock levelled his son with a chilling glare, though Fitzwilliam seemed unperturbed. "Do not speak to me that way, boy. You might have your own estate now, but you will require my help to bring it up to snuff."

"Your own estate?" queried Elizabeth, a crease of confusion between her eyebrows.

Fitzwilliam nodded, a sharp, tight gesture. "Anne left

everything to me. I do not know whether to thank or curse her for it, but Rosings is now mine to do with what I will. At the moment, I am tempted to burn the entire pile to the ground and salt the earth."

Darcy perfectly comprehended the colonel's feelings but knew that he spoke primarily out of anger and disgust, emotions which would pass with time. When he was ready, Darcy would be at Fitzwilliam's disposal to help him either repair or sell the old place; Anne's final gift to a beloved cousin would not go to waste.

"All of this plotting is for nothing until we know whether Lady Catherine lives or dies. Time alone will tell us that."

The lot of them grumbled agreement to Darcy's concise summary. Brandy was passed round to the gentlemen, chocolate—not tea, never tea—was procured for Elizabeth, and the church bells rang their heavy knells in the distance.

CHAPTER THIRTY-THREE

Mr Julius withdrew his hand from Lady Catherine's neck, shaking his head. He then grasped the edge of the counterpane and pulled it up to cover her face. When he spoke to the stone-faced housekeeper, it was with none of the good cheer he was so often characterised by, but rather a deep solemnity. "She is gone." Mrs Knight, apparently unmoved, nodded in response and began ordering the assembled maids about the business of collecting soiled linens.

If Anne still breathed, she might have sighed. In sadness for the mother who had raised her, in anguish for what that mother had done, but primarily in relief for the fact that Lady Catherine de Bourgh could never harm another living soul. "It is done, then."

"Done?"

Anne lifted her head to regard the spirit of her recently deceased mother from where she had formed on the other side of the deathbed. She stood—floated, more like—just behind Mr Julius, still robed in the mourning gown she had perished in, observing in slack-jawed outrage as he proceeded to pack away his medical bag.

"It is not done at all!" cried Lady Catherine in an echoing voice, gliding forwards to swipe at Mr Julius. Her incorporeal hand merely passed through him unnoticed. She tried again, then again and again ad nauseum, her rage rising at every impotent blow; she verily glowed with it. "Where are you going, you charlatan? Revive me! Revive me, or else I shall see you ruined! You will never practise your trade again!"

Her hands folded against her midsection, Anne patiently waited for her mother's tantrum to subside, knowing full well that there was no reasoning with Lady Catherine when she worked herself into this sort of lather. One did not rationalise with a tempest; one simply battened down the hatches and waited it out.

When Mr Julius had placed the last of his instruments in his bag, he left the room, still none the wiser that the free-floating soul of his last patient wanted a word with him. The maids and housekeeper followed him out, burdened with the detritus of their failed attempt at resuscitating the mistress. Mrs Knight, at the tail end of their procession, shut the door behind herself, leaving the dead to themselves.

"Come back here this instant!" Lady Catherine shrieked, swooping for the door like a rush of ill wind. It rebuffed her, however, per Anne's will, and she was thrown back to the centre of the room. She hovered there a moment, nonplussed, and made another attempt that met with the same result. Then another, and another, and another.

After several fruitless minutes, Anne's patience wore thin. If she were to wait for her mother to acknowledge that she was no longer in control, they would be there for ages. "You are wasting your time, Mother. Mr Julius cannot hear you, so he will never obey your commands."

"I will make him hear me!" Lady Catherine insisted, reaching for the latch. Her fingers could not so much as touch it, and she howled with outrage.

It was time to employ the frankness her mother was so fond of. "You are *dead*, madam. The living, save for a few exceptions, cannot hear us." This stark proclamation reverberated on the still air like the relentless echo of a bell.

Lady Catherine halted in her efforts momentarily before resuming her assault on the door. "That is utterly ridiculous."

"Is my presence here not evidence enough?"

"You expect me to believe myself dead on so little? If I were, I would not be trapped in my bedchamber suffering the incompetence of worthless tradesmen."

Anne scoffed, not at all inclined to allow Lady Catherine to roam the house. There was no telling what sort of mischief she could inflict upon the Darcys were she allowed free rein. "Given all you have done, I think it most generous that you were not simply left to bleed to death on the floor. The efforts of Mr Julius are better than you deserve."

Lady Catherine whipped about, her gown floating on the air at a lazier pace. It collected about her like a dark cloud ready to unleash havoc. "I have only done what was necessary, you obstinate, ungrateful girl."

Anne's iridescence, so striking a contrast to her

mother's murky aura, only brightened with her outrage. When she spoke again, her voice was more of a knell than a chime. "You *murdered* me, Mother."

"It was an accident."

"You poisoned me for years—it was no accident."

"Exactly my point." Lady Catherine lifted her chin and set it stubbornly. "You lived for nearly a decade before succumbing, so obviously my tonic did not injure you too greatly. If I had not been forced to dismiss Mrs Jenkinson, you might yet live. Better yet, if you had married Darcy and retired to Pemberley, you would never have required the tonic again."

"That is very like you, to blame others for your own malfeasance. What of Mr Stephens?"

"Who?"

"The solicitor you had burnt alive to hide my will."

"Oh, him." Lady Catherine sniffed. "He was a nobody. He did not matter."

"I should think that his family disagrees with you there. Mr Stephens was beloved in Hunsford and must be greatly missed."

"Nobodies all! Why should I care for them?"

Anne's eyes narrowed, and her aura glowed brighter. "Should you not have cared for your husband?"

Lady Catherine scoffed. "Sir Lewis was a worthless idiot, and the world is better off without him. I surely am. He thought to order me about, and I could not have that. Once he was gone, and Rosings was left to me, everything was as it should be. Really, it was for the best."

"You killed him to gain control over Rosings, I knew it. I dare say you disposed of me for the same purpose."

"I have already said that your death was an accident. Besides, my dowry saved the estate once, and it rightfully belongs to me. You were going to give it away to Fitzwilliam, of all people. What does he know of running an estate?"

"What do you?" Anne countered, wishing she were substantial enough to stamp her foot. "Rosings is in ruins thanks to your mismanagement."

"Ridiculous! Rosings is the jewel of Kent thanks to me. Your father, after wasting his own money, married me for mine, then wished to run the place like a close-fisted miser. With him out of the way, I could do as I pleased, and the estate flourished. By leaving it to Fitzwilliam, you have undone all my hard work."

"And if, without my will to provide direction, Rosings had fallen into the hands of strangers?"

Lady Catherine waved this rational concern away with an impatient flick of her fingers. "I am sure my brother would not have allowed that to happen. He would have secured it for me in the end."

What an arrogant, nonsensical presumption! Even in the absence of legal assurance, her mother had unreasonably assumed that Rosings would naturally devolve to her without Anne's will to contest it. Poor Mr Stephens had lost his life to Lady Catherine's absurd sense of entitlement.

Calming herself before her rage reduced the room to wreckage, Anne shifted the subject to one yet more unforgiveable. "Your greed, while despicable, is easy enough to comprehend. However, I still do not understand why you wished to take Mrs Darcy's life."

Her mother flew at her like the horrid ghoul that she

was, eyes alight with gleaming rage. Inches from Anne's placid face, she shrieked, "Do not call her that! *Never* call her that!"

"Elizabeth, then," Anne replied, all composure. "Was it not enough that you had already punished *me* for not marrying Darcy? Or that you schemed and murdered to illegally claim Rosings as your own? Why could you not be satisfied with that? You knew very well that she was with child, and you sought to harm her—why?"

Lady Catherine slunk back a few paces, growling. "I did it for you, of course. *You* were meant to be mistress of Pemberley, not her."

"That is both disgusting and nonsensical. It is not as if I were still alive to take her place."

"It was not *her* place to begin with—it was *yours*. She stole Pemberley out from under you, and you ask me why I needed to seek revenge? I could not allow that grasping upstart to profit from her crimes. It was in every way appalling."

"Elizabeth stole nothing from me that I did not already cast aside. Darcy asked me to marry him years ago, but I rejected his suit."

Lady Catherine was aghast. "Why in heaven's name would you do that?"

"Because I did not wish to see him beholden to you or become responsible for Rosings. Pemberley's coffers are full now, but repairing this place would have drained them."

"It is no less than his duty to assist us. We are family."

Anne, her patience again waning in the face of her mother's intractable nonsense, threw up her hands in exasperation. "He has already been assisting us for years, since his father died. You ask too much."

"Which was why I sought to unite the pair of you in marriage. It would not have been too much then. You might have lived at Pemberley whilst I oversaw Rosings Park. It was the perfect plan until that horrid girl, with her arts and allurements, interfered."

"What disgusts me most is how you absolutely disregarded Elizabeth's pregnancy in your evil schemes. How could you attempt to harm that precious, innocent babe?"

Lady Catherine's rage flickered behind her eyes like lightning strikes. "That child is a mongrel! To see the shades of Pemberley so polluted…it is not to be borne, I tell you. Even if he can no longer marry you, he can at least select a woman of excellent breeding who will do credit to his lineage. There are many young ladies who might suit—ones whom I could mould into a proper wife for my nephew. Miss Bennet is an impertinent nobody from nowhere who knows not how to take direction from her betters."

Anne's repugnance must have been clearly writ upon her face, however much Lady Catherine overlooked it. "Even were that so, that gives you no right to murder her, Mother."

"It gives me every right! If a pest, full of disease and filth, shows up on one's doorstep, does one let it inside and invite it to dine? No! One stamps it out."

"That is a horrible way to speak of Elizabeth, or any other person. I have always suspected it, but now I know for certain that you have no heart."

Lady Catherine's responding cackle reverberated off

the rafters. "I do not require a heart. It only interferes with what must be done and done for the best. What you do not understand, what you have never understood, is that you and everyone else in this house lived by my sufferance alone. I brought you into this world, and it was my right to remove you from it when you no longer deserved your place in it. You are in no position to question me, girl. I am Lady Catherine de Bourgh of Rosings Park, and I answer to no one."

"I see," replied Anne, solemn as her own grave. "Fortunately, you are now trapped here with me."

As Anne made this proclamation, chains sprouted from the floor like writhing vines, twining about Lady Catherine's ankles, creeping up her legs, and pinning her arms to her body. Her ladyship thrashed and fought, but her struggle was futile; she was subdued in less time than it would have taken her to form the intent to flee.

Lady Catherine writhed fruitlessly against her new bindings, screeching and howling to be let free. "Unhand me at once, you wretched girl, else you will learn to regret it!"

Anne, unperturbed by her mother's threats, glided forwards as if skating on a breeze. She bent close to Lady Catherine's ear and hissed, "You misunderstand your situation, Mother. As I no longer have a body for you to weaken, your power, such as it was, is gone. It is *I* who am mistress here now and *you* who have no choice but to obey."

Lady Catherine turned so they were nose-to-nose, a grotesque snarl on her lips. "Obviously, I was too kind in poisoning you. I ought to have beaten the life out of you instead so you would remember your place even in death."

Anne straightened. "Given your apparent lack of remorse, I shall take your voice from you as well." She observed with nonchalance as one of the chains lashed out from the others and wrapped about her mother's face, muffling the shout that had attempted to escape Lady Catherine's throat. Only her mother's bulging eyes were visible above the suppressive links. "As much as you have always loved doling out advice and ordering people about, it ought to be a torment to be deprived of speech. It will be a relief to everyone else."

Although Lady Catherine could neither move nor speak, the betrayal writ across her features was easy enough to comprehend. The irony amused Anne more than she liked to confess.

"You will remain here, confined to your chambers and never wailing quite loudly enough for anyone to hear, long after the world has forgotten that Lady Catherine de Bourgh of Rosings Park ever existed. I shall return eventually, though time has but little influence over me now. I dare say I shall recall my promise in a few decades, perhaps a century or two at most. If you are suitably repentant by then, I shall consider loosening your chains."

Anne concluded on a more cheerful note, "If you will excuse me, I must see off our guests. Goodbye, Mother."

As she faded into mist, Anne's last image of Lady Catherine was of her brought to her knees in a silent scream.

CHAPTER THIRTY-FOUR

Elizabeth was seated at the rosewood desk in Anne's tower, bathed in dappled pink sunlight streaming in through the window. The air seemed to sparkle about her as if infused with magic, and the breeze was redolent with flowers. Before her was a crystal vase of pink and white anemones, absolutely overflowing with verdant beauty.

Yet despite the peaceful atmosphere, Elizabeth could not help feeling unaccountably sad. Anemone, she knew, was a bloom that symbolised early death. Said to be the creation of Aphrodite upon the demise of her beloved Adonis, they were a tribute to those loved and lost too soon.

Feeling a presence at her back, she turned to find Anne standing in the centre of the room under the glittering pattern cast by the window. A tear glistened as it traced down her cheek, yet she was smiling. She was also waving farewell.

"Must we part ways?" Elizabeth asked, her voice

warbling with emotion that threatened to overwhelm her composure at any moment. "I feel as if I have just come to know you."

Anne lowered her hand and nodded, her countenance soft and solemn.

"I wish I had known you better in life. You would have been most welcome to stay with us at Pemberley and escape from this awful place."

With a hand placed above where her heart used to beat, Anne offered her a sad smile. *I would have liked that*, her expression seemed to say.

"Shall I ever see you again?"

A nod and a widening of her smile—*Yes*.

"Good." Elizabeth choked on the word before collecting herself. She was emphatic in saying, "I promise to visit often. You will be fondly remembered by all of us."

Anne opened her mouth and, with visible effort, managed to softly reply in a voice reminiscent of a spring breeze. "Thank you."

She then vanished, dissolving into a golden shimmer that faded into sunlight.

When Elizabeth woke, she was already cradled in her husband's arms, a tearful, blubbering wretch. Darcy held her to his chest, hushing and rocking her as she released her grief. Within her, the baby moved about as if offering comfort as well.

At length, the gentle thudding of Darcy's heart lulled Elizabeth into calmness and a greater sense of tranquillity. Anne had died more than a fortnight ago now, but for the first time she felt that her cousin-by-marriage was truly gone. Much as that saddened her, she could at least be content in the knowledge that Anne was at peace, no longer subject to the cruelty and neglect of her mother, or the pains of her inflicted illness.

And they would meet again, Elizabeth consoled herself. She would return to Rosings Park with her children every spring and tell them of Anne, show them her tower, and pick anemones in her memory. She felt Anne would like that. Perhaps she would make herself known now and again with the sweet chime of a distant bell, a salutation from beyond the veil.

Meanwhile, with new life growing inside her and a husband who loved her, Elizabeth would pursue her own earthly happiness. It was all anyone could do to honour those who had gone before them.

It was the first day of spring that Lady Catherine de Bourgh was laid to rest. She was interred in the family vault with Sir Lewis and Anne, which had not especially suited the feelings of those who were aware of the totality of her sins. Fitzwilliam, in particular, had advocated for his late aunt to receive the same treatment as all criminals and be denied a proper burial in consecrated ground, whereas Lord Matlock had insisted that there was no just cause to wilfully damage the family reputation out of pointless spite. It served no rational purpose to injure themselves in such a way, and so her ladyship had received far better than she deserved.

In deference to Anne's memory, however, Fitzwilliam —the newly anointed master of Rosings Park—had insisted that her ceremony be small and privately attended. One might have expected Collins, whose devotion to Lady Catherine had far exceeded what was sensible, to object, but he was much too enamoured of his new patron to contradict the colonel's directly stated wishes. He had even been convinced to keep the eulogy to what was prescribed by the Church of England only and to add no embellishments to the ceremony, though it had seemed to pain him to restrain himself on that score.

While Fitzwilliam and Lord Matlock had remained behind to squabble over the funeral arrangements, their dispute delaying the ceremony by several days, Darcy had provided whatever support he could via correspondence. Once he was assured—per the collective opinions of a midwife and two lauded physicians—that Elizabeth had suffered no lasting harm from her ordeal at Rosings, he had returned to Kent merely for the satisfaction of seeing his wicked aunt securely interred; he would sleep better at night having witnessed it for himself.

During their walk back to the manor house, with the church bells clanging behind them, Darcy bemoaned, "Finally, it is done. I shall be glad to return to Elizabeth this evening. Will you be riding with me, or do you still have some business here?"

"I shall come with you, for my most pressing business is in London," Fitzwilliam replied, his countenance weary. "I still need to sell my commission, but first I must see a solicitor and have my will written up. My father insisted on seeing it done immediately, and I find I cannot fault him for it."

Darcy glanced back to where Lord Matlock and Viscount Marbury were strolling at a more leisurely pace several yards behind. "Yes, one can understand his reasoning. It is better to know where to look for such things. I recommend the services of Mr Pickering and will introduce you to him if you like."

"I should like that very much, thank you."

"Speaking of such matters, has Mrs Jenkinson received her bequest from Anne's will yet?"

"Not yet, which is another reason for my impending journey to London. I shall see to it that the dear lady receives every penny that is due to her, though I should prefer to give her more. What with all she has done for Anne throughout the years, to say nothing of the way her service ended, she deserves it."

"Fear not, I have gifted her a trifle of my own as thanks for her devotion."

"A trifle, you say?" queried Fitzwilliam, intrigued. "What sort of trifle?"

"A small cottage—nothing much."

The colonel guffawed. "A cottage is more than a mere trifle, Darce."

"It is what Anne would have wanted," Darcy countered, somewhat defensively. "Besides, I could not countenance the thought that she must live with Mrs Younge for the rest of her days." He shuddered at the very notion. Mrs Jenkinson was nothing like her nefarious younger sister and ought not to be subjected to the impurities of Edward Street.

"Well, I thank you for your largesse regardless."

Fitzwilliam emitted a sigh. "The poor dear loved Anne like her own. It was a heartbreaking business to inform her that our cousin had died. No one had told her prior to my arriving on her doorstep. I can say with all honesty that her grief was sincere—exactly what one might have expected from her actual mother."

Darcy shook his head. *Treated abominably by her own mother, mourned by a servant. Poor Anne.*

Melancholy silence stretched between them. At length, Fitzwilliam cleared his throat and introduced a more cheerful subject. "How is Elizabeth? I know it is torturing you to be away from her."

"She was well when I saw her yesterday, and she proclaimed herself still well in the letter I received this morning. We shall both see for ourselves soon enough. By the bye, I mean to leave for town immediately after breakfast, so I hope you are ready to depart by then."

Once the roads had been dry enough to safely travel upon after Lady Catherine's sudden death, Darcy had bundled Elizabeth into their coach and carried his wife away from Rosings Park in a state of utmost relief. They had travelled directly to the Bingleys' town house— Georgiana had been staying there during her brother and sister's sojourn—where they had been greeted first with pleasant surprise then abject horror once their macabre tale had been told.

Feeling that his wife would benefit greatly from the gentle care of their sisters, Darcy had left her at Bingley's house when he travelled to Rosings for Lady Catherine's funeral, intending to spend only a single night in the cursed place. Now that this business was accomplished, he was eager to return to London, collect

Elizabeth and Georgiana, and retreat to the newly reopened Darcy House for a few weeks of the Season. He would have preferred to travel to Pemberley but felt it wise to be closer at hand for Fitzwilliam's sake as he navigated his new responsibilities and the necessary legalities. They would stay until after Easter before at last making their way back to Derbyshire for Elizabeth's confinement.

Fitzwilliam saluted him, albeit sarcastically. "I might be a landowner now, but I am still a soldier at heart. I can always be ready to travel at a moment's notice."

"Excellent. Do you mean to stay with us or your father in town?"

"If it is no trouble, I should very much prefer to stay at Darcy House. I cannot abide any more advice from my old pater on the subject of what needs to be done at Rosings. He believes that all my problems will be solved if I marry a woman with a hefty dowry."

After some hesitation, Darcy conceded, "There is something in that, you know. An infusion of funds can only help."

Snorting, Fitzwilliam retorted, "I am sure that is exactly what Sir Lewis thought as well. Look how it turned out for him."

Darcy winced. "Well, when you put it like that…"

"I would much rather marry *after* I have made the estate solvent again, not before. A heavy purse cannot replace the love and loyalty that you have with Elizabeth, and if I should ever enter the state myself, I shall settle for nothing less. I desire a bride with more principle than blunt, one who is sweet and yet courageous at the same time. Someone whom I can care for and who will care for me in return. All the money in all the banks of England cannot purchase me that."

Fitzwilliam was quietly thoughtful for a short period, and Darcy could not help but wonder whether he was thinking of Catherine Bennet. He would not presume to ask, however, and waited for his cousin to resume speaking in his own time.

He did so with a beleaguered sigh. "It is such a vast, complicated undertaking that I hardly know where to begin, only that there is not enough money for all the necessary repairs and improvements. I do not know what Anne was thinking in leaving it to me."

"She was thinking that you are deserving and capable," said Darcy, slapping his cousin on the back. "More than that, she knew I would assist you in any way possible. Come, stay at Darcy House, and I shall do my utmost to help you sort it all out."

"I shall not take your money. You have a growing family to think of."

"I sincerely doubt that my household will be adversely affected by offering you a loan, but let us see what needs to be done first before we speak in any specific terms. I am as familiar with Rosings's finances as anyone, and while there is not much capital left, there is at least a small sum that Lady Catherine did not squander. If you invest it wisely…"

The topic of investments carried them the rest of the way to the house, and after partaking of a light breakfast, Darcy and Fitzwilliam mounted their steeds and adjourned to London, where Elizabeth awaited their arrival.

EPILOGUE

July 22, 1813 Pemberley

"Relax now, Mrs Darcy. The next one'll come soon enough."

Elizabeth collapsed into her pillows in a sweaty heap, the tension in her abdomen temporarily abating. It would not last long; the contractions were, at last report, less than a minute apart. It would all be over soon, for better or worse.

Her pains had come upon her yesterday during her daily walk round the lake. She had felt miserable for some hours prior to that but had thought nothing of it; being so heavily pregnant at the height of summer meant she was thoroughly wretched much of the time. It was only when a sharp pain forced her to halt beneath the arching shelter of a willow, clutching her belly, that she suspected it was more than the usual malaise. Poor Darcy had turned absolutely white and spirited her up to the house with alacrity, shouting at the top of his voice for help.

With the mistress due at any given moment, help was quick to arrive in the form of Mrs Reynolds, who had ordered the servants about like a general arranging her troops. In short order, the master and mistress's bedroom had been transformed into a birthing chamber, the midwife, Mrs Green, was called up from the village, and her fretful husband had been banished to the library, where his sardonic father-in-law was meant to keep him occupied. The housekeeper, worth more than her own weight in gold, had even managed to keep Mrs Bennet's nerves in check by setting her up in style in the attached sitting room with a maid to distract her and smelling salts conveniently to hand.

More than a day later, the birthing process was reaching its crescendo, and a weary Elizabeth was well and truly anxious for it to be over. Her energy was flagging after labouring for so many hours together, and she was not sure how much longer she could persevere.

She turned to look out of the open windows along the far wall, where a full moon watched the proceedings with an impassive face. The wind was picking up, and she could hear leaves rustling and smell the heady perfume of roses wafting on the air. She breathed it in, drawing strength from nature as she had always done.

She would not give up. She could do this. She was eager to meet her child, to hold him or her in her arms and see their precious face at long last. She wanted to count their tiny fingers and toes, kiss their cheeks, and dote on them endlessly.

Moreover, Darcy was depending upon her to come

out of this ordeal alive and well. They were meant to grow old together and raise a whole parcel of little ones, and it would not end here.

I can do this!

Her belly drew taut again moments before Mrs Green cried, "Here it comes! Bear down, Mrs Darcy. One more good push ought to do it!"

Elizabeth gritted her teeth and put every ounce of her remaining strength into the endeavour, taking hold of the sheets with a white-knuckled grip as she curled in on herself and bore down hard. Blood thundered in her ears so loudly that she only vaguely heard the keen encouragements of Mrs Green. And then—

A cry. It warbled somehow above every other sound in the room, clear and loud as a bell.

"Congratulations, ma'am! It is a strong, healthy boy." From the next room, Elizabeth heard her mother's celebratory wail.

She gasped out a sob as she once again fell to the mattress, utterly spent. Even as she lay there panting, she reached for the squirming miracle that was her son. "Let me see him."

"Right away, missus, just let me clean 'im up first," said Mrs Green, handing the child off to a blanket that was held open by Mrs Reynolds. The dear lady's cheeks were wet with tears as the midwife tied off his umbilical cord and hastily patted him dry. The poor lad squalled mightily at this treatment.

It felt like ages, but was probably less than a minute, before Mrs Reynolds brought the child to his mother's waiting arms. Elizabeth struggled into a sitting position, helped into it by Blake, who had assisted throughout the birth, to receive him. The moment he settled against her chest, his crying ceased, he opened his eyes, and he stared at her with a stoicism that reminded her of his father. She could not help an exhausted, slightly mad, laugh at how perfectly *Darcy* he was.

Those pensive eyes were a captivating blue-grey, a shade or two darker than his father's but very much Fitzwilliam in lineage. *No one will ever doubt his ancestry.* She thought he might have her nose and mouth, but in general he was cast in Darcy's image. His dark curly hair —a whole head full of it—might have come from either of them.

Stroking his downy soft cheek with a trembling finger, Elizabeth took the liberty of introducing herself. "I am so pleased to meet you, Bennet. I am your mama."

Bennet squinted at her a long moment, then reached out to clasp her finger within his tiny fist. Elizabeth smiled at him and shook it gently, as one does with a new acquaintance. It was an odd thing, having a child; she felt simultaneously as if she had known and loved this tiny being for so long already and had only now been afforded the opportunity to truly get to know him.

I am a mother now. Dear Lord, I am a mother. She could not quite grasp the enormity of it all.

A loud bang interrupted their moment as the door flew open and crashed into the wall. Her husband, it seemed, would be kept at bay no longer and strode into the room with purpose. Just behind him, Elizabeth could see her father lingering in the doorway, chuckling and shaking his head at his hasty son-in-law. "The birthing room is no place for fathers, Darcy."

Darcy paid Mr Bennet no mind, nor the shocked cries

of the women present, from the midwife to his mother-in-law, all of whom were attempting to expel him back out into the corridor—he only had eyes for his wife. He stalked across the carpet in half the steps he usually took and was kneeling at her side within moments. "Are you well, my dearest?"

The poor man was so wan and pale that Elizabeth was more worried for him than for herself. There was no question that he had been awake, likely pacing, since her labour began, and he must have been exhausted. She was quick to put the worst of his fears to rest. "Better than well, even. There are no words to describe it." Emotion caught in her throat, forcing her to pause. "Meet our son."

For the first time since his encroachment, Darcy's gaze flickered to the bundle in Elizabeth's arms to behold their child. She witnessed the very moment that wonder bloomed across his features.

"A boy! A boy, Mr Bennet, did you hear? A boy!"

Darcy's reverence dissolved into a grimace as Mrs Bennet's voice interrupted the introduction. Elizabeth, still rather muddled, could not help a laugh. *Oh, Mama.*

"Yes, my dear, I heard. A boy at last. He is liable to be spoilt by the great number of doting aunties he has."

"Nothing you say can vex me, Mr Bennet, for I am overcome with joy. *Young Master Darcy*—how well that sounds!"

Mrs Bennet might have continued her ovation for hours were it not for the strong wind that blew into the room and flickered all the lights. Along with it came a great deal of leaves and a variety of different rose petals, raining down upon those gathered like a fragrant deluge.

Mrs Bennet somehow managed to catch a clump of them in her mouth and ran from the room coughing and sputtering. Elizabeth was pleased to see Blake follow her parents out, trusting that she would see to the situation.

A good number of the leaves and rose petals settled on the bed, while the servants dashed to force the windows closed against the wind. It somehow felt like a lovely tribute to such a momentous occasion.

ABOUT THE AUTHOR

Mary Smythe is a homemaker living in South Carolina with a rather useless BA in English collecting dust in a closet somewhere. Mrs Smythe discovered the works of Jane Austen as a teenager thanks to the 1995 BBC *Pride and Prejudice* miniseries featuring Colin Firth and Jennifer Ehle and has since gone on to read everything written by Miss Austen at least once yearly, always wishing that there were more. She has been writing since 2001, but only discovered Jane Austen Fan Fiction in the summer of 2018.

ALSO BY MARY SMYTHE

A Case of Some Urgency

A Faithful Narrative

Dare to Refuse Such a Man

Fitzwilliam Darcy, Hero

Pemberley (Happily Ever Afterlife Book 1)

Prevailed Upon to Marry

Pride Before a Fall

Rosings Park (Happily Ever Afterlife Book 2)

Welcome Home

MULTI-AUTHOR COLLECTIONS

'Tis the Season

Affections & Wishes: An Anthology of Pride & Prejudice Variations

An Inducement into Matrimony

ACKNOWLEDGMENTS

I would like to offer my deepest, most heartfelt gratitude to everyone and anyone who assisted me in bringing this novel to completion. Firstly, my husband, who did his level best to watch the kids and let me work as often as possible; thank you for keeping them occupied, I know it wasn't easy. To my kids, who are now old enough to respect a closed office door (even if they sometimes forget) and allow themselves to be distracted once in a while.

My sincere and heartfelt gratitude goes to my editors, Amy D'Orazio and Jo Abbott, who helped me prune an unwieldy manuscript into a proper novel. Amy, if this book was an overgrown garden, you helped me weed and tame it into what it is with your cuts. Jo, you are absolutely invaluable as an editor. What would I do without you to trim and nourish my manuscripts? Y'all are amazing.

Finally, I would very much like to thank Quills & Quartos Publishing, as well as Amy D'Orazio and Jan Ashton specifically, for continuing to believe in me and my writing. I am exceedingly grateful to be part of this publishing house and can hardly believe my good fortune most days.

Printed in Great Britain
by Amazon